About Us

Jon Rance

To Kristin. This book isn't about us, but this book couldn't have been written without us.

About the author

Jon Rance is the author of five novels, This Thirtysomething Life, Happy Endings, This Family Life, Sunday Dinners, and Dan And Nat Got Married. This Thirtysomething Life became a Kindle top ten bestseller and Jon subsequently signed a two book publishing deal with Hodder and Stoughton. Perfect for fans of Mike Gayle, Matt Dunn and David Nicholls, Jon's books about life, love and all the messy bits in-between have been described as hilarious and heart-warming.

Also by Jon Rance

Prologue

It's an impossible feeling to describe. That moment when you get to hold your baby for the first time. I'd spent the best part of fifteen hours in labour. I was exhausted, in pain, completely drained, but then they passed me my baby and everything else melted away. She was so small, completely helpless, her skin so fragile, her body a small, wrinkled version of what she would become in a matter of weeks. Before that I'd felt her inside of me, but in that moment, holding her, looking into her eyes, I knew my life wouldn't ever be the same again.

Her name was Alice Elizabeth Willis. Eight pounds two ounces. Eighteen and a half inches long. And she was mine. It's impossible to fathom a love like it.

Pete was perched on the side of the bed next to me, one arm around me and the other around his daughter, a tear sliding down his face. I'd only seen him cry a handful of times before, but that's what children do to you. They break you down until you're nothing and then they reassemble you in a different order. Everything you thought and felt before was different. Children do that.

My parents came into the room soon after; Mum crying her eyes out, my father, a strong, solid man, suddenly so soft and gentle. He'd been through so much in his life, but here he was at the birth of his grandchild, and when he held her in his hands, the cracked and hardened skin beneath her body, it was as if I was seeing him properly for the first time.

The day you leave hospital is one of the scariest days of your life. You'll never be ready for it. No one tells you. That moment when you get home and you're alone with your baby for the first time is terrifying. I didn't feel ready. I wasn't prepared to be a mother. I was still a child in so many ways, and yet I had my own child that needed me. She couldn't speak, couldn't tell me what she wanted, but she needed me. I didn't have a choice. I had to be there for her, for our family, and I'd go through the same thing twice more. Three children of my own. You don't get to walk away from that. You don't get to hide or take a day off because you're feeling under the weather. My family needed me, still need me, and what can you do when you feel that love? There's nothing left to do but give yourself to them. All of you. Because that's what being a mother means. It means giving yourself to them. And I have. I've given them everything.

One

Pete's still in the bathroom. He's been in there for at least thirty minutes. What's he even doing? It's Monday morning and I'm trying to get all three children ready for school. I used to think marriage was a partnership, and maybe at one point it was, but now it's more of a play that Pete's watching from afar, while I try my best to direct everyone and stop the whole thing from falling apart. I have three difficult child performers, a limited budget, and recently Pete seems to have taken it upon himself to play the role of the disappointed critic. The reviews have been scathing. It's a shambles. No one seems to know what the hell's going on. Why is Josh running up and down the stairs like that? I think Daisy might need some professional help. The set is a bloody pigsty. I don't think it's fair that by the time the curtain's gone down, you're too tired to give me anything of yourself. Sorry, Pete, I didn't realise I was meant to be keeping myself back for you for when you eventually decide to get home from work (late, yet again), moaning the kitchen's a mess, shouting at the kids, and spending half an hour complaining about your day without *once* asking how mine was. It's so selfish of me, isn't it?

I'm in the kitchen attempting to pack three lunch boxes with lots of healthy, well- balanced foods. The sort you see Jamie Oliver banging on about on the television. And I agree with Jamie, of course, he's a national treasure, but it's not always so easy in reality. My plan is always the same, get them done the night before, but for some reason after a couple of glasses of wine, and reading through another potential manuscript on the sofa, I'm too tired and so here I am, with five minutes left, shoving badly cut-up pieces of carrot and apple next to three poorly constructed ham and cheese sandwiches. At least the bread is multigrain and packed full of nutrients, if you believe the advertising and I don't have the time not to.

I worry about the amount of time I spend doing things like making lunch and pairing socks after they've been washed. Every time I read another report where they say the average person spends a year of their life on the toilet or four years watching television, I can't help but wonder how much of my life I spend doing menial chores. I'm forty now and the years are flying by. Before I know it, I'll be fifty and I'll have spent the best part of the last ten years trying to find Josh a clean pair of underpants or Pete the right sort of chorizo from Waitrose.

'Where's my homework?' yells Alice from the hallway.

'Wherever you left it,' I shout back.

Alice is my eldest at fourteen - God, where did the years go? Alice used to be the sweetest little girl. Full of hugs, kisses, and little drawings of our family with the word 'love' written over them in squiggly red crayon. She was my little angel, always hopping into bed with us in the morning for cuddles. Then she became a teenager and now it's like living with a much older woman with permanent PMT. She's still beautiful, smart, and far more savvy than I was growing up, but the sweetness has taken a backseat. Now she's sullen and glib most of the time. She can usually be found staring at her phone, a blank expression on her face that says something along the lines of: Leave. Me. Alone.

Josh is ten and in the living room playing FIFA on the PlayStation. He used to have it in his bedroom until we discovered him up at midnight on a school night, his red, half-closed eyes barely awake, but his fingers doing all sorts of finger yoga with the controller. Since then the PlayStation's been in the living room and so has Josh. He's a typical ten-year-old boy, completely football mad, a bit smelly, and his room constantly looks as though it's been burgled, although unfortunately nothing ever gets taken.

Then there's Daisy, who's seven. I do worry about her. She's what you might label a 'difficult child'. She can be fine one moment then the next she flies off the handle and has a complete meltdown. She's incredibly talented in so many ways, which is why it's so heart-breaking that she can't seem to control herself. The school keeps saying we should get her tested, but the last thing she needs is someone telling her she should go on medication or see a psychiatrist. She's just a unique child who needs lots of patience and that's the problem with the world these days; no one has any patience.

'I can't find it!' yells Alice as though I purposely hid it from her. Then she does 'the huff'. The noise that has slowly taken over the house during the last couple of years. It's lovely, obviously.

'Daisy, are you ready to go?'

Daisy's sitting at the table, her head in a book.

'Did you know that half the pigs in all the world live in China?' says Daisy.

'I didn't, love, that's brilliant, but we're leaving in five minutes and I know for a fact you haven't brushed your teeth yet.'

'Neither has Josh.'

'But that's irrelevant because I'm talking about your teeth.'

'The bat is the only mammal that can fly. Did you know that, Mummy?'

'No, I didn't, but we're going to be late. Please go and brush your teeth and maybe while you're in there you can find your father.'

'My homework is lost and no one cares!' screams Alice.

'Look in the last place you saw it,' I yell back. 'Josh, time to turn off the football and get ready for school. We're out of the door in five minutes!'

No one moves. Daisy is still engrossed in her book, Alice is huffing and puffing in the hallway, and I can still hear the almighty noise of small, digital men running around a football pitch in the living room. Why do children have no concept of time or feel the pressure of being punctual? And why do I care so much when they're the ones who are going to get in trouble? Yet here I am, jamming lunch box lids shut and shoving them in their bags, terrified they're going to be late.

'Daisy, please go and brush your teeth.'

I look across at Daisy and she looks back at me. She's so young, but already I feel like she's judging me as a mother. I know Alice has been doing it for years. Luckily Josh is far too consumed by FIFA and watching Match of the Day to care about my parenting ability. I don't know if that's a good thing or not, but it feels like it might be so I'm going to accept it like a bloody Oscar. The thing with Daisy is you can't shout at her. She's delicate and raising your voice is the very last thing you should do. So here we are with four minutes until we're supposed to be out of the door and in the car and I'm asking her ever so nicely to put the book down and brush her teeth; begging my daughter to get ready for school, terrified that one wrong move will ruin everything.

'For every human in the world there are one million ants,' says Daisy.

'OK time to go. Let's get up and brush our teeth,' I say like a CBeebies presenter.

'But I'm not ready,' says Daisy. 'Did you know…'

'Daisy!' I finally succumb to the urge to scream and the minute I do I regret it. I start apologising like an awful date. 'Sorry, it's just we're going to be late. Mummy shouldn't have shouted like that. I'm sorry. I'm sorry.'

It's pathetic.

'You shouldn't shout. You're always so worried about rushing us to school. It's going to give you a heart attack.'

Maybe a heart attack wouldn't be such a bad thing. Just a mild one so I had to spend a few weeks convalescing at home, being waited on hand and foot by Pete. Alice comes storming into the room.

'I found my homework. Not that you care,' she says belligerently.

Was I this awful at fourteen?

'Is Josh still playing FIFA?'

'What do you think?' says Alice, stuffing her homework in her bag.

'OK, let's go you two. Upstairs, brush teeth, come on, we're going to be late!'

Alice and Daisy reluctantly and with heavy sighs, start the march upstairs. As we pass the living room, I look in and there's Josh, controller in hand, a new game of FIFA started.

'Josh, turn it off now or it's going away for good!' I yell, hoping this idle threat might persuade him to finally turn it off.

'But I've just started a new game. It's Champions League.'

'I don't care what league it is, just move it!'

I follow Alice and Daisy up the stairs. Behind me, Josh mumbles something about living in Nazi Germany, which is good because at least he's learning something at school, then he tosses the controller on the sofa. We amble up past the deluge of detritus that manages to make it onto the stairs, but never actually up the stairs. Instead it gets pushed to one side so we can still walk up without having to jump over it. There's at least four pairs of Josh's trainers. How he has so many pairs I'll never know. There's books, paper, Lego, hair clips, socks - so many socks - one of Pete's jumpers, a new toothbrush still in its little box, a packet of chewing gum, the box but not the DVD of the film, Love Actually, and two hair brushes. I do try to clean this up once a week, but much like the Pacific Rubbish Island I read about in the paper last week, it just keeps growing.

We reach the landing at the top of the stairs and stand outside the bathroom door.

'Dad, we need to brush our teeth,' says Alice.

'Coming,' says Pete casually from the other side of the door.

I still have no idea what he's been doing in there for the last thirty minutes. He knows we have to leave for school. After a moment, the lock on the door clicks then the door opens and out walks Pete ever so calmly. As if he has all the time in the world. As if we're all on fucking holiday or something.

'Finally,' I say. 'What the hell have you been doing in there for so long?'

'Relax. Just getting ready for work,' says Pete, before he walks off towards our bedroom.

'Right you three, get your teeth brushed, I'll see you at the front door in two minutes,' I say to the kids, before I follow Pete into our bedroom.

We live in a four-bedroom house in Wandsworth, south London. There's two bedrooms and the family bathroom on this floor. The loft was converted into two smaller rooms before we bought the house three years ago. Our bedroom is at the front and although it's a good size, it never feels big enough for the both of us. There's a built-in wardrobe and we have a chest of drawers for underwear and so on, but there's still clothes lying on the floor and dozens of books stacked precariously next to my nightstand. When I walk in, Pete's standing in front of the full-length mirror, putting his tie on. He's dressed in his grey suit. It's early in the morning and we're leaving in a minute, so I don't want to pick an argument, but I can't help myself. All the memories and hateful comments from the other night are still churning inside my mind, maturing and festering, creating a permanent state of being I might never recover from.

'You know we have to leave for school,' I say, rifling through the wardrobe for something to wear that doesn't say, sloppy mum just out of bed, for the school drop off.

You'd be amazed how many of them look like they're off to London Fashion Week at half-past-seven in the morning. I don't know where they get the time. They must get up at four o'clock in the morning just to put on their makeup.

'And I have to leave for work.'

'Maybe don't be in there for an hour next time,' I say, realising how my voice sounds. Cold and bitter. Just like my mother's when she used to argue with my father. When she could still talk, before the Huntington's took that away.

'It wasn't an hour,' says Pete, finally getting the tie straight and looking at himself.

Peter Willis, forty-two, and still reasonably handsome. He's kept himself in good shape, mainly from playing squash with work colleagues, which is why he's late home so often, and unlike me, who's had three kids, he's got a flat tummy and a bum I'd die for. His is tight and toned, while mine seems to have given up all hope of keeping it together and has decided to go into full-scale flop mode. I don't understand. I'm only forty, surely this is too young for my body to give up on me. Pete's a solicitor and his office is only a twenty-minute walk away. This is one of the reasons why we moved house. That and the schools are better and we could just about afford it. Our old house was smaller, only had three bedrooms, and the schools were a bit more terrifying. But I can't help but feel as though we were happier there. Life seemed better then. Maybe because the kids were younger or we were younger or perhaps because Mum wasn't so poorly, but now it feels as though everything is just a bit depressing. I feel like life is full of these precious moments, these little lights, and I'm trying to hold onto them, but I can't and more and more of them are slipping away, lost forever, the lights going out one by one.

I finally find a cardigan that doesn't look too bad. It's grey and long and covers up my flabby arse. One minute until we're due to leave. I can hear the kids arguing in the bathroom. No doubt Josh is doing his best to annoy Alice, while Daisy is probably staring at something in the garden or singing a song in her head.

'Right, that's me, I'm off,' says Pete, grabbing his brown leather satchel from the bed.

Mornings are always a battleground in the house and I'm at the frontline, rallying the troops, feeding them, keeping up morale and doing my best to keep us on time. Pete is the general, miles behind the frontline, drinking whisky in his suit, keeping out of the way, keeping himself clean. He's shaved, his hair is done, and he's wearing the suit I had dry cleaned last week. He looks like he doesn't have a care in the world.

'Have a good day,' I say somewhat sarcastically, then I hear Alice.

'You're such a stupid little kid,' she yells.

'Whatever,' says Josh.

'Bye,' says Pete.

Pete walks out, giving me the briefest peck on the cheek, without an 'I love you'. He walks past the bathroom where the kids are fighting and says goodbye to them. He doesn't tell them to stop arguing or be good because that would mean him being an involved parent. He leaves that sort of thing to me.

'Right, let's go, now!' I say. 'Everyone in the car.'

The kids bundle out of the bathroom and down the stairs, past Rubbish Island, grabbing coats, bags, and shoes. I see the back of Pete walking out of the door then Josh hits Alice and Alice punches Josh and everyone is complaining and all I want to do is get them to school, drop them off, and have a moment to sit in peace and quiet. I want my husband gone and my children gone so I can be on my own because that's all I crave these days - silence.

'Bye, be good, love you,' I say to Josh and Daisy outside the school gates. 'Have a good day. Be good. See you later. Love you. Love you.'

They barely acknowledge me. I've already dropped Alice off near her school - not at school because that would be like so embarrassing - and finally after another morning from hell, I'm alone.

Back in the car, I let my head fall onto the steering wheel and I take a deep breath. I feel so guilty because I spend the morning shouting at the kids, corralling them like cattle, but once they're gone I feel awful. Why aren't our mornings more peaceful? Why aren't we sitting around the table eating breakfast together like a normal, happy family? Orange juice, porridge, freshly made pancakes, bacon, eggs, and a selection of fruit. Am I a terrible mother? It's the same guilt I used to feel when they were younger and at home, before school took them all away. The feeling of being with them all day and the guilt of looking forward to that moment when they were all in bed and I could sink into the sofa, a glass of wine in my hand, and watch television. What's that saying about being a parent? 'The days are long but the years are short'. It's so true and so many days seemed to go on forever with games, crafts, temper tantrums, just trying to survive until the end of the day, but now it feels as though the years are flying by and I'm missing out on everything.

I need to get home, but I can barely face that either because I have to clean up the devastation from breakfast, have a go at Rubbish Island, hoover, clean, then start work. Oh yes, I have a job too. It's only part-time and I'm working from home today, but I'm still at the publishers I worked for before we had kids. What was once my dream job has now become, for the most part, a bit of a headache. But at least it gives me an excuse to spend some time on my own, lost to another world. A reason not to have a go at the stairs. Because something else beyond this house, beyond this tiny bubble, matters.

I start driving towards home. It's just over a mile, but takes nearly twenty minutes. I think about riding bikes, but the image of my children being run over by a lorry fills my mind with dread so we don't do it. We could walk, but we're never ready on time and I'm sure the children would complain anyway.

I'm almost home when traffic comes to a standstill. I don't know what's going on, but there's horns being beeped and I hear the familiar sound of a siren. I have the radio on and I'm listening to Chris Evans on Radio 2. We've stopped and I'm surrounded by traffic. And sitting here I have a moment when I feel so claustrophobic that I think about getting out of the car. Instead I wind down the window and take a huge gulp of air. What's happening to me? Is this a panic attack? And this is when I realise that I'm literally and figuratively stuck, not just now, in this car, but in my life, and I'm terrified because what can you do when you're stuck? You can't go on feeling that way. Something has to give and that's why I'm scared because I know it's coming. My breaking point. All I can do is sit here and wait for it. Wait for the moment when something cracks and breaks because it's true, you can't stay stuck forever. I think back to when the kids were little and how much I loved them and how much I still love them, and I know I must keep going, keep pretending it's all fine because what other choice is there? It's just a bad day. Mondays, right? It will be OK. It will get better. I'll survive because that's something else children give you; the desire to fight. To be a fighter.

Two

North London, 1996

For the last two years of university I've lived in a shared house in Wood Green. It's your typical student digs; three small bedrooms, badly decorated, peeling wallpaper, always unwashed mugs on the coffee table, each with a puddle of cold tea at the bottom and an ashtray full of Marlboro Lights. The first two years of university have flown by and it's just after Christmas in our third and final year, which means we only have one term left before we're out in the real world. Before we have to find somewhere new to live, start careers, wear professional clothes, or in the case of my housemate, Aimee, go travelling for the year (not jealous at all). I'm studying English Literature and I want to work in publishing. I'm young, ambitious, and ready to tackle the world. I'm excited if not absolutely terrified at the prospect of becoming a proper adult.

'Right, time to rumble,' says Lauren, tall, blonde, from Manchester, and my best mate at college. 'Down this first.'

She hands me a shot glass full of something blue. It looks toxic.

'What is it?'

'Doesn't matter what it is, Rozza, just down it,' says Lauren and so I do.

It's horrid and burns my throat as it goes down,

causing me to shake my head in disgust.

'That was foul.'

'But it gets the job done,' says Lauren, lighting up a cigarette.

Lauren and I are off on a night out. Aimee's staying at home sick with a cold. She's in bed drinking mug after mug of Lemsip, watching her small portable television, wrapped in her duvet, a small hill of tissues littering her nightstand. So it's just Lauren and I, off to the student union for a drink, a dance, and a bit of fun. There won't be many more nights like this before graduation so I'm determined to enjoy it while I can. Lauren wants to be an estate agent when she graduates because she craves money and knows she can sell anything. She has the gift of the gab and an amazing pair of breasts. Her theory is that if one doesn't work the other inevitably will. You can't argue with logic like that.

We take the bus from our house in Wood Green to the university campus in Cockfosters. We have a bottle of wine on the way and smoke our cigarettes without a care in the world. It's cold outside, but warm as we walk giggling into the union building.

'Well this is shit,' says Lauren, looking around at an almost empty bar.

'It's still early.'

It's only eight o'clock, but it's supposed to be the big Friday night out on campus.

'Remember when we were first years? This place was packed every night of the week. These losers should be ashamed of themselves,' says Lauren, taking off her coat.

Lauren orders a couple of drinks and we sit down at a small table and wait for the night to kick off. The night's advertised as Friday Night Fever! One pound pints all night, one pound shots after eleven, and DJ Fuzzy will play all the hits until two o'clock in the morning. DJ Fuzzy is already in the corner playing Supersonic by Oasis, and the beer's cheap, but apart from us and a few other younger looking first and second years, it's dead. It isn't looking good for a big night out to remember. When we used to come here during our first year, a big group of us would party until two o'clock every Friday night, before bundling back to someone's halls of residence for the after party that would last until four or five in the morning. Joints would get passed around and we'd solve the problems of the world, while feasting on cheese toasties and crisps. It was only two years before, but already feels like a different lifetime.

'Maybe we should go somewhere else,' says Lauren. 'We could jump on the tube and be in central London in half an hour. I think there's a Jungle night at Bagley's.'

This is typical Lauren. She's so impatient. The first time I met her was during Fresher's Week and she had me drunk by five o'clock because she couldn't wait to get started. We were at the union bar by midday and home before seven because we were both slaughtered. After that we were given the nickname, The Lightweight Twins, for the rest of the year.

'Let's give it some time. It will warm up. Besides, DJ Fuzzy is giving you the eye.'

'Oh, shut up,' says Lauren with a smile, before she looks across and realises that DJ Fuzzy is definitely interested. 'S'pose we could give it a bit longer.'

'I'll get in another round.'

I'm not really dressed for a big night out because I

knew we were just coming to the union. I have on a pair of jeans, boots, and a nice enough top, but compared to Lauren, who won't leave the house without a full face of makeup, hair done perfectly, and preferably in an outfit that shows off far too much breast and a lot of leg, I look a bit dowdy. But this is me. I'm the girl who could be beautiful if only she 'made the effort' - that lovely two-faced compliment. I'm sure this comes from my mother who never wore makeup and told me from a young age that it didn't matter what was on the outside, but what was on the inside that counted. In contrast, Lauren grew up with a hairdresser for a mother who had her wearing 'lippy' from the age of five and made her believe that if she didn't look her best, no man would ever want her. Lauren's father left when she was young and her mother remarried twice afterwards.

Since breaking up with Alex before Christmas, I've decided I want to spend the next few years focused on my career. I have to otherwise I won't make it. I have big dreams and they don't involve a man. This is the time of my life when I need to be independent. I want to work hard, travel, and find my way in the world. I have dreams of becoming an editor at one of the big London publishing houses. I imagine a life of book launches, international travel, and important lunch meetings at expensive restaurants.

The night eventually gets going after ten o'clock, as flocks of first and second years finally begin to show up. Lauren's already pretty drunk by this point and on the dance floor making an exhibition of herself to Pulp's Common People. There's nothing quiet or dignified about Lauren. I think it was this quality that drew me to her in the first place. She's like nothing I've ever known. My own family are sort of standard issue English. Often quiet, reserved, stoic, strong, and full of self-imposed laws of behaviour that require them to get drunk before they do anything silly. From the moment I met Lauren, I was in awe of her self-confidence. Although as I've got to know her, I've realised the self-confidence is just her way of coping with the world. A mask born out of a need to show the world what she wants them to see rather than what she actually is. Inside she's far softer and like most of us, I think she just craves someone to love her.

'I'm going to talk to DJ Fuzzy, he's definitely giving me the come on,' says Lauren into my ear. 'See you in a bit.'

'I'll be at the bar,' I say as Lauren walks off towards the DJ booth.

I'm standing at the bar I've stood at so many times before. So many nights I ended up here drunk with friends, smoking, talking, and kissing boys. I met Alex here. We danced to a Smiths song and he kissed me at midnight, then we went back to his room, had sex and stayed up talking until the early hours of the morning. Alex and I went out for just over a year before things started to fall apart. We had that immediate spark, but eventually all the problems and differences started to take their toll. He changed. He became suspicious, paranoid, and slowly I started to resent him. He wasn't a bad person, he just didn't know how to love me. Eventually he became self-destructive and I knew we were over. That was two months ago and I'm finally in a good place again. Ready for whatever's next.

'Buy you a drink?' says a voice from behind me.

I turn around and this is when I see him for the first time. Peter Willis. Tall, a mop of floppy brown hair, an overly handsome, boyish face, and judging by the clothes, obviously a bit posh. You don't dress in boat shoes, a plain white Oxford shirt, and a corduroy jacket unless you've been to public school. Not in the nineties anyway. Most of the boys I dated and kissed were indie boys, all Beatles haircuts, checked shirts, Adidas trainers, and attitude.

'They're only a pound a pint,' I say rather nonchalantly. 'Hardly a big romantic gesture.'

'Two pints and a packet of crisps, my final offer.'

'Fine, but only if they have prawn cocktail.'

'Really?' says the boy. 'Prawn cocktail?'

'What can I say, I'm a classy girl,' I say and he laughs.

'It's a deal. I'm Peter, but my friends call me Pete.'

'Peter it is then. I'm Rosie.'

We shake hands in that way that English people do at the beginning of the evening, before Peter raises his hand to the barman and orders us both a pint of beer and me a packet of prawn cocktail crisps. I've already had three pints and before Peter turned up, I was considering having a couple of gin and tonics before calling it a night. But there's something about him. Something different, more grown up than other boys I've been with and I'm intrigued. I've never been approached by someone like him before.

'Cheers,' says Peter, clinking his glass against mine.

'Cheers.'

I look across for Lauren and see her talking to DJ Fuzzy. She's smiling and he's leering at her boobs. I have the feeling I might be going home alone.

'Go on then, tell me your vitals,' says Peter. 'Year,

subject of study. Let's get that out of the way first before we move on to the interesting stuff.'

'Third year. English Literature. You?'

'Fourth year. Law.'

'Law, very fancy.'

'Not really. Just a lot of hard work,' says Peter in his oh so posh voice. It's nice though. Strong, soothing, and for the first time since Alex, it makes me feel excited about the idea of someone new in my life. If only for a night.

'Let me guess, your father was a lawyer, his father was a lawyer, you've got a brother and he's already a lawyer. It's just something the men in your family do. Am I right?'

'Spot on, although no brother,' says Peter with a dangerously sexy smile. 'Let me guess: You're a writer or want to be a writer. You may or may not go travelling after university, you haven't decided yet. You'll probably get a job in either publishing or advertising, but something that lets you be creative because you can't compromise your soul for a career. How am I doing?'

'Not bad, although it's definitely publishing and I'm not going travelling yet. One day.'

'Sounds like you've got it all figured out.'

'You too,' I say, then we look at each other and in this moment, I know something is going to happen. We have the spark, the magic you feel when you meet someone special. He isn't my usual sort, who are usually a bit rougher, have lofty bohemian ideals, smoke cigarettes, and play guitar. Peter Willis is clean cut and sensible and has a career plan at the age of twenty-two. He knows who he is and is comfortable in his skin.

We sit at the bar for the rest of the evening talking,

and trading jokes and barbs about each other. Peter tells me about his life growing up in Oxford, going to public school, the rowing years, and what his plans are for the future. He already has a job lined up in London - a friend of his father's has a firm in south London. He still has lots of studying to do before he can call himself a proper lawyer, but he wants it. He craves security and money and the comfort it brings. His parents have had a long, happy marriage, and Peter wants the same. It might not be the most exciting thing in the world, but it's real and in the two hours we sit there talking, I start to realise that perhaps our dreams can coexist side by side.

For a long time, and maybe it's a symptom of my own upbringing, my friends and school, I thought I wanted a certain sort of life. Unpredictable, exciting, creative, bohemian, full of men who drank too much and caused me pain, but in a romantic way. I suppose it's the life I grew up reading about in novels; great men, full of pain and misery, but beautiful and brilliant. I thought it was the sort of girl I was. I only seemed to attract those sorts of boys. Alex was one of them. He sang in a band, drank too much, smoked too much, took far too many drugs, but he was talented and he could sing and play guitar. He looked a bit like Damon Albarn from Blur. I'd go and see his band play and he'd always search me out in the crowd and say something like, 'This one's for you, baby,' before launching into a song and I thought I was so lucky. The girlfriend of the hot lead singer. The thing is, those sorts of boys don't grow up. Alex is still the same, still searching for the dream. I saw him recently, drunk outside a pub, trying to get into the knickers of a young girl, telling her all about the band and how they'd been spotted. About how they were going to be the next big thing. He hasn't changed. His life is stuck in the same place, while mine is moving on.

Peter is already grown up at twenty-two. He isn't cool, but in a way, he's exactly what I need. He has a plan, knows what he wants and can give me everything I want too. As we stand at the bar, I know I want to go home with him. I also know that if I do, it won't be just a one night stand. It will be something bigger, something more, and although I'm not ready for a relationship or a new man in my life, there's something about Peter that makes me want to give him a chance. At least with him, I know it won't end up with him shouting at me across a pub, calling me a 'fucking slut' then turning up in the morning, still drunk, trying to apologise through my bedroom window.

'Are you sure about this?' says Peter outside the union. 'No pressure.'

Lauren told me she's going home with DJ Fuzzy, who apparently has a two bedroom flat in Enfield. I look at Peter, at his clean-shaven face with the blue eyes and floppy hair. I reach up and place my hand on his cheek.

'I'm sure,' I say and we kiss for the first time.

Our mouths taste of alcohol and mine of cigarettes, but it feels natural. He's a surprisingly good kisser. I always imagined those boys from public schools, the ones in the polo shirts with the turned-up collars, would be terrible kissers. It's all show with the; they aren't real men. They didn't grow up drinking cider on children's swings in parks full of broken glass, telling stories of girls they'd snogged the night before. But Peter knows how to kiss and we don't stop all the way back to his place.

We fall into his bed giggling, with Peter telling me to be quiet otherwise we'll wake his housemates. His room, unlike mine, has a normality about it. There are no band posters Blu-Tacked to the walls. No IKEA bookshelf half falling over with the weight of second-hand paperbacks or clothes all over the floor waiting to be washed, ironed, or worn again. This is clean and tidy. The furniture is solid and has a whiff of antique shop about it. There's a rug covering the grotty carpet, and the only pictures on the walls are framed family photos. Peter Willis isn't like other boys I've been with because he isn't a boy, he's a man and suddenly being with him, I feel like a woman for the first time in my life.

'That was incredible,' says Peter.

'It was,' I say, rolling off him. The smell of our bodies together, sweaty and alive, tickles my nostrils.

He gets up and walks off to the corner of the room, where he takes off the condom, ties a quick knot in the top, and puts it in the bin, before he comes back to bed, wrapping the duvet around us to keep out the cold. Student houses are never the warmest of places.

I cuddle into him, smelling the faint waft of the aftershave that still clings to him. His body is lean but muscular. His broad shoulders - the product of years of rowing – are hairless, and the sort of white that looks as though it's never seen the sun. There's something comforting about nestling into him in the dark of his room.

'What now?' he says after a few quiet moments.

It's almost two o'clock in the morning.

'Sleep?'

'I meant, you know, in the morning. After.'

'I usually have a cup of coffee, some toast if you have it.'

'No, no, I meant…' says Peter, sounding for the first time, slightly unsure of himself.

'It's OK, I know what you meant,' I say. He reaches his arm around my shoulder sliding a hand down over my breast. I twist my leg around his, pulling him closer to me. 'Can we just lie here and forget about tomorrow?' Forget about the world?'

'Sounds good to me. It's just, I wanted to say that I really like you. I'm not a one night stand sort of bloke. I don't want you to think…'

'It's OK, Pete, I like you too.'

'That's good then.'

'Yes, it is.'

'Do you mind if I play some music while we go to sleep?'

'No, I always do.'

'One moment,' says Pete, as he gets up and walks across to his CD player. He fiddles around for a moment before he returns to bed, his body immediately cuddling against mine again. Crowded House start playing quietly. Alex would never have listened to this. It would have been Oasis, The Jam, or maybe The Stone Roses.

'Good choice,' I say as Fall at Your Feet floats across the room, soft, romantic, and beautiful.

We lie in the darkness in his house in Palmers Green, and we fall asleep. Our bodies as one, comfortable, happy, and I know as I close my eyes that Pete and I will be having breakfast together in the morning and maybe for a long time to come. It's that sort of night. The sort of night that changes everything.

Three

One of the wonderful things about having children is watching them grow up. It's also one of the saddest and most difficult to accept. When they're babies and toddlers you applaud every achievement, every new milestone. First steps, first words, every new food they manage to keep down, every time they learn something new or say their name becomes like the opening ceremony of the Olympic Games. It's fills you with such pride and joy that any retelling of it will always sound woefully inadequate compared to the event itself. Growing up we want our children to develop, to learn, to adapt and become little people who can play independently, read books, and write words on their own. We spend our life making sure they're on track for school, that they aren't behind the other children - and little Jasper from next door who's already reading at year two level and he's only five. It consumes us because we can't stand the idea of our children not being as good as the others because we love them so much. Then one day we realise that those little children have grown up, changed beyond all recognition, and we have no idea who they are anymore. If you aren't careful, you can wake up and find yourself living in a house full of strangers.

'Come on, who fancies going somewhere? It's a lovely day outside,' I say enthusiastically.

It's Saturday morning, the sun is shining, and we're

sitting inside watching television, playing on our phones, while outside London is bristling with life. There's so much we could be doing, but instead everyone is still in their pyjamas, the blinds are closed, and no one is saying a word. There's a musty smell in the room that might be one of Josh's old farts lingering in the air, but no one seems to notice.

'Nah,' says Alice.

'Mmmph,' says Josh, who's playing FIFA on his handheld device.

Nothing from Daisy, who's too busy watching television. Pete is sitting next to her, staring at his phone.

'Pete!'

'Yes, sorry?'

'Let's do something. It's a beautiful day outside.'

Pete takes a cursory glance towards the blinds and shrugs his shoulders.

'Please,' I say, looking at him hopefully.

He seems to realise that this means something to me and turns his phone off.

'Right, kids, come on. Mummy's right, we should do something,' says Pete, standing up and turning the television off.

'I was watching that,' says Daisy scornfully.

'We're going out,' says Pete.

Alice and Josh huff loudly, Daisy tuts, and Pete looks towards me.

'Thank you,' I say.

'So, what boring place are we going to?' says Alice grumpily.

Everyone looks at me expectantly. This should be

easy. We live in London. There's nowhere in the world like it. The mix of the old and new, the beauty of the architecture, the free museums, the Southbank, the shopping, the markets, the restaurants, there's a million things to do in London on a lovely Saturday in October, but faced with the accusatory stares of my family, I can't think of one.

A few years ago, I started compiling a list of places I wanted to visit with the kids before they got too old. Because there's a timeframe for so many things and one of the hardest things about being a parent is you never know when your time is up. You think you have time to take your kids to the Tower of London and have a good time. You think you have time to spend the day with them without one of them yelling at you and calling it 'the worst, most boring day ever!' Then one day you realise the day to do those things is already gone. The time for all the dreams you had of perfect family days is over and it's never coming back. It's why days like today are so important because the kids will never be this exact age again. They can be annoying and difficult and so very grumpy, but I love them and I want to spend time with them before it's too late. Before they don't want to spend time with me.

'Well, we could…' I start to say, playing through a hundred scenarios in my mind. The British Museum - Alice would hate it and Josh would probably get lost pretending he's Indiana Jones. The National Gallery - Alice and Josh would hate it and Daisy would wander off distracted by a Van Gogh, never to be seen again. A walk along the Southbank - 'We don't want to walk. Walking's boring'. A boat trip to Greenwich - Daisy would vomit because she gets travel sickness, Josh would get in trouble for doing something dangerous at sea, and Alice would think it's a waste of time and spend the day listening to music on her phone.

'Oh God, she has no idea, sit down everyone,' says Alice belligerently.

'I have ideas,' I say, desperately looking at Pete for help.

'Maybe...' says Pete, then he smiles at me. 'How about we go and see a show?'

I look around the room and suddenly all the kids look enthused. Alice is doing her best to look ambivalent and cool, but I can tell she's excited. Her eyes give her away. Even Josh looks up from FIFA with a degree of interest.

'Yes! That sounds awesome!' says Daisy. 'Please can we see Matilda? Milly saw it last week and said it was amazing. Amazing! Please! Please! Please!'

'We'll see,' I say with a smile. 'OK, everyone get ready.'

'Yes!' says Daisy, running out of the room.

Josh follows Daisy and then Alice, who smiles at me as she walks past. It's a bloody miracle. When the children are gone, I look at Pete.

'Good choice.'

'Who doesn't love the theatre?' says Pete earnestly.

For a moment, all my annoyance and anger at him subsides and I see my husband again. The man I love. The man who wooed me into bed the first night I met him. I see the wonderful man I promised to spend the rest of my life with and I want to hug him, kiss him, and hold his hand when we walk down the street. Today is going to be a good day and I need this. I smile at Pete and he smiles back. We need this.

'I'd better get ready too,' says Pete gingerly, walking past me. I hear him skip up the stairs behind the kids.

I go into the kitchen and tidy up breakfast while everyone else gets ready and I'm excited. This is something that happens less and less the older you get. Genuine excitement. When I was younger excitement seemed to be something that happened daily. Excitement - or at least the idea of it - was never far away. There was always something to be excited about, but now weeks and sometimes months can slip by without the glimmer of it touching my life. But today it is. I'm going to get dressed up. Maybe I'll wear the new jeans I bought last week but have been too afraid to wear because they're a bit tight. We'll probably eat at a nice restaurant and we'll be out there, in London, like the sort of family I always imagined we might be - the best version of us. Perhaps we'll take a stroll by the Thames, holding hands, the kids getting along. Maybe today will make up for a truly awful month. Maybe Alice will feel something like love towards me, and Pete and I will start the rebuilding process, and who knows, maybe we'll even have sex tonight. As I pile dirty plates into the dishwasher and pop knives, forks, and spoons next to them, I'm smiling because for the first time in a while, I'm feeling optimistic.

I slam the front door shut behind me and all I want to do is breakdown and cry. I've been holding myself together the whole way home. Pete walks off towards the kitchen mumbling something about a glass of wine. The kids, probably sensing what's coming, are already heading upstairs to their bedrooms in a heavy silence. I hang my coat up in the hallway and take a deep breath. I don't want to cry, but I can't help myself. A tear leaks out and I quickly brush it away before I follow Pete into the kitchen.

I'm shaking with anger and annoyance as I walk into our kitchen. The first part of the house we changed when we bought it because the old kitchen needed expanding and updating. It had old wooden cabinets from the seventies and the floor was this horrid orange tile so we had to change it. We ended up ripping the whole thing out and starting from scratch. We added a small extension, put in new floors, new cabinets, appliances, and a nice island with a sink. It was our dream kitchen and we even managed to sneak in a built-in wine rack and this is where I find Pete. He's taking out a bottle and putting it on the side.

The day started off so well. We left the house in high spirits and headed off towards the theatre. Pete and I were laughing and joking and the kids were joining in. We decided to take the bus and it was a gorgeous morning as we drove over Vauxhall Bridge towards Trafalgar Square. We were sitting up top and I remember thinking it was the first time we'd all been on a bus together for years. The kids were talking - and not on their phones or arguing - and Pete and I were sitting together looking out across London. Josh and Daisy were sitting at the front and it reminded me of when they were little and loved to pretend they were driving.

We walked from Trafalgar Square with brief stops to enjoy the views and take in the crowds. We live so close to all of this, but rarely take advantage of it. I felt like a bit of a tourist in my own town. We walked to the Cambridge

Theatre through the back streets of Covent Garden. Pete and I bought a coffee and the kids got hot chocolate. Then we reached the theatre and this is where it started to go wrong. They had no tickets left for the matinee performance and we couldn't wait around for the evening so Daisy threw a fit in protest.

'It's not fair,' she demanded, stomping her feet on the ground.

'It's OK, we'll get tickets for another day,' I said calmly. 'How about we see another show today?'

'But I don't want to see another show,' she protested. 'I want to see Matilda.'

'Come on, Daisy,' said Pete. 'Don't be like that.'

'Here we go,' said Alice, turning away, reaching for her phone.

I looked down at Daisy and I could see what was about to happen. She was on the precipice and I knew she needed my help. Patience. I had to be calm and patient. She was annoyed, but with some carefully chosen words I could save the day. I looked down at her face and I felt sorry for her. I always did until the tantrums became too much and I wanted to put her in her bedroom and leave her there, but I feel awful because I know she can't help it. She doesn't want to have tantrums any more than we want to deal with them. It's just a part of her she hopefully grows out of sooner rather than later.

'Listen, what about this,' I said, kneeling so we were face to face. I read about this in a book. It makes me less threatening. 'What if we go inside and book our tickets for next weekend, right now? That way we'll have to come back. How about that?'

I could see she was thinking about it. Her adorable little face screwed up in deep thought. She has Pete's blue eyes, sparkling, big, always glistening and looking at the world with a curiosity I don't see as much in Alice or Josh. She's unique and beautiful and I'm hoping she smiles and says yes. I need her to keep it together. Today of all days.

'No,' she said, her face frowning deeper and those eyes, those wonderful blue eyes, looked beyond me and into the distance. 'I want to see it now, not next stupid week.'

My heart sank in my chest.

'Right, that's it no more of this nonsense young lady,' said Pete, stepping in and doing it 'his way'. The way that never worked, but which he insisted was the way children like her needed to be treated. 'Let's get going. Charlie and Chocolate Factory it is. Come on everyone.'

But Daisy didn't move. She sat down on the pavement, legs and arms crossed, her face twisted into a deep, defiant frown. She wasn't going anywhere without a fight. Pete was a few feet away with Josh and Alice and I was about to tell them to go ahead when Pete decided to take it upon himself to deal with Daisy.

'Daisy get up now! You can't sit on the pavement like that,' said Pete, his voice getting louder and harsher. I could see Daisy's face harden.

'Pete, let me deal with this,' I said.

Pete looked at me and huffed in despair.

'She can't bloody well sit there on the pavement and do what she wants. She's a child.'

'I can deal with this. If you'd like to walk ahead with Alice and Josh,' I said, trying my best to keep it together. The job of the mother is to placate everyone. Patience.

'It's fucking ridiculous,' said Pete suddenly, drawing gasps of incredulity from the children. Even Alice, who I'm sure hears that word every day at school, looked shocked.

'Daddy said a bad word!' yelled Daisy, pointing at Pete.

'I just meant...' said Pete uncomfortably.

'A really bad word,' said Daisy, trying her best to annoy Pete as much as possible.

People were walking past us and around Daisy who was still sitting defiantly on the pavement. I looked at Pete and I could tell he was losing it. He doesn't deal well with Daisy. I don't know if it's his upbringing, being a man, or going to public school, but Pete's a bit old fashioned when it comes to parenting. He isn't as Draconian as his own father - children should be seen and not heard - but he expects them to behave and not cause a fuss.

'Right,' said Pete, walking towards Daisy. He bent down and despite Daisy's best efforts, he picked her up and swung her over his shoulder. 'Let's go.'

'Pete that isn't the way. Pete!' I yelled at him, but he wasn't listening. 'Pete!'

He was marching off down the street with Daisy kicking and screaming trying her best to get away.

'I hate you! I hate you! I hate you!' yelled Daisy, who had now completely lost it.

'So embarrassing,' said Alice, who was walking behind us with Josh.

'Pete!' I yelled again.

Pete stopped and put Daisy down. Daisy lashed out a foot and kicked Pete in the shins.

'I hate you, you stupid man!' yelled Daisy, tears

streaming down her face.

'Daisy, you can't do this,' I said, grabbing her and holding her in my arms. I sat down on the pavement and hugged her as tight as I could. At first she resisted, screaming and trying to break free, but eventually she gave in and let me hold her. Sometimes this worked and sometimes it didn't. Luckily today it did, but the damage was already done. By the time her body finally succumbed and went limp in my arms, the day was over. The moment was ruined. The joyous journey on the bus forgotten as we sat slumped on the train home, none of us talking, the tension simmering just below the surface.

'What's your problem?' I say to Pete in the kitchen.

He's pouring himself a glass of wine.

'My problem?' says Pete, mock laughing. 'This is my problem now, is it? You're the one who's home with her all the time. You're the one pandering to her and making this worse.'

'What did you say?' All my anger and frustration finally boiling over. 'I'm the only parent in this house, am I?'

'That's not what I said. We just always do it your way, but it doesn't work.'

'It does work when people don't start shouting at her and throwing her over their shoulder like a bloody caveman. She needs patience, Pete.'

'Patience. You've been saying that for years and nothing's changed. She needs proper help.'

'Our daughter doesn't need help. She just needs us to be on the same page,' I say and I believe it, I really do.

'Sorry I don't have enough patience for you. Sorry I'm not good enough for you.'

'Stop being so fucking selfish, Pete. This isn't about you, it's about our daughter.'

'Who needs help!' bellows Pete, before he takes a good gulp of wine. 'I have a friend at work. His wife's a psychiatrist,' says Pete quietly, looking across at me. 'She needs this, Rosie. We all do.'

It's ridiculous because a part of me knows that Pete is right and maybe it might help, but I can't let the idea go that she doesn't need help, but time and support. It's my little Daisy. My baby. I'm her mother. I'm the one who can help her. I'm all she needs and when it's just us she's fine. It's stubbornness, I know, but she's my child and she doesn't need to see a psychiatrist because she's just a child. She'll grow out of this and she'll be fine. I know she will.

'She doesn't need it, Pete. How many times - I can take care of her.'

'But don't you see? It isn't working and days like today prove it.'

'Fine, talk to your friend. Let's do it your way. Let's take our little baby girl to see a fucking shrink,' I yell, and I'm so angry. I don't even know who I'm most angry at. At Pete for ruining the day. At Daisy for being so demanding. At myself for not being a good enough mother. At Mum for dying in that awful fucking care home.

'Rosie,' says Pete, coming towards me, trying to put a hand on my arm, but I shrug him away.

'No, Pete...' I say, wiping the tears from my face. 'Just leave me alone.'

I storm out and upstairs. On the landing, Daisy is sitting against the wall reading a book. She sees the tears and the sadness on my face.

'Mummy,' she says, standing up. 'I'm sorry I ruined the day.'

'You didn't,' I say, scooping her up in my arms. She's almost too big now, but I hug her as tightly as I can.

'Snugs?' says Daisy, which makes me start crying again. It's the word Daisy and I use for cuddles. It's our special word.

Daisy and I go into my bedroom and fall onto the bed. I lie there and Daisy curls her little body into mine and I put my arms around her. She takes my hand and pulls it tighter around her chest. We lie together and I just want to fall asleep with my baby girl next to me. Instead my mind turns to my mother and then back to Daisy and if Pete's right. What if Daisy does need help? I don't want her to think there's anything wrong with her. I want to protect her. I want her to be happy. Eventually I do fall asleep. I close my eyes and Daisy is cuddled into me and we fall asleep together and I know she's alright. She's going to be fine. She just needs some patience and she'll be OK. I just wish I could say the same thing about my marriage.

Four

I'm picking Daisy and Josh up from school. Alice is getting the bus with friends so I walked instead of driving. I'm trying to make this part of my new routine. It will give us time together to talk without the distraction and stress of being stuck in traffic. This is going to be the new start I need. 'If you aren't happy then change,' my father always told me growing up. He isn't a big believer in complaining or whining. 'If you don't like something, Rosie, change it,' he used to say to me whenever I complained. I realised the other day I've become a moaner, someone who talks about change and being better, but doesn't do anything to make it happen. 'The worst sort of people,' Dad used to say and he was right. I'd become the worst sort of person. And so I'm changing. The stairs are clear of rubbish, the house is tidy, the lunches are made the night before to give us time together in the morning, and we're walking to school. It's also some much-needed exercise for me and my flabby bottom. I've dug myself into a rut and this is me trying my best to clamber out of it.

I'm a few minutes early so I'm loitering with the other parents in the playground. I've felt like a bit of an outsider since we moved schools. So many other mums seem to know each other and stand around talking and gossiping, while I'm all alone with only my phone for company. It's fine. It's not like I need or have the time for a group of new friends, but sometimes I feel like I should know at least one mum at school. It might come in useful.

'Bit scary, isn't it?' says a voice suddenly, catching me off-guard.

I turn around and that's when I see him just behind me. Tall, dark hair, early forties, and very handsome. He's wearing a navy jumper over a white shirt, jeans, a pair of brown brogues, and a black pea coat.

'Sorry, what's scary?'

'The pickup mums. I always feel as though everyone knows each other and I'm on the outside looking in.'

'Oh, right, yes, I was just thinking the same thing,' I say with a smile.

'Do you think it's because I'm a man?'

'Definitely not. There's a few other men here and they're talking to people.'

'Right so I'm just a social leper then?' says the man and I laugh. 'Good to know.'

I turn around not sure if he's going to continue the conversation or whether that's it. Just some polite chit-chat before the bell goes and the kids come running and screaming out into the playground.

'I'm Mark.'

'Rosie,' I say, and we shake hands. 'What do you have?'

'Sorry?'

'Kids? What flavour?'

'Oh, right. Chloe's eight and Dylan's six. You?'

'Josh is ten and Daisy's seven.'

He has big brown eyes and the most gorgeous smile. He has a bit of stubble and he's wearing a pair of black framed glasses.

'So just the two? Not just, I mean, two is definitely enough,' says Mark.

'One more at secondary school. Alice is fourteen. We went the whole hog with three.'

'I don't mean to sound like a flirty black cab driver, but you don't look old enough,' says Mark, and I'm sure I'm blushing slightly.

'You know what they say.'

'What's that?'

'Makeup can work magic,' I say and Mark laughs.

'So that's what I need, makeup, got it.'

There's a delicate pause and I want to keep the conversation going. Mark is easy to talk to and he seems nice. Handsome and nice and I haven't talked to anyone else all day. Unless you count the milkman, the checkout person at Waitrose, and the wrong number who rang me earlier. Hardly electric conversations.

'Wife not around today?' I say, and instantly realise how horribly sexist that sounds. 'Sorry, I meant I haven't seen you before that's all. Not that dads can't pick up their children because of course they can.'

'No, it's fine, I understand,' says Mark, his face changing slightly, softening, his eyes looking down at the ground for a moment. 'I'm a widower, actually. We just moved to the area.'

'That's awful. I'm so sorry.'

I don't know what else to say. What do you say? What's the polite way to say I'm so sorry, I can't imagine what you're going through without sounding insincere?

'Abi had stomach cancer. She fought it bravely, but it

got her in the end. It was two years ago, and we're doing alright. I mean we're, you know, getting by. We lived in Wood Green, but I got a new job and so here we are. New house, new school, fresh start.'

I don't know what else to say. My heart is breaking for him. And those poor children.

'Wood Green. I lived there at university. Maryland Road.'

'Oh right. I know it. I have friends there.'

'And what do you do? What's the new, exciting job?'

'Nothing that exciting I'm afraid. Accounting. The job that no one grows up wanting to do, but actually pays well and you're always in demand.'

'The sensible choice,' I say with a smile.

'Something like that.'

The bell goes and our little bubble bursts just like that. Teachers appear at the door and behind them a noisy rabble of children, all eager, excited to get out. Mark and I stand side by side waiting. I want to say something before we're done, but before I can Mark beats me to it.

'It was nice talking to you, Rosie. Maybe I'll see you tomorrow?'

'Yes, yes, I'll be here.'

'Tomorrow it is then,' says Mark, and I don't know why, but I feel all flighty and silly and - that word again - excited.

The teachers stand aside and suddenly there's children everywhere. I step forward slightly to try and get a glimpse of my two. Children are running past me into the arms of waiting parents and younger siblings. Teachers are shouting, 'no running' but no one seems to be paying attention.

Finally, I see Josh walking towards me, dragging his backpack on the ground like a toddler carrying a teddy bear, then I see Daisy sprinting towards me, a huge smile on her face. I sweep Daisy up and give her a kiss, before Josh walks into my arms and gives me a quick hug. He hasn't had a great day, I can see it on his face, and I make a note to talk to him about it on the way home.

Before long Daisy is going on about her day, gabbling away without giving me a second to respond, and Josh is still looking grumpy and annoyed. As we're walking out of the playground, I look around to see Mark. He's quite tall so I should be able to spot him. Eventually I see him amongst the crowd. He's holding a girl's hand on one side and a boy's hand on the other. He's leaning down talking to the girl and seeing him with them breaks my heart. He's all by himself, heartbroken and alone with those poor little kids who have no mother. It makes me even more determined to be happy again, to not feel stuck because I'm so lucky and I love my kids so much. And even Pete and I, despite our recent problems, have generally been good. We used to be happier when Pete worked less and I wasn't always so irritable. But when I see Mark it really does give me a shot in the arm. I'm so lucky and I should be more grateful.

I walk home with the kids telling me about their days. By the time we walk in the front door, Josh is fine and excited to play FIFA after doing his homework, Daisy is in a wonderful mood, and even Alice comes home reasonably happy and talks to me while I'm getting the dinner ready. It's all going so well and it's all because of Mark. Pete comes home early for once, we open a bottle of wine, and I feel better, but it isn't until I get ready for bed, tucking myself under the duvet that I realise how excited I am to see Mark again tomorrow and my mood changes because that isn't good. It's dangerous and silly and something that will bring nothing but heartache. I know it's just a frivolous crush and maybe because I'm bored at home, haven't had sex with Pete in *forever*, and Mark is handsome and I feel bad for him, so I tell myself to stop acting like a child and pull myself together. This is a new start, a fresh beginning, and we're going to be happy again. Just like the good old days. And not just me, but all the bodies in the house, curled up in their beds, dreaming of happy days and brighter futures.

Pete rolls across and wraps an arm around me as I'm going to sleep. For a moment, I think about having sex with him, but he whispers, 'goodnight', kisses me softly on the shoulder, then rolls away again. I could make it happen. I'm sure he wouldn't say no, but I'm too tired. It's been a long day and I've already done so much, sex will have to wait for another day. Instead I close my eyes and go to sleep.

Five

Wandsworth, London, 1998

Pete and I moved into our flat just over a year ago. I never imagined I'd be able to live in a place like this so early in my life, but with both of our jobs and Pete's family giving us a helping hand with the deposit, we're here. Every day I wake up, look out of the sash window in our bedroom and down at our shared garden and the lovely big tree beyond, and think about how lucky I am. Because I am. Incredibly lucky.

Our one bedroom flat is on the upper floor of a Victorian terrace in Wandsworth. It's bright, spacious, has a beautiful living room at the front, a modern kitchen, and the use of a shared garden with an area of grass that's perfect for summer barbecues. It's on a leafy street full of gorgeous brick terraces and there's a pub at the end of the road that does an amazing Sunday roast. It all feels so incredibly grown-up after living in student digs with Aimee and Lauren for two years when the nearest we got to maturity was when Aimee bought that vintage espresso machine from Portobello Road Market. Pete and I did a huge shop at IKEA and spent what seemed like an absolute fortune on furniture and other bits and pieces from various places. I bought one of those big round paper lamp shades for the living room and we got some framed artwork and two book cases for my paperbacks. Pete picked out four nice rugs to go down on the wooden floors. It feels like a proper home.

Pete goes off to work all week at his office, which is only a short bus ride away. He works long hours and is still studying so his life is a bit chaotic at the moment. I'm at a publishers near Kings Cross and I work long hours too, but nothing like Pete. After work, I often go for drinks with colleagues or with Lauren if she's around, which she isn't much these days, while the weekends are saved exclusively for Pete and me.

Today is Saturday and Pete's already up. I can hear the low mumblings of the radio in the kitchen. It's late August and already at nine in the morning it's lovely and warm. The sun is shining in through the window and bathing the room in a lovely yellow glow. I stretch up and out from underneath the duvet and sit up. I'm in just my underwear. I love our bedroom. It's cosy and warm and I managed to salvage a few of the posters from my student house which I've framed and hung on the wall. It's nice to have this beautiful house, but feeling that connection to my past is important too.

'Coffee?' says Pete, poking his head round the door.

I yawn and do another stretch before I pull the duvet back.

'How about you get back in here first,' I say with a smile.

Pete doesn't need another invitation before he's back in bed with me, touching my body, and rolling on top of me. This is our life and I love it. Looking back at the night I met him at the union bar, I knew he was special, and I knew we had something, but I could never have imagined this. This feels like somebody else's life. A life imagined rather than lived. The weekend before we took the Friday off and spent the weekend in Paris. We took the Eurostar from Waterloo, which was incredible, and gave us so much time to sightsee and spend time eating fabulous French food and making love in our hotel overlooking the Seine. It was a magical weekend wandering through art galleries, the picture postcard streets of Montmartre, and finally going up the Eiffel Tower, which I'd missed out on the last time I'd been on a school trip when I was sixteen.

My old university friend, Aimee, is back from her travels around the world, and it's given me plenty of food for thought. We met up in Covent Garden for drinks the other night and she told me all about it. From the islands of Thailand to living in Sydney then travelling the coast in a camper van. She hiked glaciers in New Zealand, walked the Inca Trail in South America, and drank cocktails on Copacabana Beach in Rio De Janeiro. She jumped out of a plane, swam with sea turtles, and climbed mountains. Maybe before we settle down and have kids, get a mortgage and all the rest of it, Pete and I could take a year off and travel the world together. It wouldn't interfere with our careers too much and we have no other responsibilities. I'm going to talk to him about it later. I think it's something we have to do otherwise I know we'll regret it. At least I know I will.

I'm so happy and I know Pete is too, but there's also a small part of me that wonders if we're going a bit fast. A tiny flicker of doubt. I'm still only twenty-three. There's so much time for settling down, isn't there? We have our twenties to get our careers sorted, travel, and have fun before we sink into the comfort of our thirties and think about becoming parents, moving out to the suburbs, and buying a Volvo.

'That was unexpected,' says Pete, lying next to me in bed.

'Isn't that always the best sex?'

'Definitely.'

'I heard rumours about a coffee?' I say with a smile. 'And maybe some toast?'

'At your service, madam,' says Pete, pretend-cocking a hat before he gets out of bed, puts his clothes back on, and heads into the kitchen. I need to take a shower before we decide what to do today. I fancy a walk by the Thames, followed by a pub lunch, and maybe I'll broach the topic of going travelling with Pete. Or at least plant the seed because that's how Pete is. You need to plant seeds and wait for them to grow because they will. Eventually they'll grow.

I'm still drying my hair with a towel as I walk into the living room where I find Pete sitting at our small table by the window, reading a newspaper and drinking coffee. There's a plate of toast opposite him and a cup of coffee for me. There's a half full cafetiere sitting in the middle of the table because we're the sort of young professionals who own a cafetiere.

'Breakfast is served,' says Pete.

I sit opposite him, and outside birds tweet from the trees and a family walks past, the kids on their bikes, and the dad walking a dog. The sky's a deep cerulean blue with not a cloud in sight and already I'm excited. After talking with Aimee and thinking about today, I'm almost overwhelmed by all the possibilities life has to offer. Nothing is off the table.

'I was thinking maybe a walk by the Thames, and a

pub lunch?' I say, taking a sip of coffee. 'We could pop into the Tate if you like or do a bit of shopping in Covent Garden afterwards.'

'Actually, I have plans,' says Pete, looking at me from over the top of his newspaper. It's the Telegraph. My father always read The Mirror or sometimes The Sun, but never a broadsheet.

'What plans?'

'Plans. For us,' says Pete, before he looks at his watch. 'It's almost time. Get that down you and get ready.'

'Ready for what?'

'Lauren will be here in twenty minutes and you're going on a sort of spa day thing. Massages, facials, general pampering.'

'What?' I say incredulously. 'It's not my birthday, what's going on?'

'Just get ready for a fab day,' says Pete with a surreptitious smile, before he gets up, puts his coffee mug in the sink, then wanders off to the bathroom.

I'm completely gobsmacked and I don't know what to think. A day with Lauren at a spa does sound incredible, but I know something else is going on. I drink my coffee and eat my toast before I get ready. Lauren turns up, acting equally as suspiciously as Pete, and we leave for our day out. Pete gives me a kiss at the front door, but won't tell me what's going on, so I leave with Lauren and head off for a day of pampering.

We return home late in the afternoon. We had a wonderful time. We talked like we haven't in such a long time. She's living in a shared house in Finsbury Park and she's in her words, 'absolutely killing it' as an estate agent.

She's only been in the job for just under a year and already has a new car. She also has a boyfriend too. Lauren spent lunch telling me how great Neil is and about the size of his penis. It's enormous apparently. I didn't really want to know this because if I do eventually meet him, it's going to be very difficult to think about anything else. Neil and his monster cock. Lauren's happy though and that's all that matters.

I open the front door to our flat and immediately hear voices. Lots of voices.

'There she is,' says my mother, standing in my living room. I'm shocked because all my family and Pete's family are here. I love our flat and it feels enormous when it's just the two of us, but filled with both of our families it suddenly feels very small.

'Mum, Dad, James, what are you doing here?'

'Surprise,' says Dad with a smile, walking over and giving me a kiss on the cheek.

'Rosie, you're back,' says Pete, walking into the room, carrying two glasses of champagne. He hands one to his mother and the other to me.

'What's going on?' I say to Pete, a bit worried.

'Just go with it,' says Pete, giving me a kiss. 'More champagne then we'll crack on.'

'Crack on with what?' I try and ask, but Pete's already walking away.

I look at Lauren for support, but she shrugs her shoulders and smiles. I take a sip of my champagne before I say hello to all of Pete's family and my brother James. It's strange being together like this. I've met his family and he's met mine, but this is the first time we've all been together under one roof. Pete's father is a little intimidating and despite being reasonably old, still has a physicality about him that's quite overpowering. He's deep in conversation with my father. Pete's sister, Rebecca, is only eighteen and completely gorgeous and lovely. She's off to university at St Andrew's this year to study Art History.

I'm confused as to why everyone is here and why no one is giving me an answer. Five minutes later and I have a glass of champagne in my hand, when I hear the sound of a glass being chinked with a small fork. I look across and see Pete standing at the front of the living room. It goes quiet and everyone looks towards him.

'May I have your attention please,' says Pete with a serious sort of smile. 'You're all probably wondering what you're doing here. I know Rosie is. The truth is you're here for a very important moment. An important day. Rosie, would you join me up here please.'

I walk up to Pete and still have no idea what's going on. I stand at the front of the room with Pete looking out at our two families.

'Rosie,' says Pete, turning and looking at me. 'From the day I met you at university, I had this feeling. A feeling my life wasn't ever going to be the same again. The feeling I'd met someone special. Someone who made me happy, who made me better, who changed the way I saw the world. From the moment 'I' and 'you' became 'we' and 'us', my life has been nothing short of perfect. Rosie, you make me so happy.'

I'm looking at Pete, at his handsome, boyish face, at his big, blue eyes, and the floppy brown hair, my Pete, and suddenly it hits me. He's proposing. He's going to ask for my hand in marriage. Here. Now. In our flat. In front of our families. He wants to spend the rest of his life with me. Us. Pete and Rosie. Husband and wife. And suddenly I don't know how I feel about it because I do love him so much, but I'm twenty-three and I'm thinking about travelling and having fun. He wants to get married and I don't know if I'm ready. Marriage. It isn't like we can't do those other things too because we can still travel if we get married and we can still have fun and nothing has to really change if we're engaged. People get engaged and stay engaged for years. It's just a word, a promise for the future, and I do love him so much and I'm so happy with him. Yet all I can think about at this moment is how right before I met him I was so intent on being single, on following my dreams, being independent, and how since that night it's all gone so fast. Is this what I want forever? Is Pete it? Is this the life I want?

Pete reaches into his pocket and pulls out a ring box then he's down on one knee. He's looking up at me and my family and his family are breaking down with the realisation of what's happening. I'm not looking at them, but I can hear them gasping and there's tears. I know exactly what they're thinking. These two young, successful, happy people are made for each other. They're a perfect match. And maybe we are. I'm looking at him, at his beautiful face - because it is beautiful, and I think about us having sex that morning and it was lovely. I love him with all my heart. But there's a glimmer of doubt. I'll never have another first date, first kiss, first awkward night in a new bed with a new man wondering if he's it. I'll never travel the world on my own like Aimee. Saying yes to this is saying no to so many other things.

'Rosie, my love, my wonderful, beautiful, perfect girlfriend. Will you do me the greatest honour in the world and be my wife?' says Pete, a huge smile on his face because he knows I'm going to say yes. There isn't a part of him that's even considered I might say no. That I might need a bit more time to figure my life out before this. He hasn't considered it because why should he? He's Peter Henry Willis and he's a real catch and he went to the sort of school where they drilled into him that he could have whatever he wanted in life. He's special, unique, gifted, talented, and if anything, I'm just a bit plain, a tad ordinary. Why would I say no to him? So when he looks up at me it isn't with worry or doubt, but with absolute certainty that I'm going to be his wife. I think of Aimee standing on the edge of a mountain looking down at Machu Picchu in Peru and lying on a beach in Thailand and I think of me there on my own. I think of me living in my own little flat. I think of me having the excitement and gut wrenching nervousness of going on a first date again.

I look out across the room and see my family. I look at my father. The man who's always been on my side, who's taken care of me, loved me, and given me everything. Dad. He smiles at me. I look at Mum, tears in her eyes, and I know this would make her so happy. Just the glimmer of hope that grandchildren are on the way and she's already starting to melt. I smile back then look down at Pete and at that gorgeous ring with the enormous diamond that must have cost a fortune. How can I say no to him here in front of our families? Because saying no isn't just saying no to marriage it's saying no to him. I'd be rejecting him and I know it would be the end of us. Maybe I'm not ready. Maybe I need more time. But it doesn't matter because I know what I have to say. What needs to be said.

'Yes, yes, of course I'll marry you,' I say, and the room claps and cheers as Pete puts the ring on my finger. As I agree to be his wife.

I look out at the room, tears in my eyes, and the first person I see is my father. He has tears in his eyes too and I want him to hold me the way he did when I was little. He's a big man my father, but when I was little, about seven, he seemed even bigger. He'd grab me and hold me and I'd wrap my arms around his neck and I never felt safer or happier than when I was with him. I need that now. I need to feel that feeling again to know everything is going to be alright. But then I look back at Pete and I know it's going to be fine. It's Pete. It's us. I love him and he loves me and as The Beatles once sang, love is all you need. Love is all you need.

Six

The smell hits you as soon as you walk into the building. I don't know what it is exactly. A mixture of bleach, air freshener, and sadness. Mum's in a care home for people with late stage Huntington's. The home has all sorts of people with varying degrees of different illnesses, but Mum's in a special unit just for people like her. There's five of them in total. Three men and two women. One of the men is only in his early thirties. It's such a terribly sad place. I visit her once a week. She can't talk, eat, walk, and I'm not even sure if she knows who I am anymore, but I need to visit her for my own sanity as much as hers.

Today I find her as I always do these days, lying in bed. She isn't my mother anymore and hasn't been for a very long time. My mother was a creative, exuberant, dark haired lady with a full figure and she was always cooking and entertaining my brother and me. She was wonderful, but this person lying so still in the bed, their body a carcass, their face gaunt, chiselled away by the disease, expressionless and fixed, isn't her. The short, thinning, greying hair that hasn't been cut or styled in years. I don't know who this poor woman is, but she isn't my mother. Yet I still love her. I hold her hand and talk to her without the suggestion of a response. Some days, occasionally, she'll look at me and I sense a flicker of something, but I know there's nothing there. Not really. My real mother is just alive in my memories now.

Perhaps the saddest thing in the room apart from Mum is the small collection of photos she has on the table next to her bed. When she first moved into the home she had a bit more of a semblance of who she was, and she could talk. They asked me to bring in some photos of family to keep those memories alive for as long as possible. It was supposed to help. I remember searching through her things, trying to find the best pictures I could and I ended up with the three that are sitting on her bedside table. There's the photo of Mum and Dad on their wedding day. It was a beautiful day, blue skies and sunshine, and there's Mum in her white wedding dress and Dad in his tight-fitting suit and that hair, so big and long compared to the man I know now. They're standing outside a church and there's confetti falling on them. They're smiling and they look so happy and in love. I was born two years after this photo, and my brother, James, was born three years after that. There's the photo of the four of us in Cornwall. It's summer and we're playing on the beach with buckets and spades and Mum and Dad are sitting in deckchairs squinting at the camera. Lastly, I chose the photo of Mum with her grandchildren. We took it just after Daisy was born. Alice was seven and Josh was three. James's only child, Lilly, was six and they're sitting together on Mum's sofa, smiling, and Alice is holding Daisy in her arms. It's a lovely photo and it always makes me sad because it was right before she started to get worse and we had to get help. She's gone downhill so quickly since that photo was taken. It's one of the last times I can remember life being vaguely normal.

I sit down in the chair next to her bed, reach across

and hold her hand. It's just bone now and the skin doesn't even feel like skin. It's more like a crisp autumnal leaf and it feels like I could easily break it if I squeezed too hard. When I hold her hand she doesn't move. Her eyes are open, but she isn't there, she's lost somewhere inside.

'Hello, Mum,' I say, hoping for one of the days when she looks at me. She doesn't. 'It's Wednesday and I'm busy as usual. The kids are at school. We've just started walking which is nice. We should have done it a lot sooner, but you know how it is. Remember when we were kids? We always walked to school. Rain, snow, sunshine, whatever the weather, we walked. We didn't have a choice, did we?'

I always talk to her. It feels silly sometimes because she never responds, but a part of me likes to believe she can hear me and that there's still a little bit of my mother in there somewhere. A few years ago, just before we moved her into the care home, she went through a phase of mental episodes. She would be fine one moment then the next she'd try and run away or attack one of us. I remember one day I ended up sitting on her because she kept trying to escape. Dad did his best, we all did, but it was too much and that's when we knew she had to go into a home. For her own safety as much as ours. It broke Dad's heart because he wanted to do it, he wanted to take care of her until the bitter end, but it was beyond him. It was beyond all of us. But looking at her now, lying limp and expressionless in bed, I think back and at least she had some life then. At least she felt something. It took all my strength to restrain her and stop her from getting away. Now she can't even get out of bed and that's so much worse.

'The kids are fine and send their love. Alice is typical

Alice, all attitude and huffing, but she's doing well at school and there are days when I think she might not completely hate me. She reminds me a lot of you actually, Mum. Josh is Josh, football crazy and his bedroom's still a pigsty. Dad would have gone crazy. Remember how he used to shout at James when his bedroom was a mess? Then there's Daisy. I do worry about her, Mum. I wish she'd stop having these moments and Pete doesn't know how to deal with her. It's driving a wedge between us. It's all we seem to do these days, argue about Daisy. That's when he's even home. I think he's spending more and more time away from us because it's just easier. Easier to be at work than home with his family. Sorry, Mum, you don't want to hear this, do you?'

I give her hand a small squeeze then reach for my bag. As always, I've brought a magazine to read to her. Mum loved a good magazine. She surprisingly couldn't get enough celebrity gossip. This was back in the days before the internet when the only gossip you got was from newspapers, magazines, or Teletext. Growing up there was always one of Dad's newspapers on the coffee table and a women's magazine for Mum. I used to love Smash Hits and James would read comics. Today I bring out a copy of Now magazine. It has all the salacious celebrity gossip. I suppose reading this makes me feel like a piece of her is still here and it's something we're doing together. I know it's silly, but it's all I have. I take a sip of the latte I bought at Costa on the way before I open the front cover and start reading.

I go through the usual celebrity news and show her some of the pictures before I start on the latest action from the soap operas. Mum used to watch EastEnders and Coronation Street. She watched Neighbours religiously and said she'd love to visit Australia one day. Unfortunately, she never got the chance. I spend about thirty minutes reading the magazine before I pack it away in my bag and get ready to leave. Dad usually comes after lunch and spends the afternoons with her. Occasionally he comes early and we overlap so we have time to catch up with a cup of tea and a biscuit.

'I should probably get going. I still have to tidy up breakfast and do some work before I pick up the kids from school. I also have a date of sorts. It isn't a date, obviously, but I'm meeting another parent for a coffee. He lost his wife to cancer and just moved to the area. I feel so bad for him. He has two kids without a mum. It's such a sad story. I wish you could meet him. I know you'd like him. Right, I'll pop in again next week. Love you, Mum.'

I lean across and give her a quick kiss on the forehead before I make my way past the girl on reception and outside again. I always have the same feeling when I leave the home. It's a mixture of relief and sadness and I think it's how I'm going to feel when Mum's finally gone. I'll be relieved because she isn't really here now anyway and has no quality of life, but also sad because it will mean she's gone forever. At least I won't have to come here anymore because every time I do, a small piece of me dies inside. It's a constant reminder of how fragile life is and how horribly it can end. The sad thing is that Mum isn't even the worst. I see some patients and my heart breaks. At least Mum just lies there now, while others are in tears, confused, angry, and alone. I take a deep breath and watch the world going about its business. It's the same outside as it is every day; busy, chaotic, people getting on with their lives, but inside the home my mother is lying in a different world, stuck in time, never to see any of this again and this thought makes me so incredibly sad.

It's a beautiful day as I walk to my car, feeling the sun on my face, and I think about Mark. After the first couple of days of seeing him at pickup time, he suggested meeting for a coffee and a chat and I couldn't say no. He doesn't know many people in the area and I felt bad for him. Although a small part of me can't stop thinking about how handsome he is, and despite the fact I'm not doing anything wrong, I haven't told Pete about it. I'm keeping Mark to myself and I know that part may be wrong, but after seeing Mum today, the thought of seeing him gives me a little bit of hope. Hope for what, I don't know and I don't know what I expect to happen either, but it's something I know I want.

I get in the car and turn the radio on and as if by some sort of cosmic twist of fate, the Donovan song, Catch the Wind, comes on - Mum's favourite song - and I smile to myself, while holding back the familiar feeling of tears.

Seven

Mark's already sitting down drinking a coffee when I walk into Caffe Nero. My stomach's a nervous knot of butterflies and I'm barely keeping myself together. I can't believe I'm meeting Mark for a coffee, and I still haven't mentioned it to Pete. I don't know why I'm feeling so nervous about this and why I haven't told Pete because it's nothing really. Just two parents meeting for a friendly drink. I feel awful for Mark. He seems a bit lost and maybe I can help him find something. A way to move on. Although I must confess I did put a bit of makeup on before I left. As soon as he sees me he stands up.

'Hi, sorry I'm a bit late,' I say, bustling in past the other tables and chairs.

'I just got here myself.'

As I get to the table, he leans in and gives me a quick kiss on the cheek. It's over in a heartbeat, but he puts a hand on my hip to balance himself and I smell his aftershave, and I feel something. I have butterflies in my tummy and I have to tell myself to get a grip. Pete touches me - not as much as he used to - but I haven't felt like this in a long time. Like a woman.

Sometimes it's impossible to feel sexy when you're a mother. I don't blame Pete completely for the lack of spark, romance, and sex in our marriage because I'm to blame too. But it's hard. How can I feel sexy when for most of the week, all I'm doing is taking care of the kids, cooking, cleaning, and dressing as though clothes are the same as shopping bags - just something to hold a lumpy, bumpy, jumble of goods together? I never get dressed up. I don't always shave my legs in the winter as often as I should and my body is in rapid decline. I wouldn't want to have sex with me either. I often wonder how Pete really feels about me. Do I disgust him? It feels like it sometimes. The casual touches I'd get at the beginning of our relationship, the sudden kisses, the unexpected sex, the morning cuddles in bed with wandering hands, and the looks from across a room that said, 'I need you now' have all gone. I know we've been together for twenty years and like everything over time, things decay, fall apart, and change so they're almost unrecognisable from what they once were, but I still have needs. I still want to be touched by someone who wants me. I still have the desire to be occasionally fucked - not made love to - fucked. Desperately, passionately, and intensely, as though it matters more than anything else in the world. Sometimes I daydream about it between loads of washing or while I'm stopped at traffic lights.

'Coffee?' says Mark. 'What would you like?'

'Oh, no, I'll get it,' I say, reaching for my handbag.

'It's fine. You can get the next one,' says Mark standing up. 'What will it be?'

'A latte, thank you.'

Mark smiles and walks off towards the bar and I notice his bottom. He does have an amazing bum. I look away quickly and focus on my phone for a moment, trying to compose myself. I'm a middle-aged, married woman with three kids. The last thing I should be doing is looking at another man's bottom. It's ridiculous. But it is a very nice bottom and there's no harm in looking. Pete has a great bottom too. I just haven't seen or touched it for a very long time. He's too tired or I'm too tired. Trying to fit in a moment to have sex these days is like trying to complete a Rubik's Cube. The problem is I can't just peel off the stickers and pretend it's done like I did when I was a kid. And so our sex life is moved down, moved across, and has been off the calendar for months. And it isn't looking as though it will get rescheduled anytime soon. Our sex life is an unfinished Rubik's Cube shoved down the back of the sofa.

'Thank you,' I say as Mark places my coffee carefully down on the table.

'No worries,' says Mark, sitting opposite me, taking a quick sip of his coffee.

Today's he's wearing a grey jumper, light brown chinos, has a few days' stubble that darkens the lower half of his otherwise clear white face, and his soft brown eyes are looking at me from behind his black framed glasses. The more I know him and spend time with him, the more I notice how handsome he is. I'm sure he could be a model, one of those middle-aged men in a Mark's and Spencer's ad, driving a Land Rover on a rustic beach in Norfolk. The unblemished skin that looks as though he's wearing makeup because surely no normal skin is that perfect. The shape of his jawline, square and wide, only giving way to the chin that's ever so slightly rounded. The way his mouth moves when he talks, and the lips that look so soft and gentle, and the nose that fits snugly on his face. It's so much more than his looks though. He has a way about him. He's ever so

assured, confident yet emotionally raw and broken. He has a
certain something that in his younger days may have been
arrogance or vanity, but now in middle-age is just a calmness.
And when he smiles it's impossible not to smile too. He has
the most incredible smile. Mine is slightly crooked and
doesn't come across well in photos, but his is like a
Hollywood actor, with straight white teeth, and like the
wrinkles around his eyes, seems to make him look younger.
Mark Hornby is a real dish and I'm having coffee with him
while he talks about his dead wife.

'It's hard to talk about because it's been two years and
I know at some point I have to move on, the world has
moved on, but to me it still feels like yesterday.'

'It must be so difficult,' I say, looking across at him,
and feeling the deep pain within him.

'The kids are mostly alright these days. They don't talk
about her as much as they did, which should be a good
thing, I know, but I don't want them to forget her. She was
their mother. She loved them so much.'

'They won't forget her, don't worry. Just because they
aren't talking about her, it doesn't mean they aren't thinking
about her,' I say, taking a sip of coffee.

'I'm sorry, I didn't come here for a therapy session
and I'm sure you didn't either.'

'It's fine, honestly.'

'Tell me something about you. Something interesting
you haven't told anyone in a while,' says Mark and I'm
completely rattled.

Something interesting about me? I'm not sure there is
anything interesting about me anymore. Perhaps in my
younger days I was interesting, had stories to tell, dreams to

share, but now I just feel so normal, so uninspiring. The other night I watched the film, The Imitation Game, with Benedict Cumberbatch and it's the story of Alan Turing who helped crack the Enigma code during World War Two. He was deeply troubled and his life ended far too early at the age of forty-one, but his life meant something. His story is inspiring and watching the film it humbled me and I went to bed thinking how my life is so banal, so worthless compared to someone like him who saved millions of lives. Growing up I felt different. I felt as though I could achieve something important, something meaningful, and I know being a parent is wonderful and bringing three people into the world who might change it forever should be enough, but when I'm gone, what will I be remembered for? What will my biggest accomplishment be? What epitaph will be on my gravestone and who will come to lay flowers on it?

'Well,' I say, playing through every tiny detail of my life, trying to grab at something that feels vaguely interesting. 'I have an idea for a novel I might start writing soon.'

My novel. The novel I've been thinking about forever. That still hasn't happened.

'And why aren't you doing it now?'

'Excellent question,' I say. Because I'm terrified it's going to be awful. That I can't do it. That my brain has spent so long worried about washing cycles and packed lunches that anything remotely intellectual is long lost to the embers of time 'I suppose, time. Trying to fit it into my life between work, the house, the kids, and trying to maintain a marriage.'

A failing marriage. I don't say failing.

'What's it about? If you don't mind me asking.'

What's it about? My masterpiece. My contribution to

British literature. It's barely a flicker of inspiration, but I've been thinking about it for such a long time. I've even started writing a bit, but as always I'm immediately wracked with doubt and worry and it's always enough for me to stop. When I was younger I used to write all the time. Words flowed out of me as easily as water from a tap. I assumed that would always be the case and eventually I'd get around to writing a novel and it would, of course, be an international bestseller. I never imagined I'd be forty and terrified to write a sentence.

'It's just a love story, nothing exciting.'

'A love story, it sounds exciting. We all need a good love story in our lives,' says Mark, and he looks across at me and I swear I feel something sparking. Lust, desire, excitement, whatever it is, I feel it and it's dangerous. Mark smiles his smile and inside I'm falling apart.

I'm not the sort of woman who would have an affair. I love my husband, my family, and everything we have. I feel stuck and things between Pete and I are at an all-time low, but the idea of someone else is ridiculous. It's a silly, adolescent crush like the one I had on my teacher at school. Mr Hadley was young, fresh out of university and at sixteen, he was everything I thought I wanted. He was handsome, cool, talked to us like grown-ups and I convinced myself he had a crush on me too. He didn't, of course, because he was my teacher and I was sixteen, but I remember the overwhelming feeling of it and how devastated I was when I found out he had a girlfriend. I saw them together in Tesco, holding hands. She was carrying a basket with a bottle of wine and a French baguette. It broke my heart.

'We'll see. Maybe I'll start it soon,' I say, trying to

sound convincing.

'You should. I want to read it. I bet it will be amazing.'

'So, Mark, I've told you something about me, time to spill the beans on something about you. Preferably something embarrassing.'

Mark looks at me and smiles, before putting his head in his hands.

'I haven't told anyone about this for a while, so mum's definitely the word.'

'Go on.'

'When I was at sixth-form, I was in a Bon Jovi cover band,' says Mark, and I can't help but laugh.

'Oh my God, that's incredible. What were you called?'

'Bad Medicine,' says Mark coyly, cowering behind his hands.

'I would love to have seen that.'

'We were actually pretty good. I was Jon Bon Jovi. My best mate at the time, Rob Finch, was Richie Sambora.'

'Did you have the hair? Please tell me you had the hair?'

'We did,' says Mark, and we both crack up laughing.

'I need to see photos now.'

'They've all been burnt.'

'I don't believe you and I will see those pictures.'

'One day,' says Mark. 'One day.'

We sit and talk for the next hour before we have to pick up the kids. We talk about the children and school and Mark tells me about his new job. He works from home part-time so he can be there for the kids, but he really misses working in an office full-time. He gets lonely and after losing

Abi and moving to a new area, he feels for the first time in his life as though he isn't sure where he belongs. He grew up in north London and still has family and friends there, but after Abi he needed a fresh start. He needed to walk down streets he hadn't walked with her. He needed to make new memories in places that weren't already etched with memories of her. It was the only way he could move on, but now he isn't sure if he made the right decision. He wants what's best for the kids. I watched him talking and my heart sank and became heavier with every word. I wanted to hug him and tell him it would be alright, but I couldn't and so instead I sat listening, offering up platitudes and words, but nothing substantial, when I think what he really wanted was something solid to grab a hold of. Mark is lost at sea, bobbing about in a lifeboat waiting to be rescued, and the longer we talked and the more I thought about it, the more I began to wonder if it was me he was looking to. Am I the one to rescue him or maybe, he's the one to rescue me?

Eight

Wandsworth, London, 1999

I walk in through the front door, the rain whipping in behind me and I close it quickly before too much gets inside. It's a Wednesday night in late March and it's blowing a gale outside. It's been like this all day. I don't think it's been light once and I'm craving sunshine. This is the sort of day when I dream about emigrating to Australia. Pete and I could pack up and head off down under, start a new life in a country where it's warm and sunny for most for the year. Imagine having a wardrobe full of bikinis, skirts, and t-shirts instead of jumpers, coats, and wellington boots. Aimee's talking about moving there permanently one day. She said the lifestyle was amazing, the people so friendly, and the country breathtakingly beautiful. I'm sure Pete and I could have a great life there and just imagine the sunshine - I could be tanned for most of the year! I'm picturing it now as I take off my damp, wet layers in the bedroom. Despite my raincoat and umbrella, I'm soaked down to my underwear. As I'm getting undressed next to the radiator, trying to retain any sort of heat I can, I hear the front door open and close then Pete walks in, just as wet as me.

'It's like the end of days out there,' says Pete, his hair flat and wet against his head.

'I know, I'm drenched. I was just thinking about emigrating to Australia.'

'Sounds like a plan.'

I suddenly perk up.

'You'd consider it?'

'Why? Are you being serious?'

'Maybe,' I say, with a surreptitious smile. 'You?'

'Maybe,' says Pete smiling back at me.

'I think we need to get dry and talk about this over dinner and a bottle of wine.'

'Now that sounds like a plan,' says Pete. 'I'm going to jump in the shower.'

'I'll get started on dinner.'

'Love you,' says Pete, giving me a kiss.

I put on my pyjamas, while Pete has a shower, before I go into the kitchen and start on dinner. I rummage through the fridge until I find a pizza and a bag of pre-prepared salad. I open a bottle of wine and turn on the oven. This is an average meal for us during the week. I wish we ate better, and I have good intentions, but honestly most nights we don't get in until seven or sometimes later, so spending an hour cooking dinner just isn't feasible. I'm too tired and usually too hungry. We need to eat quickly and easily. To be fair, I do try and buy as much healthy food as possible - hence the salad. And the pizza has vegetables too.

Pete eventually walks out in his pyjamas, his hair damp from the shower. I pass him a glass of wine and we sit down at the table. The pizza is almost done. I'm excited to talk to Pete about Australia because it's something we've never discussed before. I'm sure if we wanted to we could do it, but Pete's never struck me as the adventurous type. He's

English to the core and it's hard to imagine him living in shorts and surfing. It's hard to imagine him outside of London if I'm being honest. It's something that really appeals to me though; the idea of moving across the world and living somewhere else, if only for a few years. I've always felt this need to travel, to explore, and to do more than the average person. Maybe that's what terrifies me most of all - being average.

The pizza is done and on the table along with the salad. Outside the wind and rain continues unabated. It's howling and the rain is lashing like whips across the window.

'So seriously, Pete, would you consider living abroad? I've always wanted to go to Australia and Aimee says it's amazing.'

'I'd consider it. As long as it didn't interfere with my career. I've put in too much effort to jeopardise that.'

'Wow, I'm amazed. I never took you for the adventurous type.'

'I'm not,' says Pete, before taking a bite of pizza. 'But if you wanted to, I'd do it for you.'

'That's lovely,' I say, taking a bite of salad.

I sit for a moment and imagine us moving across the world to Australia. Us. Pete and me living in the land of Neighbours and Crocodile Dundee. OK, we'd definitely be living much nearer to the Neighbours version than the Crocodile Dundee version - I'm terrified of spiders and living in the outback does nothing for me - but I could picture us living in Sydney or Melbourne near the beach and having sun most of the time, having a better lifestyle, being outdoors, and going on the adventure of a lifetime together. I know it's just an idea, a dream, and I need to do some serious research into whether it's even possible, but just the idea of it makes me giddy with excitement. I'm sure I could get a job in publishing over there and Pete could continue his studies and become a lawyer. I know it's easy to be excited on days like today when it's hell on earth in London, and we probably won't do it, but it's just the idea of doing something with Pete. I've talked to him about having a gap year and he isn't against it in theory, so maybe we'll do that first, spend six months in Australia to see if we really like it.

We finish our dinner and decamp to the sofa to finish our wine and watch television. It's almost eight o'clock and this is always one of my favourite parts of the day, slumping on the sofa with Pete. He's sitting at one end of the sofa and I have my feet up on his lap. He's giving me one of his legendary foot massages. I realised very quickly after we moved in together that Pete was rather adept at rubbing feet so now it's one of the things I look forward to every evening. By day, I'm on my feet a lot from getting to work, walking around the office, popping out for lunch and getting home again. It all involves walking and I'm not usually in the world's most comfortable shoes so by the end of the day, my feet are quite sore. I'll never get bored of Pete's foot massages.

Our wedding plans are slowly gathering pace. We don't have a date yet, but we're planning on next summer. I'm excited to marry Pete. When he proposed, I did have some doubts, but since then things between us have just got better and better. My job's going well, and I love living in our flat. I love living in London. Yes this weather is awful and the idea of being somewhere warm is very enticing, but right now, at this moment in time, I'm happy where I am and happy about where we might be going. Spring is just about here and summer is around the corner. Pete and I will be able to spend the summer weekends in London enjoying the sunshine and all this wind and rain will be a distant memory.

It's just before ten when we decide to go to bed. We brush our teeth before we get into bed. I don't know about Pete, but I'm too tired for anything sexual to happen. This happens to every couple, I'm sure. We've been together for a while now and the early enthusiasm has waned and I know we're in a bit of a sexual rut. Pete's working longer and longer hours and I'm working hard too, so the last thing I'm thinking about at night time is having sex. A part of me feels bad because he must be thinking about it, but it's hard to feel sexy when you're exhausted. To be fair, it isn't like Pete's desperately trying every day and I'm saying no. He isn't trying either. This is just one of those phases you go through in a relationship. There was a spell during the honeymoon phase when we were doing it almost every day. Now it's been over a week and it's on my mind. I don't want to bring it up in conversation because it will be fine. We'll have sex soon. Maybe at the weekend when we both aren't so tired.

I cuddle into Pete, feeling his body against mine. It feels so nice as outside the wind and rain keep bashing against our flat. I feel his body in my arms, the bare skin of his back against my fingers and I still feel the same excitement. If I wasn't so tired, I'd have sex with him right now, but as it is I'm happy to cuddle up with him and listen to the weather outside.

'Australia then,' says Pete. 'That's the dream?'

'Maybe. I would definitely like to live somewhere

warm and tropical one day.'

'Me too,' says Pete sleepily.

We both lie like this for a while before Pete rolls away and goes to sleep. He always sleeps on his side nearer the window and I sleep on my front nearer the bedroom door. We have our routines and we know how things work between us. We're settled in our relationship, in our life. I'm trying to go to sleep, but I'm thinking about work because I'm working on a big new author. Every now and then a manuscript comes along that blows me away. I read a lot of very average manuscripts and some that are just awful to be honest, but occasionally I get one that really excites me. This is one of those manuscripts. Alison, my boss, thinks this one could be huge and she's letting me do a lot of the work on it. It's my first really big project and it's both terrifying and exhilarating. It gives me faith I'm heading in the right direction and I'm being trusted to take on more responsibility. Between that and thinking about our wedding my mind is full, but in a good way. Life is busy but with things that make me happy.

Pete is snoring within minutes - something that doesn't make me happy - and I push him a few times, but he just grumbles something before snoring again. I love Pete, but his snoring drives me around the bend. Even with the sound of the wind on the window all I can hear is Pete. After ten minutes of trying but failing to sleep, I decide to get up and do some work.

I walk into the living room via the kitchen. I make myself a cup of coffee, before I fall onto the sofa and read through another couple of potential manuscripts. It's something that never ends in publishing. We get over a hundred manuscripts every week and it's up to people like me to have the first read through. I usually read between ten and twenty a week. I don't get past the first few pages of some, while with others I read the first three chapters at least once or twice. I give the best ones to Alison to look over. I'm the filter so I do end up reading a lot of rubbish, but it gives me the confidence that maybe one day I can write my own book.

I'm on the sofa, sipping my coffee and reading through another not so good manuscript, when my mind starts drifting and thinking about Australia again. Could we really do it? Would safe and cautious Pete take such a huge leap of faith? There are definitely more questions than answers, but we're young and we have all the time in the world to figure them out. I get back to the manuscript and before long it's past midnight and I'm really starting to flag. I have to wake up in six hours and head off to work again. Life and time feels so strange sometimes. It's only been three years since I met Pete, but it feels as though it's been a lot longer. Life felt so easy and comfortable back then. We lived in the moment because it's all we had to think about. Despite our career goals, we didn't have any real long term plans because we were students. The only things we thought about in the future were deadlines for essays and when our next student loan payment was going to be put into our bank accounts. Life was simple, but now despite being happy, I find myself thinking wistfully about the past and pondering the future. Three years ago, I could barely comprehend beyond the end of the week, but it's the opposite now. Maybe that's just what happens as we get older.

Eventually I slip back into bed again, beneath the

warm sheets and duvet. The rain seems to have let up a bit and the wind isn't howling quite as loud. Pete is still snoring, but this time I'm so tired I fall right to sleep, all my thoughts dissolving into dreams.

Nine

It's almost six o'clock by the time I get dinner on the table. Since the kids finished school it's been a disaster. Daisy was in a foul mood at pickup time and Josh had a rough day too. Something about the football team and being played out of position. The walk home wasn't much fun and they both complained all the way about being too tired and why we couldn't just drive like everyone else. Alice came home shortly after, huffing and puffing about homework and why Claire Bates is being such a bitch. I have no idea who Claire Bates is, but apparently, she's like a total nightmare. I tried talking to her about it, so she knew I understood and could relate, but Alice looked at me as though I was completely mental. Apparently, things are different these days and it's not the 19th century anymore. I was going to correct her on my birth date, but I already felt as though I was sinking fast and it wouldn't have helped. I ended up letting it go and she went off to her bedroom to do her homework.

Rather than start an argument, I let Josh play FIFA because he needed to unwind and I could tell he was on the edge. I tried talking and reasoning with Daisy, but she was looking for a way to get in trouble and Pete's texted and he's going to be late home. He's supposed to finish at five so he should be home by five-thirty at the latest. Instead he's 'stuck at the office' until about seven. It seems a bit too much of a coincidence that the exact time he'll be home is the exact time all the madness ends and it's time for bed. As usual, when I really need him he isn't here, but as soon as the chaos is over he'll saunter in and take over. Bedtime is the one time of the day that isn't too chaotic and is quite nice, especially with Daisy who loves to read a book before going to sleep. Thanks, Pete, you're an absolute star.

Dinner was supposed to be amazing. I had a vision of us sitting around the table together, eating a delicious, healthy meal and talking about our day. Instead it descended into anarchy. I thought I had it all together, and I did, but then it all fell apart at the last moment. Happiness was snatched from my grasp when I wasn't looking.

I went out this morning and bought all the ingredients for a meal that everyone would like. Daisy won't eat anything remotely spicy or anything she considers bland, which leaves me with a very narrow flavour window to aim for. Josh doesn't like peas and can't have dairy. Alice doesn't like tomatoes, red meat, fish, asparagus, carrots, sweet potato, or broccoli. I usually end up making them separate meals because finding something for them all is a nightmare. Today, however, I was ready. I was going to make chicken pies from scratch without vegetables in a dairy-free sauce. I made mashed potatoes - fake ones from the packet because Alice won't eat real ones - and green beans because they're the only vegetable everyone will eat without complaint. I also made a dairy-free chocolate mousse for dessert. I thought I had a solid plan in place, but then the pies burnt and Daisy had a freak-out, which led to me dropping the green beans on the floor, and consequently, we're sitting down for a dinner of scrambled eggs on toast. It was the only thing I could whip up quickly. Only Alice doesn't want it, Daisy is complaining the eggs are too runny and the wrong colour, and Josh doesn't care about dinner because dinner's stupid. We're at a standoff and Pete isn't coming home. The cavalry has decided to fight a different fight leaving me exposed on all sides.

'I'm not eating it,' says Alice, pushing her plate away.

'Me either,' says Daisy. 'Eggs are for breakfast.'

'I'm sorry about the pies, but this is what we have,' I say desperately.

We're sitting round the dining room table. I'm at one end, Alice is on her side and Josh and Daisy are opposite her. I can feel a huge argument coming on and I'm not ready for it. Why for once can't they just do something without complaining? Without treating me as the enemy.

'Can I be done?' says Josh, who's eaten perhaps two small bites of toast.

'You have to eat more than that,' I say. 'And Alice, Daisy, this is dinner. If you don't eat this you're going to be hungry.'

'Fine, whatever. I'd rather go hungry than eat this,' says Alice, folding her arms across her newly formed chest. She's always been small in the chest department - just like her mother - but recently there have been drastic developments that worry me. I know what boys are like with breasts at that age.

'I want something else,' demands Daisy.

I look at the clock on the wall. It's five minutes past six. Pete won't be home for another hour and a half. What am I going to do? Argue about this or give in for an easier life? I'm too tired for an argument. I can't spend the next hour and a half shouting at my kids. And it's just dinner.

What's worse? Spending the rest of the day at war with each other or not having something nutritious to eat? Pick your battles, Rosie. Bugger it. I'm going to give in for once. I spend so much energy locked in battles with my children. Today I'm going to let them win. We all need a win now and again.

'Fine, what do you all want to eat?' I say, looking across the table at my children.

'What, like anything?' says Josh, a small smile replacing the sullen frown.

'Yes, Josh. What do you want to eat?'

'Cereal!' yells Daisy, who a moment ago wouldn't consider eggs because eggs are a breakfast food. 'A big bowl of Crunchy Nut Cornflakes.'

'Fine, go and get it. Josh?'

'Toast with peanut butter and jam!' says Josh. 'Like in America.'

'Deal, get out the peanut butter and jam. Alice?'

'Really? Anything we want?' says Alice disbelievingly.

'Yes, whatever your teenage heart desires,' I say, and a smile spreads across her face.

'McDonald's. Cheeseburger meal,' says Alice, taking me by surprise.

It's not what I meant.

'Oh yeah, can we?' shouts Daisy from the kitchen. 'We never get McDonald's.'

I think about this for a moment. It's against everything I believe in. We never get fast food because I've always tried to give my kids a healthy diet. Whenever we go out for the day, I always try and find somewhere healthy for us to eat. Something organic, local, and sustainable.

Everything McDonald's isn't. Yet here we are and I'm tired of the same old arguments. I think back to when I was growing up. We always ate at the table and Mum cooked, but occasionally Dad would come home with fish and chips and I remember those days with such fondness. The joy when Dad would come walking in with a hot paper bag of salt and vinegar covered fish and chips that you could smell all the way from the front door. James and I would run to the table excitedly, while Mum would butter half a loaf of white bread. Sometimes we're so afraid our children are going to go off the rails we shelter them from too much. Sometimes you need to give them what they want. Let them be kids. Let them eat McDonald's.

Josh and Daisy are in the kitchen, frozen like statues as if they're at a birthday party playing a game, and Alice is staring at me, waiting for an answer. Surely she won't say yes. I think of Mum lying in her bed unable to move, her mind who knows where, her body disappearing beneath the duvet, her life all but over. I think of Mark, and his wife dying and his children who don't have a mum because of a cruel twist of fate. I think of my father smiling as he opened the bag of chips on the table. I think of Pete at the office, apart from his family again. Well, bugger him!

'Get your coats,' I say with a smile.

'Yes!' screams Josh from the kitchen, charging to get his coat and shoes on.

'Best dinner ever!' screams Daisy, following Josh out of the room.

I look across at Alice and she's smiling at me. She's actually smiling.

'Thanks, Mum,' she says and I'm almost in tears.

'You're welcome.'

I realise I'm buying my kids off with McDonald's. I'm a McMum. A McFailure. A McSellout. But at this moment I don't care because my children are happy and no one is yelling at anyone else. In this moment, we are happy and maybe that's all we can hope for in life. To be happy in the moment. I realise it won't last and maybe before bedtime there'll be another breakdown and I'm setting an unhealthy precedent going to McDonald's on a school night, but it doesn't matter. Sometimes we need to stop worrying about the future and all the repercussions of our actions and do what feels right in the moment. Sometimes it's the only way.

It's cold and dark outside, but we rush out of the house together, giggling, pulling on our coats and bundling quickly into the car - the old Volvo estate we've had for years. Pete and I bought it after Alice was born. Before that we had a small Volkswagen, but we panicked about driving our children around London so we decided to buy the biggest, safest car we could find. After a day spent searching the used car dealerships around London, we found 'the beast'. A light blue nineteen-ninety-five Volvo estate that's big, square, and despite being hit three times, doesn't have a knock on it. It's our car and there's always jumpers and coats thrown in the boot, children's books, balls, and shoes in the back, and up front there's a floor full of mix CDs packed full of 90s classics along with children's albums we used when the kids were little. There's a feeling of real excitement in the car. Josh and Daisy get in the back and put their seat belts on without me having to ask. Alice is up front and everyone is happy. We're changing the routine. We've gone rogue.

'Ready?' I say.

'Ready,' they all say back to me and we set off to McDonald's. Another disaster averted. Another fire put out. A day maybe my children will remember when they're older. The day Mum gave in and we had dinner at McDonald's. On a school night!

'This is so fun,' says Daisy from behind me and I smile because it is. It is fun.

Alice pushes play on the radio and the Take That song, These Days, comes on and Alice and I sing along with it together. A rare moment of closeness and camaraderie breaks out in the car. It's one of those spontaneous moments of joy like the time Cliff Richard sang at Wimbledon and before long we're all singing together as one. These days.

Ten

Kew and Chiswick, London, 2000

There are glorious days and then there are glorious days. This is a truly glorious day. It's my wedding day. It's eight o'clock in the morning and already the sun is shining and the sky is a brilliant pastel blue. It looks as though the weather is going to be on our side. I'm staying in a hotel near the church with my family and Lauren. I barely slept a wink last night because I'm too excited. Today's the day I get to marry the love of my life.

I'm at breakfast, sipping on a cup of coffee, when my father comes walking into the room. Lauren, my bridesmaid, is still asleep. She drank a bit too much last night, while I could barely drink anything. She fell into bed at just gone one, while I lay there thinking. I'm nibbling on toast when Dad sits down opposite me.

'Morning, love.'

'Morning, Dad. Sleep well?'

'Like a log. You?'

'Barely a wink.'

'Ready?'

'For what?'

'For the biggest day of your life, Rosie.'

'I know, and yes, I am. I can't wait,' I say and Dad smiles.

The waitress comes over and Dad orders a cup of tea and a full English breakfast. The girl takes his order then wanders off towards the kitchen. The small, boutique hotel is in a lovely old pub, just over the Thames from Chiswick, in Kew. It's a beautiful setting, just off Kew Green and a short walk to the river. We took a stroll down there last night. It was wondrous watching the sun going down over the Thames, while rowers glided past and dogs chased sticks. The pub is over two hundred years old and I can't help but wonder how many other brides have stayed here the night before their wedding over the years. How did they feel? What was their wedding like? Are they still alive and do they remember their big day? My parents and Lauren are the only ones who stayed here. Pete is staying at his parents' house with his best man, Ralph, and everyone else will meet us at the church at two o'clock this afternoon. Two o'clock, and then I'll be married. I'll be Mrs Rosie Willis until the day I die.

'I remember my wedding day like it was yesterday,' says Dad, a wistful smile on his face.

'Even with your memory?'

'Yes, even with my memory,' says Dad with a little laugh. 'It's something you never forget, love. The day you get married will stay with you forever, so make sure you enjoy it. Savour every moment because it will be over before you know it. It goes so fast.'

'Thanks, Dad,' I say, reaching across and giving his hand a squeeze. 'How's Mum?'

'She'll be fine. Just a bit under the weather, but she'll be alright,' says Dad, trying to smile, but I know the look on his face. He's worried and so am I.

Mum's been having some health problems recently. She's always been a bit clumsy - something that seems to have been passed down to me - but recently it's been worse. She's dropping things with increasing regularity. She's also been having some uncontrollable twitches and spasms, which seem to have come from nowhere. It's a worry because her doctor doesn't know what's going on, but something is changing and I know Dad's worried about it. We all are. It's Mum.

Dad's breakfast comes and he looks over the moon about it. It does look wonderful. I'd order it myself, but I'm too nervous it might come back up again.

'Any last-minute nerves?' says Dad, taking a bite of a huge Cumberland sausage.

I've been nervous about this day since I agreed to marry Pete. Not because I'm not sure about him because I love him with all my heart, but because it's marriage. It's so final. So definite. I'm only twenty-four. Maybe things will change, maybe we'll grow apart, but because we got married, that's it. I know it's silly to think this way because I have no doubts about Pete, no doubts about spending the rest of my life with him, but I suppose I'm nervous because I want it to be perfect like my own parents. We have a lot to live up to.

'Just the usual ones,' I say, taking a bite of toast. 'Nothing serious.'

'Do you want some last-minute advice?' says Dad, smiling his smile at me. His dad smile. The one he used to put me to bed with at night. That smile. 'Love is wonderful. It's the most wonderful thing in the world. It brings us together. It makes us who we are. Love defines us. Embrace it. Hold onto it because marriage isn't always easy. It isn't smooth and it can be hard work, but always remember, it's about love. Nothing else matters, Rosie, but love.'

'And love is all you need,' I say, tears suddenly prickling my eyes.

'That's right. Love is all you need.'

Dad looks at me and I can see his eyes glistening in the morning sunshine that's coming in through the window. His little girl is getting married. I love him so much and I know how much he loves me. All my nervousness and doubts are sinking away as I look at my father, knowing that one day, my own children will be looking at Pete in the same way. Pete will be someone's dad and I'll be their mother and we'll have this. This love.

Dad and I continue with our breakfast and after a while Mum comes down and so does Lauren. Lauren looks terrible and is apologising for getting so drunk last night, while Mum starts on her breakfast. We sit together in the hotel, the calm before the storm. We drink tea and talk. I tell them about when one of Pete's cousins got married in Edinburgh last year. It was a gorgeous day and I remember standing next to Pete at the church, looking at him and thinking about our wedding day and getting so excited by it because Pete's perfect and I can't imagine my life without him.

The opening bars of Fall At Your Feet by Crowded House ripple around the marquee. It's our first dance to the song we fell asleep to on our first night together. We're surrounded by family and friends. Pete and I move slowly around the dance floor, his hands around my waist, my arms around his shoulders, and we're looking into each other's eyes, husband and wife, married, and so in love. Moments don't get a lot more perfect than this.

"Till death do we part,' says Pete.

'In sickness and in health,' I say.

'I love you so much.'

'I love you so much.'

We kiss and a cheer goes up from the crowd, before other people start joining us on the dancefloor. My parents, Pete's parents, family, friends, and we're all dancing together to a song that means so much to us. It's our song on our special night and it means the world.

It's just after ten o'clock in the evening and the night is a dreamy wonderland of lights, decorations, music, flowers, friends, and that word again...love. The wedding ceremony passed without a hitch, but I was glad to move onto this. All our friends and family are here in this giant marquee at Chiswick House. It's a strange wedding because we're the first of our generation to get married. Our friends from school and university are still finding their way in the world and this feels ever so grown up in comparison. I would have been happier with a slightly less formal wedding, but Pete's family insisted. Pete's their only son and they wanted him to have the perfect wedding. It is nice and the main thing is that everyone's here.

We had a lovely meal earlier, but before that we had the speeches. Dad's was brilliant, touching, funny, and only a tad embarrassing, but it was Pete's that really had me in tears.

Hello. Thank you all for coming today. It's been a magical day so far and long may it continue. Thank you to everyone that's helped and to all the bridesmaids, who look gorgeous, and to my best man,

Ralph. Rosie, you look more beautiful today than I ever imagined possible. I always knew I was the luckiest man from the moment I met you at the union bar. You know, and I've never told you this, but I wasn't going to go out that night. I wanted to stay in and study, but my friends dragged me out with the promise of a life changing night. Little did they know how right they were. The last four years with you have been the best of my life. I love you so much and when we're together everything just feels right. I feel right. You make me a better man, Rosie. You make me complete and I promise to spend the rest of my life trying to make you the happiest woman in the world. Whatever comes our way we'll tackle it together. Whatever ups and downs we may have, we'll always have each other. Will everyone please raise their glasses in a toast to the most beautiful wife a man could wish for, Rosie Elizabeth Willis.'

I cried, he kissed me, and the day's been like a dream ever since. I'm standing watching all my friends dancing on the dance floor. There's a lot of drunk people out there and it makes me happy they're here to celebrate us. I've had a few glasses of Prosecco, but I don't want to drink too much because I want to remember every moment of this day. I'm trying to catch all the moments, all the little lights, and hold onto them.

'Fancy seeing you here,' says Pete, sliding an arm around my waist then giving me a kiss on the cheek.

'Yeah, you know, just seeing what all the fuss is about.'

'And what do you think?'

'I think,' I say, turning to face Pete, giving him a kiss on the lips, 'that marriage is the best thing I've ever done.'

'Good because I was just thinking the same thing.'

'Great minds.'

'Exactly.'

We stand together watching our nearest and dearest giving it all on the dance floor. There's a few people snogging and I notice Lauren is all over Ralph. Lauren's single again and so is Ralph so good luck to them. Although I fear she might eat him alive. After a moment, Pete leans in and whispers in my ear, 'Ready to get out of here?'

'Sorry?'

'Let's sneak off now. We have two weeks in Portugal to look forward to and I'm ready.'

I look at him and smile. It's been a long day and I haven't had much of a chance to spend time with him. There's only a few hours left anyway and most people are too drunk to care whether we're here or not.

'I just need to say goodbye to my parents.'

'Fine. See you back here in a minute, Mrs Willis.'

'OK, Mr Willis,' I say, before giving him a quick kiss then heading off to see my parents.

I find them sitting down at a table by themselves. Dad's sipping on a beer and Mum has a glass of wine. They both look so smart; Dad in his best suit and Mum in her dress with the cream hat. It's funny seeing them at my wedding. That's an odd thing to think, I know, but it reminds me how old I am and how old they are. I think I felt like a kid for so long, but suddenly it's like I've grown up and the dynamic between us has changed. It's changed how I see them. They did this once, a long time ago. Before James or I were born, they stood facing each other and agreed to be husband and wife. Then they had us and a whole lifetime has passed, and now here they are watching me getting married. Watching me start my life.

'Here you are,' I say, sitting down next to them.

My wedding dress isn't that big, but it's still uncomfortable beneath me. I try and flatten it down with my hands, but it doesn't really work.

'Rosie,' says Dad. 'How are you, love?'

'Good. We're going to sneak off I think. Get to bed. We're exhausted and we have an early flight tomorrow.'

'It's been a lovely day,' says Mum.

'Yes, it has, really lovely,' I say to Mum.

I notice the twitch. Her head moves quickly for a split second, I see her wince, and it breaks my heart. I hope she's alright. I hope it's nothing serious.

'Where's Pete? We should say goodbye,' says Dad.

'He's over there, but look, we're going to sneak out quietly. I just wanted to thank you.'

'What for?' says Mum. 'We didn't do much and Pete's family paid for all of this.'

'Not for today, Mum. For everything. For having me, raising me, giving me the chance to have this. I love you.'

'Love you too, love,' says Dad.

'Love you,' says Mum, as I get up and give her a kiss on the cheek.

I give Dad a hug too before I join Pete and we sneak out of our wedding. We have to leave for the airport at eight in the morning, so leaving early gives us the chance to get back to the hotel and relax, and maybe have sex for the first time as man and wife. Man and wife, it almost seems ridiculous. Just kids playing at being adults.

We hold hands as we walk off towards our waiting car. I take one last look back at the marquee before we get in. It's lit up from inside by a thousand lights. The Robbie

Williams song, Angels starts playing and I hear a cheer go up. Inside a hundred and twenty-five people are dancing, singing, drinking, and celebrating love. Our love. I get inside the car next to my husband and we start the drive back to the hotel to start our wonderful life together.

Eleven

I'm standing in front of the mirror in our bedroom looping a pair of silver earrings through the small holes in my ears; the silver earrings Pete bought me for our fifth wedding anniversary. Tonight we're going out. Technically we're going in because we're going for dinner with Lauren and her boyfriend, Dave, at her flat in Balham. But it's a night out without the kids so I'll take it. I'm wearing a dress, I have makeup on, and my underwear is matching. I've already had a glass of wine so I'm feeling a bit calmer than I usually do on a Friday evening at six o'clock. Pete's already home and downstairs taking care of the kids while I get ready. This is practically a holiday for me. I might not be lying on a beach surrounded by tropical foliage, sipping on a fruity cocktail, but this is as near as I'm going to get. It's nice to have Pete home early. I didn't even cook dinner because he brought home a pizza for the kids.

'Wow you look…' says Pete walking into the room.

'Like a dog's dinner? Mutton dressed as lamb? Too fat for this dress?'

'I was going to say beautiful,' says Pete, coming up behind me.

In years gone by, he would have reached his hands around me, squeezing my waist then sliding his hands up and over my breasts. I used to love it when he did that. It reminded me I was still an object of lust; a sexy woman to

Pete at least. I loved it when he wanted me so badly it was an ache, a desperate need. He would have kissed my neck before turning me round; tongues lashing in and out of each other's mouths, hands moving quickly, grabbing, touching, and then we'd stop, knowing we couldn't go any further, but the seed had been planted for later. That's what would have happened in years gone by, but we aren't like that now. A thin layer of uncertainty, resentment, and annoyance is there. We haven't managed to get past it and so his words, nice though they are, don't mean as much. If anything, they're more of a reminder of how far we've fallen. He doesn't wrap his arms around me. He doesn't kiss my neck or tell me he loves me. Instead he sits on the bed and puts his socks on.

I know he doesn't really want to go tonight. He agreed because he knew I wanted to go, but he isn't excited about it. He's doing his best impression of a man happy enough to go out, but he's never been a very convincing actor. The only thing he does well is posh and repressed. I think the truth is he's never really loved spending time with Lauren. She's too loud, too brash, and too much to take for Pete. When we were younger he did better, but as he's aged he's become grumpier and less tolerant of anyone who doesn't fit in with his strict criteria for friend material.

'I'm looking forward to tonight,' I say, taking one last look at myself in the mirror.

'Yes, fun,' says Pete unconvincingly.

'Look,' I say, turning to face him. 'I know this isn't your idea of a fun night out, but please for me, can you at least pretend to enjoy yourself?'

'I'll do my best,' says Pete, smiling a not very convincing smile, before grabbing a jumper and walking off towards the bathroom.

I finish getting ready on my own, excited about the night, and hoping we can start healing this rift, this chasm of uncertainty between us. I know he isn't excited about seeing Lauren and meeting her boyfriend, but maybe we'll have fun and it will help. Perhaps he'll get drunk and be more like the old Pete.

'OK kids, be good,' I say.

We're in the living room and the babysitter, Ellie, seventeen, from five doors down, is with us. Josh is playing FIFA, Alice is on her phone, and Daisy is reading a book about dinosaurs. Not a single reply comes back.

'Did you hear your mother?' says Pete.

'Yeees,' the kids say in dull unison.

'And you have everything?' I say to Ellie.

Ellie is tall, slim, has long, straight brown hair, a pretty face, and is off to Exeter university next year to study medicine. She's bright, funny, and I trust her completely.

'Yes, Mrs Willis, we'll be fine. Just have a lovely night,' she says.

When I look at seventeen-year-old Ellie, so gracious, polite, and with a beaming smile that lights up the room, and compare her to a sullen, glib, fourteen-year-old Alice, I can only hope this is what she becomes. Hopefully the angst of her early teens breaks and she washes up as this wholesome, intelligent, inspiring young woman.

'All the numbers are on the fridge. Josh and Daisy need to be in bed by eight at the latest and Alice by nine, nine-thirty if she's being good,' I say, rattling off all of my worries in a second.

'It's fine, honestly,' says Ellie, smiling at me. 'Just go.'

'Come on then,' says Pete, inching towards the door.

'There's food in the fridge and help yourself to drinks and anything from the cupboard.'

I dash around the room and give all my children a kiss on the head before we leave the house and set off towards Lauren's flat. It's funny, so many days I crave time away from the kids, an evening to play at being proper adults, but when I get it, I find it incredibly hard to leave.

Outside it's cold and there's a drizzle of rain in the air. Pete ordered a taxi and it's already waiting for us. We could drive, but then we can't both drink and as we get so few nights out together, we decided to indulge and really enjoy ourselves. We get into the taxi and Pete tells the driver where we're going. And then we're off, the street lights showing us the way through the darkness towards Balham.

Pete and I sit in the back of the taxi, our hands softly touching on the seat between us, although it feels more like an act of hope than genuine affection. I want tonight to go well. I want us to feel connected again; to be on the same page, whatever that page is, because it feels as though we've become strangers to each other and it's exhausting to live with a stranger. I want us to laugh again, to touch each other without it feeling awkward or contrived, and I want to feel like his wife. Because I haven't felt that way in a long time. Having coffee with Mark the other day, I realised how much I missed talking so intimately with another adult. I loved talking with Mark, it was refreshing and felt new somehow, but I should be feeling that with Pete. We need to get that feeling back or what else is there? A break? Trial separation? A loveless, benign marriage of convenience? Divorce? I don't know what the options are, but I do know this, something has to change.

Lauren's been going out with Dave for six months. They met through work. He's an estate agent for another company, so technically they're rivals, but according to Lauren, this just makes the sex better. I don't see her as much these days. Certainly not as often as I'd like. Our lives are so different and have been for a long time. In our twenties, we still made the effort to meet up once a week, clinging onto the dying embers of our student days, but as our thirties stretched towards our forties, we seem to have lost the closeness we had and now we can go for a month or two without seeing each other. I met Dave once before at a pub and he was exactly how I imagined: tall, dark, handsome, slightly arrogant, and he drives a sporty two seater BMW.

Pete and I are standing on the doorstep. Pete's holding a bottle of wine, and the rain's getting heavier. I'm already considering calling home to make sure everything's alright, which I know is ridiculous. I keep telling myself to stop worrying and just enjoy myself. Ellie is wonderful and despite being a pain in the neck for us, I know my kids and they're generally brilliant for other people. I also read them the riot act and promised to take away their pocket money for a month if they weren't perfect. This is one of the differences between Pete and myself. I know he's not even thinking about it. He isn't worried about the kids. Out of sight, out of mind. All he's thinking about is having a few drinks and an Indian. Meanwhile I'm terrified one of the kids, probably Josh, will get injured and break something and end up at A&E, Alice will start smoking cigarettes in our absence, and Daisy will have a breakdown and burn the house down. There's far more irrational thoughts shooting through my mind too; electrical currents of terror and despair connecting throughout my body, sending shockwaves of fear to my brain, but I'm doing my best to suppress those. This is what being a mother is like. Exhausting.

Lauren's flat is gorgeous. I suppose it's one of the advantages of being an estate agent, she knows how to buy property. It's a two bedroom with a large open plan living, dining, and kitchen area. It's decorated beautifully. Lauren has always had very good - and expensive - taste. It's the flat of the single woman without children and every time I come here I feel slightly jealous. Our house, as nice as it is, is always in a state of disarray. We have three children and so have enough stuff for a house twice our size. I sometimes look at houses online, the clean, well-designed, beautiful houses, just like ours in theory, but ones either without children or with full-time cleaners and nannies. The houses of the rich. Lauren isn't rich, but she is single and so her flat is immaculate. There's no pieces of Lego on the floor, no piles of books stacked in a corner, or rogue teddy bears hiding in the airing cupboard. Her house is like a catalogue - all wood, marble, and black and white photos on the walls. It's a thing of beauty and there are days when I wish I could stay here on my own for a week; sit in the clean, minimalistic space and just exist. No clutter, no stomping feet on the stairs, raised voices, unexpected presents in the toilet or husband's socks lying on the floor like roadkill that died on their way to the washing basket. Just the smell of cleanliness, fresh coffee, and magazines to read in front of the flat screen TV she has mounted on the wall.

The front door opens and stood there is Lauren, overdressed as usual in a little black dress, hair done, and makeup applied liberally. She looks amazing.

'Hello, hello, hello,' says Lauren. 'Rozza, you look gorge, babes, and who's this handsome man on your arm?'

'Lauren,' says Pete dryly.

'You look incredible too, as always,' I say, giving Lauren a kiss on the cheek and a hug as I walk in. I instantly smell it; The Single Life, by Lauren.

Pete gives Lauren a kiss on both cheeks and hands her the wine, before we walk into the flat. Dave is in the living room and stands up when we walk in.

'Alright, Rosie,' says Dave in his broad Essex accent. When I first met him I thought he was putting it on a bit because it's very strong, but it's just how he is. 'Great to see you.'

'Yes, you too. And this is my husband, Pete.'

I do a half turn and introduce Pete, who steps forward with the handshake.

'It's a pleasure,' says Pete, sounding far posher than he is next to Dave.

'Alright,' says Dave, who's dressed in trousers, shirt but no tie, and a pair of shiny shoes.

'They brought wine,' says Lauren, holding up the bottle.

'Wicked,' says Dave. 'Although I've just started on a beer. Fancy a cold one, Pete?'

'No, it's fine, I'll have some wine,' says Pete.

'No worries,' says Dave, his Essex accent for a second wobbling towards Australian.

We stand around for a moment, before Lauren ushers

us over to the kitchen, where an island dominates the centre of the space. There's stools along one side and we all sit down. She's put a few bowls of crisps and snacks on the top and serves us all a drink. In the background, there's some music playing quietly. I think it's Robbie Williams. She's always loved a bit of Robbie.

'To mates,' says Lauren, holding up her wine glass.

'Mates,' we say clinking glasses together.

'Lauren tells me you're a lawyer,' says Dave to Pete.

'I'm a family and divorce solicitor,' says Pete.

'You don't want to piss this one off,' says Dave to me.

Dave's laughing, Pete's smiling, and even Lauren's giggling, but I'm not because it's crossed my mind a few times recently. Not that we're on the verge of divorce, but what if things don't get any better? What if at some point I do want out? I wouldn't stand a chance against Pete. He does this for a living. He meets couples and families in turmoil every day, who see no other way out than divorce. Couples who once upon a time loved each other enough to stand in front of their friends and family and say their vows, who now want to destroy each other. This is his bread and butter and it makes me wonder whether he sees it in us or whether because he spends his days amongst it, wrapped up in it, he doesn't notice it at home. Pete looks across at me and I pretend I'm smiling along with everyone else, while trying to hide the pain and uncertainty I feel from my face. I've become rather good at this these days.

We sit around the island drinking and talking, nibbling on snacks, before we finally get around to ordering food. Just in the short time we've been here I can see that Pete doesn't particularly like Dave. Dave is brash and loud where

Pete is humble and quiet. Dave is arrogant and cocky, while Pete is self-assured but restrained. Dave grew up in working class Essex, went to the school of hard knocks and the university of life, while Pete went to public schools and studied law. They're very different, but the good thing is that Dave doesn't seem to notice and neither does Lauren. It's only me who can see the contortions on his face, the eyes that glaze over with mild contempt, and the way he drifts off mid-conversation idly looking around the room. Pete wasn't like this when we were young. He was open, easy going, relaxed, and social. But over the years - and maybe it's because of his job - his circle of friends has shrunk to the point where he only associates with old friends and a few carefully chosen work colleagues. Anyone else is only allowed into the circle by appointment only.

'Right, boys, go through into the living room, I need to talk to my bestie,' says Lauren ordering Pete and Dave out of the kitchen while we wait for our food to be delivered. Pete gives me a momentary look of frustration, but follows Dave anyway. I'm sure I'll hear all about it at the end of the night.

'What's new?' says Lauren, filling my glass up again.

I'm already onto my fourth glass of wine and I'm feeling it. Unlike Lauren, who probably drinks like this on a regular basis, the way we both did in our twenties, I've slowed down and although I do drink most days, it's usually just the one glass. I can't remember the last time I was properly drunk. It's been a while.

'Not much.'

I could tell her about Mark, but what would I say? I've met a man, a widower, a handsome, sad man, and I want to help him. That I want to be there for him probably more than I should. That he makes me feel something I haven't felt in such a long time. That he gives me hope, makes me feel like a woman again, and he makes me laugh. Yes, that's right, he makes me laugh, which Pete hasn't managed to do in a very long time. You should never underestimate the importance of laughter in a relationship because it covers up all manner of other failures.

'Not much, sounds exciting,' says Lauren. 'How's things with you and Pete? Still, you know…?'

I've mentioned to Lauren a couple of times about my relationship problems with Pete. She's the only sounding board I have except Mum. Only Mum doesn't offer anything in reply.

'About the same. Still working on it. Anyway, that's enough about my shit life, what's going on with you?'

Lauren looks at me, huffs at my complete lack of conversation, then launches into her usual 'how's my life' preamble. If there's one thing Lauren loves more than shopping, it's talking about herself. Not that she's self-obsessed because she isn't, she just loves a good gossip.

'Things with Dave are hotting up. We're off to Croatia next week for a few days before Italy for a week. We're driving down the Amalfi coast in one of those convertible Mini Coopers, Dave's idea not mine, but it sounds good to me. Food, wine, and you know, plenty of sex. He's an animal, Rozza, honestly,' says Lauren, looking at me with raised eyebrows. 'For the first time in my life, I can hardly keep up!'

I really don't need to hear this after my answer, but Lauren continues unabated. She tells me all about work, the house she sold in Putney for two million. The weekends away with Dave, the fancy restaurants, and the fast-paced life that's always on the go. The girl at work who's having an affair with their boss. It makes my life seem not just dull in comparison, but old and out of touch. She's out there every day, making money, living her dream, in London, and doing what she loves. I definitely can't say the same. I'm not even close.

Eventually the doorbell goes and the Indian arrives. I'm not sure who's more relieved, Pete or me. We reach into cupboards and get plates, knives, forks, more drinks, and sit down at the dining room table to eat. This is a proper grown up night in. The sort of night we tried to do as students, but never quite managed to pull off. Back then it was candles, cheap cutlery bought from IKEA at the beginning of the year, all sitting around a chipped wooden table, on an array of eclectic chairs because there were never enough matching chairs for a proper dinner party. There was beer and cheap wine next to baked baguettes with hummus, olives, and a lasagne served with a bag of salad dumped into a bowl. We listened to soul music or jazz, smoked cigarettes while we ate, drank wine, and played at being adults, talking about the world as if we knew what the hell we were talking about. What we didn't realise then was that playing at it was a lot more fun than being it. Then it was a fun game because we knew we were still kids, but now when the end of the night comes, we have to go home to reality. No more playing.

'I was telling Pete about Italy and that,' says Dave, shovelling a mouthful of curry into his mouth. Dave ordered a hot madras because men like Dave can eat spicy food and drink ten bottles of lager and still get up for work in the morning. Pete ordered a Korma because he gets indigestion at the sight of anything slightly hot. 'About the Amalfi Coast in the Mini.'

'Sounds delightful,' says Pete.

'Yeah, we're excited aren't we babes?' says Lauren, looking at Dave and winking.

I look across at Pete and he's inspecting a piece of chicken as though he's looking for germs. I do love Pete. I love who he was and even what he's become up to a point, but I wish we could get some of that spark back. When I look at Lauren and Dave I can see it. It's electric. I have no doubt after we leave they'll probably jump into bed - or maybe do it on the dinner table for all I know - and have their animal sex. I want that with Pete, but I don't know how we get that back. How do you go from this to that? Because we had it once, it's still there stuffed under the layers and years of marriage, of arguments and repressed thoughts and feelings we've kept hidden to keep the peace. It's there somewhere, we just need to find it.

'Bye, Rozza, it's been great,' says Lauren at the front door. It's just past eleven o'clock. Not that late really, but late when you have three kids. 'See you soon, yeah?'

'Definitely,' I say, giving her a hug and a kiss on the cheek.

Pete and Dave give each other a solid handshake and Dave suggests going for a beer sometime. Pete smiles and says yes, of course, but I know he never will. We all say goodbye, before Pete and I jump in the waiting taxi and head off home. The kids should all be asleep by now. I've had seven glasses of wine and I'm feeling looser and ready to try something. I want Pete to feel something too. I want him to get me home, grab me, and fuck me on the sofa or against the wall. I just want to feel something for once. You can't go through life not feeling because eventually you become numb. I'm tired of feeling numb.

'That was a good night,' I say to Pete in the back of the taxi.

I reach a hand across and place it at the top of his leg. I feel it flinch beneath me.

'If you say so,' says Pete.

'What? You didn't love Dave?' I say, giggling slightly. I always laugh more when I'm a bit drunk. Pete used to love that about me.

'What do you think?' says Pete, not detecting my tone, not feeling my excitement at the possibility of having sex. He isn't feeling any of it. 'It was fine.'

I reach my hand a bit further up his leg and squeeze it. Pete finally realises what's going on. He looks at me and I'm smiling back at him. Surely he must want it too. It's been months and the last time I checked he was still a man.

'What's going on?' says Pete.

'I just thought. The kids will be asleep when we get back, we've both had a few drinks, maybe we might…'

I leave the question hanging in the air, hoping he'll lean across and kiss me. Maybe put his hand between my legs like the time in Dublin just after we graduated from university. But he doesn't. He doesn't kiss me and he doesn't touch me. He doesn't do anything.

'What's the matter?' I say, moving my hand back to my own lap.

'Nothing's the matter.'

'Then why don't you want to have sex with me?' I say

perhaps a little bit too loudly. The driver looks at us in his mirror and I can feel Pete tense up in horror. He does a lot of tensing these days. Just like his father.

'Rosie, please keep your voice down,' says Pete quietly. 'It's embarrassing.'

I'm fuming on the inside and disappointed, but now isn't the time to let all of this out. I don't know when will be. And so as usual I keep it in. I sit back and look out of the window at London shooting by. At people laughing and walking towards pubs for drinks. I'm not numb though. I'm not. Pete maybe but I refuse not to feel. I refuse to give in and remain stuck. I can't because it isn't me. That girl who sat at those student dinner parties, laughing, joking, and talking about big things, life changing things, she's still inside of me and she isn't leaving. She won't give in.

Pete pays the driver while I walk into the house. Ellie is sitting in the living room watching television and the house is quiet. She packs up her stuff and Pete pays her and we both thank her ever so much before she leaves. Pete, ever the gentleman, walks her home despite it only being a few houses away and I go straight upstairs. I'm so angry with Pete, but I can't talk to him now because I'm too upset. It will have to wait. Instead I brush my teeth, get undressed, and into bed alone. I turn over and pretend to be asleep. Pete comes in and I can feel him get into bed next to me, not touching me, not talking, and he goes to sleep too. Two people so close and yet farther away than we've ever been.

Twelve

It's Wednesday morning and I'm ushering the kids out of the door on the way to school. Pete left about twenty minutes ago, a piece of toast hanging from his mouth. Today we're out of the house on time and no one is freaking out or threatening to stay at home because school is stupid. Everyone is in a good mood. Especially me.

It started on Monday while I was talking with Mark. He happened to mention he was popping into London on Wednesday and visiting the National Gallery. I said it had been years since I'd been and suddenly he was asking me if I fancied going and I was saying yes and now we have a whole day planned. A whole day with Mark in London and I still haven't told Pete and I don't know why. In my defence, Pete and I are hardly talking about anything at the moment. Since dinner at Lauren's, things have been so tense between us. I tried talking to him about it. I asked him what the problem was and why he's being so off and not present in our life, but he didn't want to talk. Nothing's wrong, he's fine, just tired, he said, but it's more than that and I can feel it. He's coming home from work even later and even when he's home the tension is eating away at us. I can feel him slipping away from me and me away from him. Luckily, the children don't seem to be noticing, all too occupied with their own lives, their own dramas. Today is going to be a good day. A holiday from my own life. A day to remember what it felt like not to be Mum and to be me. Rosie.

We're meeting at school then we're taking the train in together. We're going to get a coffee and a croissant before heading to the National Gallery for a few hours, before a late lunch and home in time to pick up the kids. I've been thinking about it since Monday. It's all I can think about. What am I doing? My marriage is falling apart, crumbling like an old wall, brick by brick, stone by stone, and I'm off gallivanting around town with a handsome, single man. And there's something between us. I can feel it. As much as I can feel the tension, frustration, and anger between Pete and I, I can also feel the pull of attraction with Mark. I realise it's a dangerous game we're playing, but for some reason I keep joining in, keep wanting to be a part of it. Maybe it's the feeling of being alive, of feeling special, wanted, and attractive again. Pete makes me feel none of these things and Mark does. We all need to feel wanted now and again. We all need to feel special to remember that life is special.

'Have a great day, love you,' I say to Alice at the bus stop.

I think about giving her a kiss, but I know better than that. I dream about the future when Alice is in her twenties and we can meet for coffee like friends and she'll give me a hug and a kiss on the cheek. We'll talk about our lives, share gossip, and we'll feel so close we'll be able to tell each other everything. The future, when my children are happy and healthy and we all get on like the best of friends, as though none of their childhoods, all the shouting and arguing, tears and tantrums, ever happened.

'Love you,' says Alice quietly giving me a half-smile and this is as good as it gets right now. If she's saying, 'love you' and smiling at all, it's a huge win. She might as well be taking out a full-page advert in every national newspaper and proclaiming her love for me.

'Come on you two,' I say to Josh and Daisy. 'Let's go.'

Daisy holds my hand and we walk along the pavement to school. Josh walks just ahead of us, kicking a small stone like a football. His shirt is untucked at the back and his hair is a bit of a mess, but that's Josh. He's ten. In a few years, he'll probably start caring about how he looks. He'll go through puberty. I'm not that excited to have a pubescent boy in the house though. All the fluids and hair and pornography. At the moment, all he cares about is his mates and football. In a couple of years, once the lure of the fairer sex starts to pull him away, dragging him by the shirt collar into the unknown land of lust, sex, and relationships, he'll be changed forever. There are times even now when he still seems so young, still so innocent and pure against the murky and complicated waters of the world Alice inhabits. I want to hold him back, grab him and hug him, and tell him not to get any older. He doesn't realise, but this is as uncomplicated as his life is ever going to get. Right now it's simple and straightforward, but once it starts, once the wheels of puberty begin to turn that's it. Life will be complicated forever. There's no going back.

'Today's going to be a good day,' says Daisy from next to me. 'A good day, Mummy.'

'I hope so,' I say, squeezing her hand three times. She squeezes it back three times. This means, I love you. She looks up at me and smiles, her bright blue eyes glistening in the early morning sunshine.

Daisy's been having trouble at school. Twice in the

past week she's ended up in the head's office for fighting. It isn't her though. Not really. She gets annoyed and frustrated and doesn't know how to connect the emotional dots to escape so she resorts to hitting. I feel so sad for her because she isn't that little girl. She's kind and lovely and has a beautiful soul. She's creative and I know that once her demons go away she's going to be brilliant. At the moment, it's a struggle.

We reach the school gates and I say goodbye to Josh quickly. He's always in a hurry to get inside for a kickabout on the playground with his mates. As soon as he's gone I kneel in front of Daisy and look at her face. Her beautiful, gorgeous little face. The big, blue eyes, and the freckles that run across her nose. The gaps in her teeth where the baby ones have fallen out and the new ones are still coming in. My baby girl.

'Today's going to be a good day,' I say.

'Today's going to be a good day,' repeats Daisy.

'If you get angry what do you do?'

'I take a deep breath and think happy thoughts.'

'And if that doesn't work?'

'I tell the teacher I'm having a hard time and need help.'

'Good girl. You know Mummy loves you very much,' I say, holding her face in my hand.

'I love you too very much,' says Daisy with a smile.

I give her a kiss and hug her tightly, before she turns around and walks off into school. It breaks my heart saying goodbye to her sometimes because I want to protect her, help her, but I know at some point I have to let go and she has to help herself. When she's inside the gates she turns around, gives me the biggest smile, and waves and I almost start crying, but I don't. Instead I wave back and blow her kisses and watch her walk into the school, into the melee of children that are already running and screaming, then she disappears. Gone from view. And that's when I hear his voice.

'Morning,' says Mark.

He's standing next to me in a long wool coat, a scarf around his neck, looking at me from behind those black framed glasses. He says goodbye to his children with kisses, hugs and promises of the park after school. He stands in front of me with a smile, bouncing up and down on his heels.

'What?' I say smiling back.

'Nothing. Just excited for the day. Shall we?'

'We shall,' I say with a giddy excitement, before we start walking off towards the station.

The journey in is comfortable and we talk about the sort of art we like. Mark did an A Level in Art History and despite being an accountant, is a bit of an expert. It's refreshing to talk to someone about art who knows something about it. Pete can't stand art galleries and the times we have been, he tends to mope around looking at his watch. We took the kids to the Tate a while ago and he spent most of the time on his phone. All these little things, these differences between us, never seemed to matter before. They were tiny flecks of paint on an otherwise perfect canvass, but now they're everything. They're all I can see.

We eventually reach Charing Cross and grab a coffee and a croissant from Costa before we walk down Villiers Street and find a bench facing the Thames. It's a chilly morning, but bright and sunny and it's nice to sit and watch the world go by. I'm always amazed that no matter what the month, London is packed with tourists holding up maps, following tours, and taking photos with their large, professional looking cameras. To our right and across the river, the London Eye is still and the Southbank is busy with people walking to work and joggers enjoying an early morning run. We sip our coffees and eat small chunks of croissant. We could almost be in Paris.

'This is nice,' I eventually say.

'It is.'

We're so comfortable together. There isn't that need to talk, to say something. Instead we sit in silence together. No pressure.

'I was just thinking we could be in Paris sitting here with our coffee and croissants.'

'That would be nice. I love Paris.'

'Me too,' I say, and we look at each other and smile self-consciously.

It's comfortable, but then we have the occasional spark of something and this is when I know we need to stop this before we do something we can't take back. Before we go too far. Not that I think I would or Mark would either, but the possibility is there and surely that's enough to push the stop button now before we have to make a decision either way.

'I went to Paris with Abi as part of our honeymoon. Paris, Venice, and Rome. All of the most romantic places on one holiday.'

'Sounds magical.'

'It was,' says Mark, and I can almost hear the sadness

in his voice.

I can't imagine Pete dying. The pain Mark must have gone through and is still going through breaks my heart. Maybe it's why I keep playing this game, because I want to help him. I want to be a part of his life. He has a pain in his heart and maybe, just maybe, I can help mend him. God that sounds terrible because what can I do? He lost his wife and his children are without a mother. What good can I possibly do?

'I went to Paris with Pete before we had kids. When there was still some romance left. It feels like a lifetime ago now.'

'I know what you mean. Sometimes when I close my eyes, I can barely picture Abi's face. If it wasn't for the kids, it would feel as though she never really existed.'

'You'll always have the memories,' I say, standing up. 'Fancy a walk, I'm getting a bit chilly?'

'Sure,' says Mark, standing up, and we start walking along the Thames. The National Gallery opens at ten and it's only half-past nine so we meander along, sipping our coffee, and talking. 'Do you ever wish you could go back in time to remember what it felt like to be young?'

'God, all the time,' I say and Mark laughs. 'I'd give up one of my kids to be a teenager again for a night.'

'Eighteen, the summer before university, I went with four friends to Newquay in Cornwall for a week. I remember it so vividly. We camped, went to the beach, met girls, drank too much and listened to music. Life doesn't get a lot better than that and the sad thing is we had no idea how good we had it. All we had to worry about then was which girl we were going to try and pull that night.'

'I know what you mean. Some days I want to say bugger everything, jump on a train, and go somewhere far away for a few days. Just for some peace and quiet.'

'Where would you go?' says Mark, looking across at me with a smile.

'Maybe Edinburgh. I went to the Fringe Festival in ninety-seven. I had such an amazing time and Edinburgh's beautiful. I haven't been back since. God that's so sad, isn't it? It's only a few hours away.'

'The same with Newquay. I have such fond memories, but I haven't been back since.'

'We should make a pact right here, right now,' I say, stopping for a moment and turning to face Mark. 'In the next twelve months you have to go back to Newquay and I'll go to Edinburgh.'

'It's a deal,' says Mark, and we shake hands, holding on just a little bit too long, before we let go with slightly bashful smiles. I suppose this is as near to feeling like teenagers as we're going to get.

We finish our coffee, before we head off to the National Gallery. I'm excited as we walk in and grab a map each. The last time I came here was when Alice was eight. Six years ago. Daisy was only one and Josh was four. I remember it was a bit of a disaster and we were only in there for about an hour and we didn't see an awful lot of art. It was one of my last attempts at bringing culture into our lives. Today feels very different. Today I'm only here with Mark and we can take our time. We start off wandering through the early and high Renaissance rooms. Mark talks to me about the paintings and points out a few of the more famous ones. We discuss what sort of art we like and how it affects us. It feels incredible to be talking about such highbrow things because I used to do this all the time.

When I was going out with Alex at university, before it all fell apart, we used to go to art galleries, music nights, and comedy gigs above pubs in London boroughs we'd never normally visit. We'd be forever searching out things to do. We used to get Time Out religiously and we'd scour every page looking for things to do throughout London. We'd spend the day in Camden, going to the market by day, then disappearing into pubs in the late afternoon, only resurfacing to head off to a club after closing time. We found small music venues to watch obscure bands and visited museums we only heard about by word of mouth. I remember one day he took me to the Hunterian Museum, which is a museum of anatomy and surgery. It was incredible. They had all sorts of body parts, including deformed ones in little jars. Alex and I wandered around in amazement. I'll never forget those days, always running onto and off tubes - we hardly ever paid back then. Under Alex's brave and careless leadership, I got used to following people quickly through the ticket machines so we never paid for a travel card. Now the idea terrifies me and the thought of my children doing it fills me with worry, but back then it was how life was. We lived, we saw things and talked about things, big things. Ideas, philosophy, and life. I miss it. I miss the feeling of it. The excitement of it.

Mark and I walk around taking in all the incredible works of art, surrounded by other people, tour groups, children, and in the middle of it all, us, in our little bubble. We eventually make it into the impressionist's room and this is where Mark comes alive. The impressionists are his favourite artistic group. We stop in front of a Paul Cezanne called Hillside in Provence, and he starts telling me about it.

'Look at the brushstrokes, the way he simplifies nature to its natural forms.'

I'm watching him talking and the way his face lights up with excitement and wonder. It's obviously something that's important to him and perhaps helps him stop thinking about Abi for a moment. In this second, I feel both jealous I don't have that myself and it makes me like him even more. More than I should. The more into it he is the more handsome and attractive he becomes and I have to look away. I distract myself because I suddenly realise I am falling for him. That I have feelings for him that go beyond mere friendship and wanting to help him. I want to know him, know what's inside of him, and I'm thinking about what it would feel like to kiss him. I know I shouldn't have these feelings but I do. They're there. I suppose they've been there for a while, but suddenly they aren't in the distance, at the back of my mind behind everything else. They're front and centre and I have the sudden urge to get away. To run away and be as far away from here as possible.

'It's wonderful,' I say, trying not to let him see the look on my face. The slight redness of my cheeks, the way I'm running my hand through my hair, and the smile that suggests something. I know this smile. Fortunately, Mark doesn't and we move onto the next painting.

The National Gallery becomes a trip not about the paintings, but about us. We start talking and meandering off into conversations about each other. There are smiles, and gestures, and he puts his hand on my arm, my shoulder, and my back. It makes me stop for a moment and realise I like the feeling of him touching me. It's wrong, I know, but in this giant building in the centre of London, I feel like we're in our own little world. It's exactly how I used to feel when I was with Pete.

After the National Gallery, we wander outside and drift off towards the street. It's just after twelve o'clock and I'm feeling hungry. We mentioned getting lunch, but I have no idea where. We stand and look at each other when suddenly Mark gets a smile on his face.

'What?' I say, feeling the sunshine that's now reaching through the clouds and basking us in a warm glow.

'There's a pub I used to go to when I worked in the City. The Fox and Anchor. Fancy a quick pint?'

A pub lunch with alcohol on a school day. I feel like a naughty schoolgirl playing truant. What can I say but yes? Mark flags down a black cab and the next moment we're sitting in the back, driving through the streets of London towards a pub for lunch. I should feel guilty about this and I shouldn't be encouraging it, but I'm enjoying myself. If it wasn't for Mark what else would I be doing? Washing, cleaning, visiting Mum, or reading another manuscript. Everything else in my life I'm doing on my own. I have no one to talk to, interact with, but with Mark it's like I'm alive and we're doing things I haven't done in twenty years. It might be wrong and I'm sure if Pete found out he'd go ballistic, but at this moment, in the back of a black cab with Mark, I don't care. For once I'm thinking about me and about what I want and that's it. No compromise, no placating, and no patience needed. This is about me and for once, I don't feel stuck.

It's almost seven o'clock and I'm in the kitchen

washing up. Pete's in the living room with the kids and we've just had dinner. I'm washing dishes and daydreaming about my day with Mark. The pub was lovely. It was just like he said. A beautiful, old, Victorian pub in the City and the food was fantastic. Mark had a pint of beer and I had a couple of glasses of wine. It was wonderful. We talked, laughed, and I truly felt twenty years younger. It was like going back in time and all the while we were in the pub, I didn't think about anything else. I didn't think about Mum dying or my problems with Pete or the kids. I was living in the moment and it felt truly magical. Eventually it was time to go and the spell was broken. We took the train back and picked up the kids from school, before we said goodbye. Mark texted me twice afterwards to say what a great day he'd had and how he hoped we could do it again soon. I replied and said yes, but I know deep down we can't. It isn't right and if we keep doing it, keep spending time together, something is going to happen. I'm daydreaming about the best day I've had in years, but I'm also sad because I know it can't happen again.

'How was your day?' says Pete walking into the kitchen.

He starts pouring himself a glass of wine. He's trying. I can see he's trying.

'Fine. Nothing special,' I lie. 'You?'

'The usual.'

We smile at each other, but it's etched with awkwardness and we both seem unsure what to say next. Rather than make small talk, Pete wanders off back to the living room while I finish the washing up, trying to remember every moment of my day with Mark, catching the little lights and holding onto them for dear life.

Thirteen

Railay Beach, Thailand, 2001

The heat is different here. People say that, don't they? The sun is different when you go abroad and they're right, it is. We've only been here for two days and I never want to leave. It's paradise. We spent the first week of our holiday in Bangkok and the north before we flew south for the next two weeks. Bangkok was a real culture shock and it took us both a few days to adjust. The madness of it was quite overwhelming, but it was wonderful and I loved it. Pete had a harder time adjusting, but now we're here he's starting to relax.

This was our alternative to going travelling. We talked about it, but Pete just didn't want to go away for a year. His career was too important, he couldn't risk taking a year off, and what would we even do for a whole year? I said maybe six months, but even that was met with the same lack of excitement and so here we are. Three weeks in Thailand. Pete said we can do all the countries, but just in little holidays rather than one big adventure and I agreed. This is Thailand and next year we're going to do Australia. It's better than nothing and as Pete pointed out, we can still do everything without losing money and ruining our careers in the process. It's the practical solution to my wildest dreams. I understand how important Pete's career is to him and I'm enjoying my job too. I've been promoted and as Pete said, this makes sense. Plus, if we left for longer we'd have to give up the flat. I know it's a compromise, but isn't that what you do when you really love someone?

We're lying on the beach, on top of our towels, and it's a glorious morning. Pete's reading a book and I'm listening to music and reading a magazine. I should be reading a novel, but I'm taking this holiday as a chance to get away from everything. I read enough for my job and so for the next two weeks all I'm going to read is mindless magazines and menus. We're staying at a nearby resort and it's amazing. I suggested staying somewhere a bit more rustic like a hostel so we could sort of live the backpacker life for a few weeks. The deal we struck was that I chose the destination and he chose the accommodation and he didn't want to stay in a 'dingy hostel' when he could stay somewhere with proper showers, a comfy bed, and real food. Pete isn't a traveller. So here we are. We have trips planned to the Phi Phi islands and another into the jungle to ride elephants, but otherwise it's going to be beach, snorkelling, kayaking, and riding mopeds to the different bars Aimee told me about.

The beach is beyond perfect. It's golden and soft and leads into turquoise blue water where soaring limestone rocks jut out from each side of the bay. The greenest palm trees and jungle sit behind us and all we have to do is lie here. It's like a dream and to make the whole thing even better, I'm turning twenty-five in two days. I'm turning twenty-five in Thailand.

'Fancy lunch soon?' says Pete, looking across at me.

It's just after twelve and we've been sitting out here

for most of the morning. Despite applying factor thirty sunscreen, I can feel my skin beginning to burn. It's probably best to head back and grab something to eat before we do something else this afternoon. I'm not sure what Pete's planning, but I'm going to get a massage. I've already had a couple since I've been in Thailand and they're amazing and so cheap.

'Sure, I say, wrapping my headphones around my CD Walkman and putting it back in my beach bag. We pack up our stuff and start walking back to the resort. I can see Pete's chest is burnt and as we walk along, holding hands, a sense of calm and tranquillity, I'm suddenly overawed by a sense of happiness. 'Thanks for doing this.'

'Doing what?' says Pete, giving me an inquisitive smile.

'Coming to Thailand. I know it isn't really your thing.'

'Please, I love it here. Look at me in my flip flops and shorts. I could be a local.'

I laugh.

'Right,' I say, giving his hand a squeeze. 'A real local.'

We get back to our room and Pete immediately jumps in the shower, while I walk out onto the balcony and sit down. The views from here are incredible. I can see the sea glittering in the sunshine. Tall trees litter the resort as well as groups of monkeys that sit waiting for scraps of food to eat. They also make quite the racket first thing in the morning.

As I'm sitting here, sipping on a bottle of water, I feel a real sense of calm that I've never really felt before. I remember Aimee telling me about this. When she was away, she said how she felt a freedom she hadn't experienced back home. We go from school to sixth form to university then into work without often questioning what we're doing and taking a break. I suppose it's this sense of freedom I'm missing out on by not going travelling. Pete says we have freedom because we have money, but I think what he's talking about is security, not freedom. One of the nights we were in Bangkok, we met another couple in a backpacker bar. They were the same age as us and travelling the world for a year. They were only a few weeks in, but listening to their stories and plans, I felt so jealous. They were really doing it, while we were just on holiday. They had that sense of freedom, of letting go and really being in the moment. You don't get that being on holiday because you know that in a few weeks, you'll be home again, back to work, and life will carry on as it did before. And I'm not unhappy. I'm not. But despite never really having that freedom, I miss it. I miss that Pete and I will never have it. We still have so much time in our twenties to travel and be free together in London, but it isn't the same.

I'm listening to the noises surrounding me, closing my eyes, and savouring the moment so I can remember it forever, when Pete walks out onto the balcony and sits down opposite me. I open my eyes and see he's just in a towel. His hair's wet and he's smiling at me.

'This is nice,' he says.

'Yes, it is,' I say, feeling the warmth on my face and listening to the sound of the waves and the monkeys in the trees. Somewhere in the distance I hear music. I think it's Coldplay. 'Changing your mind?'

'About what?'

'Travelling,' I say with a hopeful grin.

'No, just enjoying the moment,' says Pete, putting out

any semblance of the flames that were beginning to catch hold. 'And I'm sorry.'

'What for?'

'For not wanting to go travelling. I know you do, but it just isn't me. I love this, being here with you, but I couldn't do it for a whole year. I need structure, security, and despite the sunshine being lovely, I'm not sure my pale, English skin could deal with a whole year of it.'

'I understand. Let's just enjoy this shall we.'

'Yes, and with that in mind,' says Pete, getting up. 'You know I'm not wearing anything under this towel.'

And on the balcony, I grab the towel and whip it off, so Pete's completely naked. I can't help but laugh. Pete runs back inside quickly, falling on the bed and I follow him, jumping in next to him. This is amazing and I'm so thankful we get to experience this. This small holiday from our otherwise incredible life. We might never get to travel the world for a year, but what we have is amazing and Pete's right, we do have a lot of freedom. Weekends away, holidays like this, and with no plans to have kids and settle down anytime soon, we have all the time in the world. Pete and I. Me and Pete. Life really is good. And who knows, if we love Australia next year, maybe that dream will become a reality.

We make love on our bed in Thailand and afterwards we fall asleep, napping with the balcony door open, the warmth filling our room, the sound of the ocean slipping into my dreams, and Pete's naked body wrapped tightly around mine.

Fourteen

Rain is lashing against the windows and the sky is dark with heavy grey clouds. It's thoroughly miserable outside. Luckily, I'm inside attempting to give the house a bit of a clean before Dad shows up. Dad's coming over and I'm trying to make the place look vaguely presentable. Not that Dad cares, but I don't want him thinking we live in a complete shithole. Dad doesn't come that often. He still lives in the house I grew up in near Woking. He used to come into London all the time when Mum was fine, but recently he's been coming in less and less. He can't stand the traffic, the people, the chaos, and it's too much for him. He hasn't been here for six months now, but today he's making the effort. Today I get to make my father lunch.

I can't stop thinking about my day in London with Mark. I'm running the hoover across the carpet on the landing and I'm thinking back to our day together. God it's so sad, isn't it? It excites me and I know it's all so wrong and silly, but Mark makes me giddy. He just does. There's something about him that makes me feel young again. He makes me want things I don't have in my life, that I haven't had in a long time. He brings something out in me I thought was lost, gone forever in a cloud of kids, housework, and middle-age. I keep thinking I should talk to Pete about him, explain myself, because maybe he'll be a bit jealous and it might give him a kick up the bottom, but what would I say?

Do I think about him? Do I imagine myself kissing him? Do I feel a connection with him? You can't explain these things without it sounding awful. In my head, it's just fanciful dreams, but when I think of the actual words, it sounds more like an affair. But it isn't. It's something else. Its two people lost in life, in London, trying to grab hold of something to keep them from disappearing forever.

When I open the door, Dad's stood there underneath his umbrella, the rain lashing down behind him. It's big fat rain that smacks against the ground and splatters up.

'Come in, quick, out of the rain,' I say, stepping aside to let him in.

'Hello, love,' says Dad once he's inside. 'It's raining cats and dogs out there.'

He gives me a quick kiss on the cheek, before he takes his coat off and hangs it up, propping his soaked umbrella against the door.

'The kettle's just boiled.'

'Oh, lovely, I'm gasping,' says Dad, following me through into the kitchen.

I walk into the kitchen, quickly boiling the kettle again to make sure the water's hot enough before I pour the water into the teapot. Dad insists I use a teapot and 'proper tea'. He can't understand the modern fascination with tea bags in cups, it drives him crazy. Dad sits down at the table and I walk across and sit next to him.

'How are you?' I say.

'The traffic getting here was terrible. It's getting worse,' says Dad, ignoring my question. 'I don't know how you can live here. It would drive me round the bend.'

'You get used to it.'

I know Dad would never get used to it. Not now anyway. Once upon a time maybe, but he's in his sixties now and the man I knew growing up has changed so much. He looks old. The big strong body, the body of a manual worker - Dad was a plumber for forty years - is wasting away and he's ever so slightly bent over, his back a constant reminder of the years he spent working in difficult positions, fixing leaks and pipes. His face, once handsome and full, is now thin and the hair is grey and he has a bald patch at the back that gets bigger every time I see him. The heavy bags under his eyes because he doesn't sleep - hasn't slept since Mum moved into the home - because they shared a bed for so long he can't sleep without her. Today he's wearing trousers and a shirt under a brown jumper. The brown jumper he's had for years, bought for him one Christmas when James and I still lived at home. There's a small hole in one elbow, but he doesn't care. Hasn't cared in a long time.

'Check on the tea, it's done. You don't want to over stew it,' says Dad, nodding towards the tea pot.

I get up and take care of the tea without mentioning I'm the sort of heathen who usually makes tea with teabags in the cup. The teapot only ever comes out when he's over. I pour us both a cup of tea and bring them to the table with a couple of biscuits. Dad takes a sip like someone tasting wine in a restaurant and I'm the waiter hoping to get his approval.

'Very nice,' says Dad. 'So, how are the kids?'

'Yes, all good. No complaints.'

'Daisy's doing alright?'

'She's in a good phase at the moment, we're hoping it's going to last this time.'

'And what does Pete think?'

'Pete thinks she should see someone, but it's like I said Dad, she just needs a bit of patience that's all. Time, love, and patience and she'll be fine.'

'Let's hope so, eh,' says Dad, taking another slurp of tea and a bite of a chocolate covered digestive. Dad only buys Rich Tea biscuits and occasionally Hob Nobs, but never chocolate covered biscuits. Too sweet he says, but he never has a problem eating them at my house.

'And how are you?'

'Fine, all things considered. Back's been giving me a bit of jip. It's the cold, love. Winters are always worse.'

'Have you been to see the doctor like I said?' I ask, even though I already know the answer.

'No point, they can't do anything. I'm just getting old,' says Dad with a thin smile. 'You can't do anything about that.'

He is getting old and it's terrifying to watch. I can see the life slowly leaving him, the pain of losing Mum etched across his face, touching every word, and squeezing him dry of the love he felt for her. Because that's what's happening to me too. The love I had for Mum, for my mother, is slowly dripping away like water down a drain. Going around and around it's draining away because she isn't here anymore and so the body we go to see, the woman who is lying in that bed, is taking away bits of our life. Of our love. I see it in Dad every time we're there together. He sits watching her, looking at his wife, knowing she's already gone, but hoping for one last moment together before the end. One last look or smile that's never going to come. It's draining him. He's a shell of the man he was. He probably imagined his retirement with Mum, happy walks into town, day trips to the beach, ice cream, coffee and cake, surrounded by their grandchildren. But it was taken from him and now he can't enjoy any of it, even his grandchildren, because she should have been with him. His wife should have been there too and because she isn't he can't be either. I've seen him with the kids, trying his best to play grandfather, and if you didn't know him you might think he looks happy, you might think he's coping, but I know better. I know different.

'You aren't old, Dad. Not yet.'

Dad laughs and I smile back, but we both know the truth.

'How are you? How's my little girl?'

I love that he still calls me his little girl. Even now. I like the thought of being little to someone. When I was a kid and going to bed, Mum would always read me a book then Dad would come in after and sit with me. I didn't see him all day because he worked long hours, but he'd always be home in time for bed. Looking back now with the hindsight of being a parent and knowing how life is, and how life was back then, I'm so thankful he always made the effort. So many other men of his generation might have gone to the pub, been absent, but not my father. Whatever sort of day he'd had he would make it home to say goodnight to his kids. I'd be in bed, tucked up under my duvet, and he'd lean down and give me a kiss on the head and say, 'goodnight little girl, my Rosie'. It always made me smile and I'd go to sleep with the feel of his kiss on my head and his words in my ears.

'I'm fine, just fine, you know, plodding along.'

'Be careful with that, love.'

'With what?'

'Plodding. Sometimes you can be plodding along then the next moment ten years have gone by and you're still plodding. Life isn't for plodding. It's meant for running, for skipping.'

'But sometimes as much as we want to be running or skipping, life makes us plod.'

'You know, your mother and I plodded along for too many years. We got bogged down by life too, love, but you know what? I'd give anything to have just one more day with her. These were supposed to be our years. When we thought we'd have the time and money to really enjoy ourselves. Don't waste time plodding, Rosie, start skipping because one day you might wake up and find you don't have any choice.'

I look at Dad and smile, but I'm thinking about Mark because he makes me feel like I'm skipping. He makes me want to stop plodding.

'More tea?' I say quickly.

'Please,' says Dad, passing me his empty cup.

Dad and I spend the next hour talking, drinking tea, and finally the rain lets up. Dad does his usual walk around the house, looking for any jobs that need doing. Despite Pete's many incredible qualities, household repairs and DIY aren't amongst them. When there's a problem with the house either I find a way to fix it or we get a man in. Dad never got a man in. If the washing machine broke or a wood panel in the garden fence needed replacing, Dad would do it. He once built a wall in the front garden and he took care of the car himself. I don't think we ever went to a garage. When our car needs a service, it goes to the garage, but Dad is a man from a different generation, the generation that fixed things. Everything had value to them. If things broke they got repaired. Now we just buy something new, even when the old one isn't broken, because we can. We're the IKEA generation; cheap, flat packed and replaceable. It's no wonder marriages don't last either because they're becoming as dispensable as everything else. Instead of trying to fix them, we chuck them away and get a new one. The thing is, I don't want to be like that. I want to be like Dad. I want to fix what I have, work on it until it's not broken anymore because true love should last a lifetime.

'The upstairs tap's leaking, I'll have a look at it,' says Dad.

'Dad, it's fine, honestly,' I say, but I know it doesn't matter.

'Where are your tools?'

'Good question,' I say, feeling slightly embarrassed I don't know where the tool bag is.

Growing up, the shed was Dad's little world. He kept his tools and things in the shed. He had lots of tools and if you ever went into the shed, you'd better not mess them up. He kept everything in its place and knew where everything was. Every nut, bolt, or washer had a spot. The shed was Dad's retreat. He used to go out and smoke cigarettes, clean things, make things, and if you didn't know where Dad was, the shed was the first place you'd look. Pete and I just have a tool bag, and I don't even know where that is. I think it's in the cupboard under the stairs.

'Don't worry, love. I'll get mine from the car,' says Dad because he keeps one there just in case.

'I'll put the kettle on,' I say, doing the only thing I know will help.

'Perfect,' says Dad smiling and I know this makes him

happy. Helping and feeling helpful makes him happy.

Dad goes out to his car and gets his tools, while I make another pot of tea. When it's ready I bring a cup upstairs to Dad. I find him sitting on the floor, a wrench in his hand, and he's fiddling under the sink.

'Tea,' I say, setting it down next to him with another chocolate biscuit.

'Thanks, love.'

I can't stop thinking about what Dad said about plodding through life. He's right and I want to stop plodding. I want Pete and I to start running again, together. Mark does make me feel giddy, he makes me skip, but he isn't my husband. He isn't the man I love. And the more I think about it, and think about Mum and Dad, the more I realise I need Pete and I to work and it's up to me to make it happen.

'How's it going?'

'Fine,' says Dad from underneath the sink.

'Can I tell you something?' I say, realising I need to talk to someone. I need to talk to my father.

'Of course, love.'

'My marriage is in trouble, Dad. Pete and I have been drifting apart for a long time and now we're so far apart, I don't know if we'll find each other again. There's a hole in my marriage and I want to fix it, Dad, I do, but I don't know if I can,' I say, then I find myself crying. I don't mean to, but for some reason the tears just come and I can't stop them.

'Hey now, come on,' says Dad, coming out from underneath the sink and holding me in his arms. I sink into my father and let the tears out. I think I've needed this for a long time. I just need to cry and there's nothing like crying into my father's shoulder. I did it when I was little and it always helped and it helps now. It soothes me. Dad rubs my back and eventually I stop crying and he gets me some tissues so I can blow my nose.

'Sorry,' I say between heavy sighs, trying to regain some composure.

'It's alright. That's what I'm here for,' says Dad, looking at me with a smile, rubbing a tear away from my cheek. 'Now tell me what's going on.'

I tell him everything. I tell him about the arguments, the tension, and how Pete and I don't see eye to eye on anything these days. I tell him about Mark and how he makes me feel and it scares me because I want my marriage to work, but I'm worried Pete and I are beyond repair. I tell him I'm scared for the kids and I want everyone to be happy, just like the good old days, but that everyone and everything is moving on and I'm not ready and I don't know how to keep my family together. Dad listens patiently then he looks at me as only my father can.

'Rosie, marriage isn't easy. It isn't. Kids aren't easy either. You and James were good kids most of the time, but you had your moments. Trust me, your mother and I went through a lot of bad times, but through it all, we loved each other and we knew this was it. We knew we had to make it work because there wasn't any other option. And you might think this Mark fella is an option, he might make you happy right now, but you have to work on your marriage because otherwise I know you'll regret it. Sometimes it's easier to think that something new is better, but the grass isn't always greener. It isn't.'

'I know, Dad. I want Pete and I to work, but it feels

like the more I try the worse it gets.'

'You can't give up, Rosie. You can't. Just remember the good times. Hold onto them and keep going and it will get better. I promise,' says Dad, before he leans across and gives me a kiss on the head. 'Don't give up on Pete.'

'I won't,' I say, and I mean it. I'm not going to give up on Pete. I'm going to make it work. I have to. For the kids, for us, and for my parents because they would never have given up. Dad still hasn't given up. Despite everything, he keeps loving Mum and won't stop until her last breath is gone. I don't need any more inspiration than that.

Fifteen

London, 2002

I didn't believe it at first. It couldn't be true. How had it happened? We were always so careful. Except that one time. That one night when we weren't, but thought it would be alright because it was just once. What were the chances? As Pete and I looked down at the pregnancy test and at the lines that said we were having a baby, we were both in complete shock. I wasn't supposed to be pregnant. It wasn't in the plan. We'd been to Thailand and we were going to go to Australia next, our careers were both going so well, we loved our little flat, our life. Everything was going along ever so nicely, just as we wanted, but then one night of carelessness, and everything was out of the window. All our plans were put on hold. Life wasn't ever going to be the same again no matter what we decided to do.

'Fuck,' is all I could say between the tears. 'Fuck, fuck, fuck, fuck.'

What were we going to do? How could we have a baby? How could we raise a child when we were still trying to figure ourselves out? I wanted to stop life and get off for a moment. I wanted a timeout. I wanted Pete and I to be travelling the world together; young, carefree, and no worries, lying on a beach in Australia, drinking late into the night because we could, with nothing to get up for in the morning. And yet I knew straight away without having to think for a moment that I was going to have it. It was our baby and no matter what plans they ruined, what changes they would bring, it was our mistake and not theirs. I didn't have a choice in the matter. We were going to have a baby.

'It will be alright,' said Pete, his arm around me. 'We'll make it work.'

I'm three months pregnant now, and I feel it. My belly is getting bigger and I know in reality I don't look significantly heavier, but I feel enormous. I've had some awful morning sickness and I'm tired all the time. We've already made new plans; changed everything we were going to do because we're starting a family. We're looking at somewhere bigger to live, maybe even a small house. Pete's family have mentioned helping us buy somewhere and Pete just got a pay raise, which will help tremendously, especially if I end up not going back to work full-time. Pete and I have talked about it and I'm still not sure what I'm going to do. I could take maternity leave then go back to work full-time and put our baby in a nursery. I think about this and it terrifies me. Shouldn't I be at home with my baby? Shouldn't I be the one taking care of them, looking after them, and being there for them? The way my mum was for me. I understand some women don't have that option, but if I can, shouldn't I? We have a few months to decide, and I still have no idea what I'm going to do yet. One thing I do know is I'm scared and worried. But today isn't about me. Today is about Mum.

Pete and I are driving to my parents' house in Woking. They have something to tell us that Dad wouldn't tell me over the phone so I know it isn't good. It's about

Mum. Her involuntary movements are getting worse and more frequent, her clumsiness, moods and memory are deteriorating. Her body is more fragile and she's looking older. I still don't know what she has, but I know it isn't good. It can't be. We're driving along the A3 and it's a nice, warm day outside. Snow Patrol are playing on the radio and Pete has his hand on my leg. He's driving and I'm looking out of the window at the world passing by.

I realise how lucky I am in the big scheme of things. I've had a wonderful life so far, with no serious problems or setbacks. My childhood, teenage years, and university were all incredible and since meeting Pete, it's only improved. When I look back on life, all I see is fun, laughter, and love. I've been incredibly blessed and I know it. But this year all of that has changed. First getting unexpectedly pregnant and now Mum. For the first time in my life, I'm feeling the pressure of sadness, of bitterness and of doubt. When life is going well, when it's easy, we don't doubt ourselves or what we can do, but things can quickly go wrong and when they do, you suddenly start doubting everything. It's human nature I suppose.

I'm staring out of the window, watching the trees fly by. At the green fields and hedgerows that haven't changed. They're the same as the first time I did this drive with Pete in my old Mini. It was during the last term at university when we popped back for the weekend. A few clothes tossed in a bag along with a bottle of wine and packets of crisps for snacks. Blaring Oasis from the CD player with the windows down. When Pete and I were just starting out and Mum was fine and I, as Liam Gallagher sang, would Live Forever.

'Are you alright?' says Pete looking across at me,

squeezing my leg.

'Yeah, fine, just thinking.'

'About?'

'About us, our baby, about Mum. How life used to feel so easy and fun, but now feels complicated and difficult,' I say, realising I sound a bit melodramatic, but I can't help it.

'Everything will be OK, Rosie. I promise I'll make everything OK,' says Pete, squeezing my leg again and it feels nice. He always rests a hand on my leg when he's driving and I love it because it makes me feel like I did back when life was uncomplicated. I think it's why we love tradition and going back and doing the same things again and again because it reminds us of a time when things were easier. Even going home reminds me of times gone by when I first went to university and drove home for the weekend. Weekends to get my washing done, eat Mum's Sunday roast, sleep-in and watch television, just like I did when I was younger. You see without even realising it, and despite being so incredibly happy at university, I still longed for days gone by. I still needed to feel the comfort of my childhood home to remind me of who I really was. We can get lost in the world and it's nice to have somewhere to go back to. To remind us who we are.

'Here we are,' says Pete, pulling up outside my parents' house. I see my brother's car parked outside too. 'Ready?'

'What if I say no? What if I'm not ready?' I say, looking at Pete, feeling the pressure of tears not far away.

'Whatever happens, I'm here for you and will always be here for you.'

'Love you.'

'Love you too.'

I lean across and give Pete a kiss, before I take a deep breath and we get out of the car. Dad answers the door and as soon as I see his face, I know it's bad. His face is flat and looks shaken. It's white and cold and his eyes look so terribly sad. I'm doing my best not to fall to pieces and keep the tears in.

'Alright, Dad,' I say, leaning in and giving him a kiss on the cheek.

'Hiya, love,' says Dad softly. 'James is already here, come on in.'

Dad says hello to Pete then we walk through into the living room. James is sitting down with his wife, Sarah, and Mum's on the sofa looking a bit shell shocked. I say hello to everyone then sit down next to Mum. I immediately reach across and hold her hand. It's cold and I can feel the bones beneath.

'Alright, Mum?'

'Yes, love,' says Mum smiling, but her face isn't happy. It isn't a nice smile. It's not one of Mum's lovely big smiles. 'I'm fine.'

Dad finally comes into the room and sits on the other side of Mum. Pete's sitting by himself and I look across at my brother, James. He looks the way I feel. Scared, humble, and small. I remember sitting here with him when we were kids. Whenever we were in trouble, Mum would say, 'get in the living room and sit down'. And we did. Mum had quite the temper on her when she needed it. Most of the time she was happy, smiling, and packed full of love for her family. She loved being a mum. Being a parent is all she ever wanted. She didn't have career dreams or aspirations like me, her only wish was to be a proper mum. She got involved at school, spent hours and hours trekking us around to football, gymnastics, ballet, rugby, girl guides, friends' houses, birthday parties, or whatever else we needed. She was the best mum because that's all she ever wanted to be. A wife and a mother. And I think we sort of look down on that these days. We think women should be able to have a career and a family, but maybe that's the problem. Can we do it all and still be as good as our own mums? And it scares me because I want to be as good a parent as my own mother, but I know I can't. Not without giving up work. I want to be like her because she inspires me, but I don't know if I'm good enough for it.

'Thanks for coming,' says Dad, and I can tell he's falling apart inside. He's a simple man and I can see it on his face. The pain of what he's about to say. He's holding Mum's other hand in his. 'The thing is, we finally know what's going on with your mother, and it isn't good I'm afraid. I don't really know how to tell you this, so I'm just going to say it. Your mum has Huntington's disease,' says Dad, and immediately I'm wracking my brains trying to piece together everything I know about it. I don't know all the details, but I know it's bad.

'What, umm, does that mean?' says James after a moment. 'I mean, how bad is it?'

'It's a hereditary disease that slowly kills the body. It breaks down the nerve cells so she's going to gradually lose a lot of her mental and physical self. It's going to be tough for all of us, son, especially your mother, but we need to be strong. We need to stay together and be here for her because she's going to need us.'

'How long?' I say.

'It's hard to say. The doctor said ten to fifteen years from the first sign of symptoms, but she's going to get worse. Slowly, gradually, she's going to get a lot worse,' says Dad.

'Is there anything they can do?' says James, starting to tear up.

'Not really, son. No cure, just drugs to make it easier, that's all.'

I give Mum's hand a squeeze as the first tear slips out and down my cheek. I remember reading about Huntington's when I was researching possible reasons for her health problems. I know it's horrible and people go through many mental and physical challenges before death. I don't want my mum to go through this. She doesn't deserve it. It's Mum. My mum.

'Oh, Mum, I'm so sorry,' I say, turning and wrapping her body in my arms. I hug her and I can't stop the tears. I feel like if I squeeze her hard enough it might somehow help.

'It's going to be alright,' says Mum, as always putting us ahead of herself. 'I'm strong, Rosie. I'm going to fight this.'

James gets up and gives Mum a hug too, both of us kissing her and letting her know just how much we love her, how much we're here for her the same way she was for us for so many years. Eventually the tears stop. James is rubbing his eyes, as am I, Pete is next to me holding my hand, and Dad has one last thing to say.

'It's just, and there's no easy way to say this,' says Dad, his voice cracking, before he finally breaks and starts crying too. 'I'm sorry, I thought I could do this, but I can't. I'm sorry.'

'It's OK, Frank, I'll tell them,' says Mum.

'Tell us what?' I say.

'One of the hardest things about Huntington's is that it's passed down through generations so there's a fifty, fifty chance that you or James are carrying the gene too. You need to get tested as soon as possible to find out,' says Mum, and without even thinking about it, my hands go to my stomach and I'm holding my unborn baby.

I've just had the worst news and I'm overcome with emotion and sadness, but my first thought is with my baby. I want to protect them. I want them to be alright. It doesn't matter about me, but them, and I realise I'm a mother. It's the first time I feel like a mother, a proper mum, and it's at this moment - this horrible, horrible moment - that I know I can do it because I feel it. I suddenly understand what my mother feels for me and for James. It's unconditional and it's forever. It isn't a love I've felt before, but it's so strong it takes me a moment to come back to reality. I'm holding my baby and I realise they're the most important thing in the world. I don't want to let them down. I can't. I have to do my best to protect them and give them the same carefree wonderful, happy childhood I had.

The next few hours feel numb and dreamlike, full of long silences, tears, hugs, cups of tea and biscuits, and we do our best to comfort each other. James and I talk and do some quick research online about getting tested for Huntington's. It feels good to do something positive and practical in a moment of helplessness. We look through photo albums together: The holiday in Cornwall, Uncle Ray's wedding when James was the usher, album after album of James and I growing up, the childhood years of bad clothes, dodgy haircuts and funny poses for the camera, followed by the grumpy teenage years with James and I looking annoyed we were even alive. The holiday to Spain when Dad got food poisoning, and the trip to Scotland when we got lost during a snowstorm. We look at all the memories and laugh together and cry together because this is what families do. We feel everything as one.

I finally get a moment alone with Mum in the kitchen. I'm making a cup of tea and she's putting some biscuits on a plate. For some reason, I'm finding it hard to look at her because knowing she has this disease means knowing what's going to happen to her. She's going to lose the ability to think rationally, she's going to have mental episodes, not know who we are and forget all those wonderful moments we had. She's going to lose the ability to walk, to talk, to eat, and be herself. She's going to become someone I don't know and she isn't going to be my mum anymore. It's hard to look at her because every time I do, I feel like I'm going to burst into tears which I know it isn't helping, and I want to help her.

'Love you, Mum,' I say, stirring the tea in the teapot.

'I know, love.'

'And I'm going to be here for you every step of the way.'

'I know,' says Mum, walking over and standing next to me. 'Look at me, Rosie.'

I turn and look at her, feeling the overwhelming weight of tears beginning to take over.

'The one person who's going to need you the most is

your father. He isn't good with this sort of thing. I'm not going to know what's going on one day, so please, if there's one thing you can do for me it's take care of him. Will you do that for me?'

'Yes, of course, Mum,' I say, feeling the slow plod of tears trickle down my face. Mum wipes them away with her sleeve the way she always did.

'That's my girl,' says Mum with a smile. 'You always were the strongest one.'

Eventually we all leave, giving Mum and Dad tearful goodbyes on the doorstep, before heading home. Pete and I are back on the A3 driving back into London. The sun has been replaced by a foggy greyness now and there's no music on the radio. I'm looking out of the window and Pete has his hand on my leg again. Just like before, but it's different now. Everything is different now. Life can change in a moment and it has. It's twisted and contorted, and everything I felt and thought is different now.

'I'm going to stay at home,' I say without looking at Pete.

'Sorry?'

'I'm going to be a stay at home mum. When they're born. I want to do it properly, Pete.'

'Of course, whatever you want,' says Pete, squeezing my leg.

Before it felt like a choice. I could stay at home or go back to work, it was my decision to make, but as soon as Dad told me about Mum, it wasn't a decision anymore, just something I had to do. I don't know why exactly, but I know it, I can feel it inside of me, and I know it's something I have to do. For me, for my baby, and for Mum.

Sixteen

'Can you pass the bread?' I say to Daisy, who's nibbling on a slice and licking off the butter, a habit she's had since she was little that has yet to go away.

'Here you go mother,' says Daisy in a posh accent.

'What was that?' says Pete.

'T'was my voice for the school nativity play, dearest father,' says Daisy. 'I'm in character.'

'But the play isn't for another month. That's a long time to be in character,' I say, smiling and looking across at Pete. We give each other a look, a parent look that makes me happy because it's been so long since we've been like this. I feel relaxed and optimistic for once.

It's a Friday night, Pete's home early, and we're all sitting down for a proper family dinner. I made fresh lasagne, a salad, and bought a lovely fresh baguette from the bakery this morning. Pete and I have a bottle of wine to share and even the kids seem to be enjoying the novelty of a proper family dinner.

''Tis not a problem for I,' says Daisy theatrically.

'Blimey, she's really into this,' says Pete, before taking a sip of wine.

'I can't wait to see her on stage,' says Josh. 'I bet she's going to mess it up big time.'

'Josh that isn't nice,' I say. 'Apologise to your sister.'

'Sorry,' mumbles Josh.

The old Daisy might have reacted to this. She might have started an argument that would have resulted in her crying, screaming, and being sent to her room. But this is a new Daisy. Daisy the actress.

'Miss Hollingshead said I'm going to be a star,' says Daisy. 'She says I'm a natural.'

'OK, darling, that's wonderful, but we shouldn't brag,' says Pete.

'Not bragging, Daddy dearest, but speaketh the truth,' says Daisy.

'We're all very excited about it, aren't we?' I say, looking towards Alice.

'Yeah, can't wait,' says Alice, smiling at her little sister, but I can tell there's something on her mind. She's been in a strange, distant mood all week. I've been meaning to talk to her about it, but the moment's never been quite right.

Daisy getting a part in the school nativity play has been brilliant for her. We were so worried about her going for the auditions because she would have been devastated if she didn't get a part. She practised and practised and we read lines with her because she was desperate to get one of the lead roles. I'm not sure where this great desire came from, but it's like a light went off in her head and she decided she wanted to be a performer. She's always been creative, loves singing and dancing, but it's suddenly this thing she loves and she wants to be great at it. I've never seen her so happy as the day she got the part. We're all so proud of her and it's wonderful to see her really coming out of herself. Maybe this is what she needs to channel that anger and frustration into something worthwhile and meaningful. Perhaps one day she'll become an actress and it will have stemmed from this.

Miss Hollingshead has been in touch and mentioned that Daisy is doing remarkably well and is a natural performer. She already knows all her lines and doesn't have the slightest bit of nerves about performing in public.

'This lasagne is amazing,' says Pete, looking at me across the table.

'Thank you,' I say, taking a sip of my wine. 'I must say it's nice to all be around the table together.'

'Daisy's licking the butter again,' says Josh.

'Daisy, please don't lick the butter,' says Pete.

'I just like it,' says Daisy, before she gets 'in character' again, 'What can one say, it's delightful.'

I can't help but laugh and neither can Pete. Even Alice chuckles and Josh smiles at his little sister. This is so nice. Just what I need. We sit together and talk about our days. Pete and I watch, drinking our wine, while our children talk and argue and do their best to get one over on each other. Sometimes, most days actually, this annoys me and ends up with me shouting at them to stop, but today I let it go. Today I let them joke and try to wind each other up and I sit back and drink my wine and eat my lasagne, and it is a great lasagne. I spent most of the afternoon making it so it had better be amazing. Like the atmosphere around the table, it's filled with love and that's something every recipe needs. Fresh organic tomatoes help too, of course.

Eventually we finish eating and Josh needs to desperately finish a game on FIFA, Daisy wants to go over her lines with Pete because I've been doing it with her all week and she needs something to 'freshen it up'. Meanwhile, and sensing a moment with Alice, I ask her to help me tidy up.

'But I've got things to do,' moans Alice. 'Important things.'

'Come on, it won't take long,' I say enthusiastically. 'And I don't think going on Instagram or Snapchat is that important.'

'Fine,' huffs Alice, while everyone else rushes off to the living room.

Alice and I start collecting plates and putting them on the side in the kitchen. Working together we get the table cleared in no time and I take the opportunity to talk to her. Despite being fourteen, she's still my little girl and I can tell when something's on her mind. Her face gives her away. I worry it's something awful like she's being bullied and doesn't know how to talk about it. Whenever I read about another teenager committing suicide because of bullying I want to keep my kids in the house under lock and key and never let them leave, but I know I can't and so instead I worry. It's why I always force my kids to talk to me because I can't stand the idea of them being in pain and not being able to help. I need them to know that whatever's happening, whatever's going on, I'm always here for them.

'Is everything alright?' I say to Alice, while she's putting dishes in the dishwasher.

'Yeah.'

'I know something's bothering you,' I say, standing against the side and taking a sip of wine. 'I can tell, you know. I'm your mum.'

Alice stands up and looks at me.

'And like I said, I'm fine.'

I look at Alice and I know she's lying. Alice is just like her father in so many ways. Josh is more like me and Daisy is a mix of the both of us. Just like Pete, who hates to discuss anything personal or emotional, Alice doesn't like talking about her life. I also realise she's a teenager and I'm probably the last person in the world she wants to confide in, but it's hard for me to stay out of her business. Whether she likes it or not, I'll always want to know what's happening in her life.

'Alice, please, if there's something on your mind you can talk to me. I do understand what it's like to be a fourteen-year-old girl, you know.'

'Right,' says Alice. 'Are we done here?'

'No we're not. Let's sit down at the table for a moment.'

'Really? You're going to make me do this?'

'Alice, please,' I say, sitting down and Alice reluctantly sits down too. 'I'm worried about you. Are you being bullied?'

'What? No, that's mental,' says Alice laughing.

'Then what is it?'

Alice looks at me and for a moment I think she's going to break and let herself go. Maybe we'll finally have one of those magical mother, daughter moments I've heard so much about. But she doesn't. This isn't one of those syrupy American family TV shows.

'It's nothing. I'm fine.'

'But if there's a real problem, if you need me, please talk to me. OK?'

'OK,' says Alice forcing out a smile. 'Can I go now?'

I want so much to know what's going on with her and I want to be the sort of mum she can talk to about anything, but I suppose just like with Daisy, I need to be patient. I have to trust she'll come to me when she's ready.

'Sure, love.'

Alice gets up and heads off upstairs to her bedroom.

I finish tidying up then go into the living room where Josh is playing FIFA and Daisy is running lines with Pete. I sit down and watch Daisy and Pete for a moment. Pete's sitting on the sofa next to Daisy, who's looking very intense. Daisy's teacher, Miss Hollingshead, has written her own modern version of the traditional Nativity play. Daisy is playing the role of Mary or as she's called in the play, Molly, and along with her husband, Joe, the call centre manager, they live in a flat in Basingstoke. The scene she's doing is the opening scene where she tells Joe she's pregnant. Pete's playing the role of Joe.

'I have some news,' says Daisy.

'I have to get off to work at the call centre, Molly, can it wait?' says Pete, holding his script.

'I don't know, Joe, can the fact I'm pregnant wait?'

'Pregnant!'

'Yes, Joe, I'm pregnant and you aren't the father!'

'Blimey,' says Pete, trying to stifle a laugh.

'What's funny?' says Daisy looking annoyed. 'You can't laugh, Daddy.'

'Sorry, love.'

'Let's go again,' says Daisy, closing her eyes, taking a deep breath, before she opens them again and looks at Pete seriously. 'I have some news.'

I look across at Pete and smile. He gives me a little smile back then I sit for a moment and watch Josh playing FIFA and I'm happy. I'm still worried about Alice, but hopefully she opens up soon and talks to me. I'm happy because this is my family and through thick and thin we stick together. This here, right now, is us. It might not be perfect, and it definitely isn't the perfect version of us I have in my head, but I don't think that really exists. But this us, sitting in the living room with Daisy running lines with Pete and Josh playing FIFA is the real us and it's enough.

'Fancy a game?' I say to Josh.

Josh looks at me as though I've gone crazy.

'Seriously?' says Josh incredulously. 'You want to play FIFA?'

'Why not?'

'Because I'll beat you like fifty nil.'

'I know, but it might be fun.'

'Alright,' says Josh. 'I'll set it up. Be prepared to lose!'

'Let's do this,' I say, getting up and walking over to where Josh is. He hands me a controller. I really have no idea how this works, but I'll give it a go. Josh spends a minute setting everything up. He picks teams and goes over the controls with me then we're off. It takes about ten seconds before he scores his first goal. It's actually a lot harder than I imagined. Trying to get the little men to do what I want is impossible and before long Josh is five nil to the good. Despite the score line and the fact I can't seem to keep the ball for longer than a second, it's fun. It's fun playing with Josh and even Daisy and Pete stop rehearsing and start watching us. Daisy starts supporting me and yells at Josh to stop showboating. The game eventually finishes fifteen nil then Pete gives Josh a game while I help Daisy with her lines. Apparently, I'm a lot better than Daddy, who couldn't do the voice properly and kept smiling at the wrong times.

We spend the evening in this small bubble of bliss. Alice eventually comes down too and joins in. Pete and I drink wine, while the kids play video games and we talk like a real family, like the family I always wanted us to be, and I even start to feel differently with Pete. I'm having so much fun I don't think about Mark or Mum once. I'm too busy enjoying a precious night at home with my family.

Seventeen

I usually end up going into the office once or sometimes twice a week if it's busy or I have a particularly good manuscript. To be honest, it's nice to feel a part of it. It's also slightly depressing to spend time with people whose whole life doesn't revolve around children and cleaning up the mess on the stairs. Don't get me wrong, there are women at the office who have children, some grown up and at university, but there are also quite a few who are still childless and hearing their tales of the single life can be a bit depressing. There's Georgie, a blonde, twenty-seven-year-old, editorial assistant who loves a good chat, and she's lovely, but hearing her talking about her life, about the endless holidays, the weekends away, the Sundays at the pub with mates, makes me feel quite old and past it. We're friends on Instagram and it's like following a celebrity. Her super tidy flat is gorgeous and like something from Homes and Gardens magazine. She loves sourcing her furniture from markets and salvage yards. It's all about upcycling and recycling. I wish I had the time. The only recycling I do is taking out the rubbish. The worst part is when she asks me the same question every week, 'So, Rosie, what's new with you?' And every week I give the same stilted, drab reply. 'Nothing'. Nothing is new with me because I'm forty and I have three kids and a marriage. And it's not that I want her life because I don't, but I wish that just once I could say something to her about my life she'd think was remotely exciting. It would be nice not to see her pitying face when I say, 'nothing' because it makes me feel like a sad, unwanted puppy in a dog home.

Today I'm in the office and I'm meeting with my boss, Alison. She's the commissioning director who oversees everything I do. I've been reading a wonderful manuscript she sent me a few weeks ago and I'm here to give her the thumbs up. We're meeting in fifteen minutes so I'm in the break room making a last-minute cup of tea and grabbing a biscuit. We have the best biscuits at work. I think it's the result of having an office full of women. I'm nearly finished when Georgie walks in.

'Hi, Rosie,' says Georgie, walking across and flicking the switch on the kettle. She brings in her own special green tea.

'Georgie, hi.'

She looks absolutely gorgeous as always. I try and make a bit of an effort when I come into the office, but most of my work clothes are about ten years old so I look a bit frumpy. Georgie, on the other hand, looks stunning. It's cold today and she's wearing a figure hugging knitted dress with a long cream cardigan, and a lovely scarf that wraps around her neck and down towards her perky young chest. Her blonde hair is immaculate in pigtails and she's wearing a beautiful pair of suede boots. I'm wrapped up in an old jumper, plain black British Home Store trousers, and the scuffed boots I bought five years ago in the January sales.

'It's chilly out there today. How's things? What's new?' says Georgie.

'Oh, you know, not much. What about you?'

The familiar feeling I have around Georgie of being the most boring person in the world sinks through my body, deflating me so I feel even shorter and more hunched over than I normally do. I notice her flat tummy and the long, slim legs, and I can feel my own stomach getting visibly larger as a result. The extra roll of fat like a small inflatable travel pillow that sits just below my belly button that refuses to budge no matter how much weight I lose elsewhere.

'Not much,' says Georgie, much to my surprise.

'Really? That's not like you.'

'Lying low, trying to write that novel.'

'You're writing a novel?' I say, trying not to sound too surprised. Not that I should be because it's Georgie and this has probably been in her big life plan since the age of ten. She's going to write a bestseller and be all over the Sunday supplements within a year.

'Trying, but it's hard going. Didn't you once mention something about writing one?'

'Oh, that old thing,' I say with a nervous laugh. 'Just mucking about, nothing serious.'

The truth is I've been trying to write a novel for years. It was supposed to be something I did while I was at home with the kids. I've started more than a few, but none were finished and now I can barely finish a shopping list let alone a full-length novel. Another pipedream to add to the pile.

'You'd be great. You're so funny and wise and you must have so many stories to tell. I bet it would be amazing,' says Georgie, making me gush with gratitude.

'Thanks, it's just trying to fit it in,' I say. The usual lie. 'Anyway, what's yours about?'

'It's a story about a girl like me, trying to navigate her

twenties, dating and so on. A sort of modern day Bridget Jones for Millennials. I love Bridget Jones, it's amazing, one of my fave books, but it was published in the nineties and feels a little dated now. Do you know what I mean?'

'I know exactly what you mean,' I say, feeling a little dated myself. I remember when it came out. I was twenty years old and living in London. It spoke to me then and still does now.

'I feel like the twentysomething girls of today need a new voice. A new hero.'

'And that voice is you?'

'Hopefully.'

'Well good luck,' I say, grabbing my cup of tea and another biscuit.

'You too,' says Georgie with a gorgeous smile. 'There's always time to write.'

I give her a sort of, OK then, laugh and head nod, before I take my tea and biscuit and head off for my meeting with Alison feeling much worse about myself. Why can't I be more like Georgie? I'm sure that's how I used to be. She's so driven and dedicated and she lets nothing stand in her way. I used to feel that way, but now it's as though all of that drive and energy has been turned off or dimmed down, and it feels impossible to get it back again. I'm the new low energy version of me.

The meeting goes well and Alison's happy with my work. We talk and it's nice because I've known her for a long time and we're good friends. She loves the manuscript too and wanted another pair of eyes on it before she took it further. It's nice that despite working from home, she still trusts me and values my opinion. After we're done talking about the book, I'm about to get up and head off for lunch when she stops me.

'One last thing before you go,' says Alison.

'Sure, what's up?'

'Naomi is leaving us. She's moving to Scotland with her family.'

'Wow, God, good for her. I know she talked about it, but that's great.'

'Yes, it's wonderful and we're all super happy for her. The thing is, it leaves us with quite a large gap and it's a gap I was rather hoping you'd fill. I want you to come back full-time, Rosie. Commissioning editor for commercial women's fiction. What do you say?'

I'm flabbergasted and I don't know what to say. Of course it's something I've thought about and I love the idea of being a full-time worker again, but there's the kids and the house and Pete. How can I do it all? I don't want to be one of those women who try to have their cake and eat it, but end up with a face full of cream. I've gone backwards and forwards on this for the last few years as the kids have grown up and need me less. Maybe I could make it work and perhaps I'll be happier and a better mum as a result. I need time to think about it though and I need to talk with Pete.

'Can I have some time to think about it?'

'Of course. Just a few days though because Naomi is leaving at the end of the month and we need to fill that role as quickly as we can.'

'A few days, no problem.'

'I'd love to have you back, Rosie.'

I thank her for thinking of me and we chat a bit more, before I leave. I feel excited and nervous and full of adrenaline as I walk out of the building and towards lunch with Lauren. This could be my life. Working lunches, meetings with authors, and everything I wanted before we had kids, before Mum got sick, and when Pete and I were happy. Maybe this is what we all need to get life back on track again. A reset button. There's just something I need to talk to Lauren about first.

I'm meeting Lauren in a pub nearby called the Grafton Arms. It's a nice little pub with good food and it's where I find Lauren, in her dark blue business suit, drinking a glass of wine. She's talking on the phone when I sit down, putting my handbag next to hers on the table. Lauren looks at me, pulls a face, then pretend shoots herself in the head.

'They won't go lower than one point seven. Yes, yes, I know it's a lot of money for a two bed terrace, but it's in Notting Hill. I'll talk to them, but look here's the thing, if you go in a hundred grand under, it's going to be gone because someone will pay it and they know it. If you really want it, we need to go in strong. I'm telling you it's the way to go. OK, let's talk later. Bye, bye.'

She puts her mobile down on the table.

'One point seven million?!' I say. 'For a two bedroom. Jesus.'

'It's in Notting Hill and you should see it, Rozza, it's incredible.'

'But one point seven million, that's crazy!'

'This is my life. How are you, babes?'

She gets up, leans over and gives me a kiss on the cheek. I swear she gets taller every time I see her, although when I look down I notice the huge heels she's wearing.

'I'm fine, great, actually. I just got offered a full-time job at work and I'm in a bit of a tizzy about it and need your advice.'

'Then you're in luck because advice is my middle name.'

'I thought it was Ann,' I say, and Lauren laughs.

'Oh, Rozza, you've still got it. Let's get some food and drinks and we can knock this out in thirty minutes,' says Lauren, grabbing menus and passing one to me.

We study the menus for a minute before I decide to go for a salad because I really should be watching my weight. I can't get the image of Georgie in that dress out of my mind. I quickly change my mind though when Lauren points out it's bloody freezing outside so I get the shepherd's pie instead. Lauren gets a burger and orders us both a glass of wine before we're back at the table ready to sort my life out.

'Pros and cons,' says Lauren. 'No wait, we don't have time for that. Just take the bloody job and stop being such a Bridget no balls about it. The old you would have taken that job on the spot.'

'I know and I want to, it's just the kids and the house...'

'Bugger the kids and the house. It's time you thought about you for once. The house will be fine, just get a cleaner, and the kids are all grown up. They don't need you around all the time crushing their mojo.'

'Thanks for that.'

'You know what I mean. They're not babies anymore, Rozza, they can survive without you and you can survive without them.'

'I haven't talked to Pete about it yet.'

'And what's he going to say? It's your life. You need to decide what's best for you.'

'And you think me going back to work full-time is what's best?'

'Of course, don't you?'

'Maybe. Yes. No. I'm not sure.'

'Look at me, Rozza Louise Willis. You've given the last fourteen years of your life to your husband and kids, and no offence, but it's made you quite boring.'

'Wow, offence taken.'

'This is your chance to get out there again. This is your chance to be you again. The old Rozza. We could be doing this on a regular basis.'

'So, you're only saying this so we can get slightly pissed during lunch more often.'

'No, I'm saying it because I think it's what you need.'

'Mm,' I say hesitantly.

'What does that mean?'

'It means there's something else I want to talk to you about first because it's why I'm so worried about taking the job.'

'Go on,' says Lauren as our food arrives and we start tucking in.

I had such a wonderful time with my family the other night playing games and going over lines with Daisy. I felt, for the first time in a long time, a real closeness with everyone. Sometimes our lives are so disjointed and fractured it's hard to feel that bond that keeps you together. It's almost as if after a while you stop feeling it then it's hard to remember what it was that brought you all together in the first place. That might sound a bit silly because we live together, but being close to someone physically doesn't mean you're close emotionally and as the kids have grown up and Pete and I have had our problems, I was starting to feel as though I was living in a house full of strangers. But then you have nights like last Friday and it reminds you who you are and why you're so important to each other. It was wonderful, but once the kids went to bed and it was just Pete and I alone, it changed. The frostiness, the sense of fracture and aloofness returned, and we felt a bit like strangers again. I don't know what it is, but there's something between us, a buffer that's keeping us apart.

I explain this to Lauren and tell her how I'm worried if I start working again, the chasm will only get wider. Pete and I are already in such a precarious place that if I start working full-time, I'm worried we'll never be able to find each other. I wish I knew how this wedge between us, this gaping hole, became so big.

'Look, Rozza, I get it. I totally understand, but do you think not taking this job is going to help? Maybe if you're happier it will help your marriage because you unhappy, definitely isn't helping,' says Lauren, before she takes a big bite of her burger.

'So what should I do?'

'Talk to him. Talk to Pete and get everything out in the open. Explain how you feel about you, about work, about your marriage, and maybe talking everything through will help.'

'You do know, Pete, right? Pete who hates talking about anything slightly serious or emotional.'

'Then you have to make him. Your life depends on it,

Rozza. Trust me, nothing gets fixed until you really open up and let everything out.'

'Speaking from experience?'

'What do you think? You've met my mum.'

'Fair enough,' I say, putting a fork full of hot shepherd's pie in my mouth, and it is exactly what I needed.

I know Lauren's right. I suppose I'm just worried about what happens when we do finally get everything out in the open. Do I tell him about Mark? And what do I say? I'm meeting Mark for a coffee tomorrow, something I really shouldn't be doing, but he sounded like he needed to talk. But Pete and I need to talk. We've needed to talk for such a long time and I know I've been putting it off, but now with the job offer on the table, it's time. There's no more time for delays, for procrastinating. If I'm going to take this job, save my marriage, and move forward the only way is with honesty and openness. I only hope Pete feels the same.

Eighteen

Chelsea and Westminster hospital, 2003

Nothing can prepare you for motherhood. Literally nothing. And nothing can prepare you for going into labour either. Especially the first time. Pete and I were in bed trying to sleep, but I wasn't because I was the size of a whale and I hadn't slept properly for months. The last month of a pregnancy is merely a constant struggle to be comfortable. That's it. Lying in bed for eight to ten hours is impossible when you're so big. I roll around, mumbling, groaning, keeping Pete awake, who bless him has done a remarkable job of keeping me and himself sane. He gets up in the night and gets me water, helps me in and out of bed, and still goes off to work in the morning and rings me all day to make sure I'm fine. I stopped working a month ago on doctor's orders. I'd planned to work right up until the baby was due, but I had high blood pressure and my ankles were the size of footballs, so I was ordered to stay at home. I bought a stack of magazines to read, watched hours of television, and read a few novels, waiting for my baby to come. Pete was wonderful the whole time, cooking dinner, getting me whatever I needed, rubbing my feet and helping me up to go to the toilet. I really couldn't have done it without him.

Two hours ago, I was sitting up in bed with Pete and I

said I felt something.

'Is it a contraction?' said Pete.

'How the hell am I supposed to know? It's not like I've had one before.'

'What does it feel like?'

'I don't know, it hurts. Like I have a giant poo that won't come out.'

'Oh, ok,' said Pete, sounding a bit disgusted.

'You asked.'

'Let me time them. I think we're supposed to time them. Shit, why didn't we pay more attention in those classes instead of messing about and giving all the other couples funny nicknames?'

'Because they were boring and if I remember correctly, it was you who said, it will be fine, women have been doing this for thousands of years, I'm sure we'll figure it out.'

'But you listened to me,' said Pete with a smile.

'Fine, you start timing and I suppose we'll just figure it out.'

And we did. I still had the pregnancy book his mother had brought us and we looked it up. We started timing my contractions and when they were at ten minutes we decided to make the trip to hospital. The drive Pete had practised and practised time and time again, just to make sure he knew exactly where to go and the quickest route. Luckily, it was the middle of the night and so the roads were empty.

'But what if this is nothing?' I said. 'They'll think we have no idea what we're doing.'

'Rosie, we do have no idea what we're doing!' said Pete, before he helped me off the bed, downstairs, and into the car.

I'm lying in a bed now and we're waiting. Pete's still timing my contractions and the midwife has been in and checked how dilated I am - not enough apparently. Pete rang my parents and his parents and everyone is on their way. It's code red.

'How are you feeling?' says Pete, sitting on the chair next to the bed.

'I must say, not great,' I say, the huge, deep pain in my belly, the heavy feeling of a baby pressing itself against my cervix. My body is getting itself ready to deliver a baby, but my mind isn't on the same page. There's no way I can do this.

'Can I get you anything?'

'How about a time machine to take me back to the night we had unprotected sex after a few too many glasses of wine?'

'Hilarious, Rosie,' says Pete, reaching across and holding my hand.

'Oh, fuck, here comes another one,' I say, feeling the ever-increasing pain shoot through my body. It's like the worst period pain times a hundred.

I've read so many articles about labour and about the joy of it. How wonderful it is and the sheer majestic beauty of it. These women who want no drugs or to deliver in pools because it's more natural. Gosh, it's just so lovely and there's absolutely nothing disgusting or difficult about the whole thing. All I can say to them is fuck off with your hippy bullshit and give me the drugs. Nothing in the world is worth this much pain.

'Get the midwife now!' I scream to Pete. 'I need more

drugs!' Pete looks momentarily shocked by my sudden outburst and just sits there. 'Pete, fucking go now!' I've seriously never sworn so much in my entire life.

'Right, yes, of course, sorry, sorry,' says Pete apologetically, running out of the room in search of help.

After they administer the drugs my mind is awash with relief and I'm feeling a bit lighter and certainly fuzzier. I tell Pete to sit next to me. He sits on the edge of the bed, holding my hand and rubbing my head.

'Love you,' Pete says, looking into my eyes.

'Love you too.'

'I can't believe we're about to have a baby.'

'Yes, about that,' I say, squeezing his hand a bit tighter. 'Look before I do this, I need you to promise me something.'

'Anything.'

'No I mean it. I need you to look me in the eye and promise me.'

'Rosie, you're about to have our baby...'

'Promise me!'

'I promise,' mumbles Pete uncertainly.

'The thing is, Pete, I'm about to give birth and you're going to see things. It's going to be horrible down there and there's a good chance I might poo while I'm doing it. I need you to promise me that whatever you see, whatever happens, you'll still love me and want to have sex with me afterwards. Promise me.'

Pete laughs, leans down, and kisses me on the lips.

'Rosie, you could do the biggest, smelliest poo in the world and I'll still love you and want to have sex with you afterwards. You're my wife and I love you more than anything else in the world and despite what you think, pregnant you is bloody sexy.'

'Maybe it's the drugs talking, but I'd have sex with you right now if I could.'

'Me too, although probably best we don't.'

'Right, time for another look downstairs,' says the midwife, walking into the room, slapping surgical gloves on. She's down there for a minute before she comes back up with a smile on her face. 'I think we're about ready.'

'What? Really? She's coming?' I say, tears suddenly stinging my eyes.

'She's coming,' says the midwife. 'And once they're ready, there's no going back.'

'Bloody hell,' says Pete, gripping my hand even tighter and taking a deep breath. You'd think he was the one having the baby.

It's an amazing experience and something that changes you, both physically and emotionally. Pete is amazing the whole time and despite the pain, the exhaustion, and everything else, eventually she comes.

'I can see her head,' says Pete from somewhere below me. 'I can see our baby girl's head and it's incredible, Rosie.'

'Another big push,' says the midwife. 'You're doing really well.'

And I push and push and Pete's down there watching our baby girl being born. I still can't see anything or hear anything because all I'm doing is focusing on the midwife. I'm trying to recover some energy between each last push because I'm exhausted, but I know I have to do this. I have no choice.

'She's almost here,' says Pete, his voice breaking.

'One more push should do it,' says the midwife and so I do.

One last push then I feel it. I feel my baby come out of me in a release of energy and pain, but she's here. My baby girl is in the world and a few seconds later I hear her voice. Her cry. Pete is crying and I'm crying, before Pete cuts the cord and she's being passed to me. She's lying on my chest. This little baby covered in blood and her face is scrunched up like the oldest person in the world, but at this moment, in this exact moment in time, she's the youngest person in the whole world. And she's mine. Ours. We created her and it's the most incredible feeling I've ever known.

'We did it,' I say to Pete, who has tears rolling down his cheeks.

'You did it,' says Pete, looking down at his daughter.

'She's perfect.'

'She is.'

And we sit for a moment together, holding our daughter, and for the first time in my life I truly understand love. Not just the love I feel for Pete or my parents, or the love I felt for previous boyfriends and friends, but the love you feel for a child because it's the most powerful feeling in the world. It goes beyond everything else. It physically changes you and makes you a better person. It's also terrifying because now I have this girl who needs me to protect her, to care for and love her and there won't be a second for the rest of my life when I'll stop worrying about her. It's the single most profound moment of my life and it makes Pete and I closer than we've ever been before.

My parents come in first, after the baby and I have

been cleaned up. Seeing them makes me start crying all over again. I can't help it. Seeing Mum is especially emotional because of the way she's declined over the last nine months. It's almost as if my pregnancy has been a mirror to her own struggles. While my baby grew inside of me, the disease grew inside of Mum, and now the woman who's seeing her granddaughter for the first time, is already different from the woman I told I was pregnant. The tics and involuntary movements have become worse, but more than that she's changing. She's quieter, more reserved and often drifts off and when I look at her. I still see my mum, but also someone who won't be herself for much longer. I won't get to see her into old age, she won't get to be a proper grandmother to our baby, and these thoughts seep deep within my soul and break my heart. James and I were both tested for the Huntington's gene and luckily, we're both fine. It was a tense and worrying time, especially being pregnant, but when we got the news on the same day, the whole family celebrated. We're going to be fine and our children will be too, but Mum is already starting to fade and there's no telling how quickly or slowly she will go.

'Here she is,' I say, passing her to Mum, who's sitting on the chair next to me.

'She's a real little smasher,' says Dad, tears in his eyes.

Mum holds her and we take photos and it's bittersweet because I have a baby and she's perfect, and Mum's still here, still with us, but I know my daughter will never know her. She might know a version of her, but she'll never know the real Mum, her proper grandma. And that thought makes me so sad. But today isn't the day for sadness, it's a day to be happy and reflect on how lucky we are. Pete and I sit together on the bed watching my parents with our baby before Pete's parents make it in too. They're over the moon and there's soon talk about drinks in the nearby pub to celebrate. I need my rest and so does our baby.

'So, what's her name going to be?' says Dad, before they leave.

I look across at Pete and he smiles at me.

'We were thinking Alice,' I say. 'Alice Elizabeth Willis.'

'That's lovely,' says Dad.

'Very pretty,' says Pete's mum.

'Mum, what do you think?' I say, looking at Mum, stood closely next to Dad. 'We had to slip Elizabeth in there.'

'It's lovely,' says Mum. 'Thank you.'

Elizabeth is Mum's name and it's been either the first or middle name for all the women in my family for generations. It feels especially poignant given Mum's condition. The parents eventually leave and Alice is asleep. I'm tired too and I need to sleep, but for a few moments at least, it's nice to cuddle with Pete and enjoy our baby daughter. It's an incredible feeling and one that although unexpected and life-changing in ways I wasn't ready for, I wouldn't take back for a moment.

Nineteen

I'm meeting Mark for a coffee at our Caffe Nero. I shouldn't say 'our', but it's become the place we go. It's nice. We talk, drink coffee, and eat the occasional pastry, and it's something I've come to really enjoy. There's very few people in my life I can talk to so openly and Mark has become one of them. It's something I'm so conflicted over because I know we're too close and especially so considering how things are with Pete. But it's not like anything is going to happen with Mark and I intend to tell Pete everything when we eventually do talk.

I've decided I want to take the full-time job. I want to go back to work and I'm terrified because it's such a big change, but I think we can make it work. Talking to Lauren I realised she was right. The children don't need me as much as they used to and maybe not being there all the time will improve our relationship. The same with Pete. Perhaps if I'm happier and more fulfilled, we'll be able to repair our marriage and be happy. I've thought about it a great deal and I've decided that Pete and I need to have a big talk about everything. We need to get everything out in the open, talk through our problems, and really figure everything out. I'm nervous but excited to be moving on. After fourteen years of being a mother, wife, chief cook, washer, and taxi driver, I'm going back to work in the job I wanted all those years ago. I'm only forty, maybe I can still achieve all my dreams. As the saying goes, It's never too late.

When I get to Caffe Nero, Mark is sitting down and he's already bought me a coffee.

'Good morning,' I say, walking in.

As usual he gets up and gives me a peck on the cheek. It's something that's become so familiar and comfortable between us that I don't think anything of it anymore. Even the hand on my waist that used to make me slightly uncomfortable and anxious is now routine. Mark and I are good friends and there's nothing wrong with that.

'How are you?' says Mark, looking dashing in a turtleneck jumper.

'Really good actually. I have some news.'

'Sounds exciting.'

'I'm going back to work full-time,' I say, unable to stop a huge smile from spreading across my face. 'I haven't discussed it with Pete yet, but I think he'll be fine and I'm so looking forward to it.'

'That's great. I'm so excited for you,' says Mark, but there's something in his eyes, in the way he's sitting, that tells me otherwise.

'But?'

'But what?'

'You said you're excited for me, but you don't look that excited.'

I take a quick sip of my coffee. He even put in the one sugar I have with my latte.

'I'm sorry, it's just, I'll miss our coffee mornings,' says Mark, and I'm trying my best not to blush, but I can't help it. 'I'm excited for you, Rosie, but a little sad for me if I'm being honest.'

'Then you'll have to make it into town for lunch, won't you?' I say without really thinking it through properly.

'Definitely,' says Mark, looking at me and this time it's him that's blushing slightly.

I need to change the subject quickly because this conversation is going somewhere too difficult and challenging to even comprehend. I know Mark and I are close, and there are feelings simmering between us that are more than just friendly, but I'm determined to fix my marriage with Pete and besides, Mark's still grieving for his wife. He's probably just lonely. It must be so difficult for him. I want to be here for him, but I need to take care of my own marriage first. I'm about to change the subject and move on to something less inflammatory, when Mark reaches across and places his hand on mine. For a second I flinch, about to pull it away, but I don't. It feels warm and comforting. I look across at Mark, at his handsome face, at his eyes that are looking into mine.

'Mark, I…' I stutter.

'Rosie, I'm sorry, I know this is wrong, and I'm not trying to put you in a difficult situation because I know you're married, but I have to say this. I've been thinking about it for a while now, and I think it's best to get it out in the open. I care about you, Rosie. You're an amazing woman and if there's any chance, at all, of us becoming more than just friends, I want you to know it's something I've thought about.'

Mark looks at me, his hand still on mine, and I don't know what to say or what to feel. I'm so conflicted and confused. I didn't want or mean for this to get so out of control. Mark and I have a connection, I've known that for some time, but to act on it or admit it, is something else entirely. I'm completely thrown because I wasn't expecting this. What does he want me to say? How can I respond? I'm getting hotter and redder and I need to get away. I need some fresh air. I can't handle this.

'I'm sorry,' I say, pulling my hand away and standing up.

I grab my coffee and coat and start walking out.

'Rosie, please,' says Mark, but I'm not listening and soon I'm outside and walking as quickly as I can towards home. Away from Mark and away from temptation.

As soon as I get home, I sit down at the dining room table, my warm coffee still in my hands, and I start crying. I don't know why I'm crying about this, it's daft, but I'm feeling emotional and this put me over the edge. My phone rumbles with a text and when I look down it's from Mark and it says, *I'm sorry*. I feel awful walking out on him like that, but I couldn't deal with it. I'm married to Pete and I want us to work, for my family to be closer and stronger, and today I felt something for Mark that threatens to destroy that. This is why I'm crying. Not because I'm sad but because I'm scared. I'm excited to start working full-time again. I know I can make my home life work and I can do better with the kids, but the one thing I still don't know if I can fix is my marriage. I want to and I hope we can, but I don't know and hearing Mark today, it threw me because for a moment I felt something pulling me to him and it scared me.

I finish my coffee and start tidying the house before I have to get the kids. I lose myself in thoughts about my new job and what I'm going to say to Pete, and I imagine our family happy again. I daydream about holidays together, exotic beaches and warm sunshine, the kids playing, Pete and I having the time of our lives. I'm hoovering and picturing the happiest family, the family I always wanted us to be; together, solid and full of love. This is what I need to focus on and this is what I want.

The kids bundle into the house after school. Coats get hung up in the hallway, shoes get kicked off and bags dumped on the floor. The previous quiet of the house is destroyed as Josh turns on the television, Daisy is pestering me about a school drama trip, and Alice is playing music in her bedroom. I saw Mark briefly after school, but I came late on purpose so I could pick up the kids but have no time to talk to him. He looked sad and lost and I felt sorry for him, but I need to focus on my family and not his.

I'm making fish, chips, and mushy peas for dinner and Pete has promised he'll be home on time. I want tonight to go well. Once the kids are in bed, I'm going to talk to Pete about everything. I'm ready to move on and I need to know Pete's on the same page. All of this can only work if he feels the same. I feel a deep pain in my heart because despite knowing that everything I dreamed about earlier is just that, a dream, I also realise it could be a reality and I want it. I want it so badly it hurts. One of my plans is to ask Pete if we could have a proper family holiday. We need it and we haven't been away for so long. Pete works long hours and always feels guilty about taking time off. I was looking at brochures in Tesco the other day, at all the places we could go, and I got excited. I always thought we'd be the sort of family that travelled a lot, but we don't and it's something we have to change. I want us to go away, maybe this Christmas, somewhere abroad, somewhere different and warm. The kids would love it and I think it would bring us all closer together. It's about getting the work/life balance that right now we don't have. Now it's all work and life is suffering.

Dinner is in the oven and Josh and Daisy are doing their homework at the table. Pete will be home soon, so I head off upstairs to see Alice. I don't know why but I've been thinking about her a lot today. I'm still worried because I know something's wrong. When I get to the landing, I go to knock on her bedroom door when I hear a noise. She's crying. She's trying to be quiet, but I know when my daughter's crying. My heart immediately starts to throb because my little girl is upset and I can't stand it. I knock on the door, but instead of waiting for a reply as usual, I go straight in.

'Alice, what's the matter?'

She's sitting up on her bed. I'm waiting for the argument, the shouting, her telling me to go away and leave her alone. I'm expecting her to turn me away, tell me I have no idea what her life is like. I'm waiting for the cold shoulder, but today it doesn't come. Today she melts and I go to her, grabbing her body, as she falls into me, crying uncontrollably into my shoulder. My poor baby girl. What could have happened for her to react like this? My mind is awash with all sorts of thoughts and theories, none of them good.

'What's up, love?' I say, stroking her hair and feeling her body shudder against mine.

She's so grown up now. The small, thin body I used

to hug is now growing and becoming that of a young woman. She has breasts, hips, and she's fleshy. When she was younger and I used to hug her in bed, she was all bone, but now she feels so different, so alien.

'I thought he liked me,' says Alice between tears. 'I'm so stupid, Mum.'

'If there's one thing you definitely aren't, it's stupid.'

She pulls away so I can see her face. Her cheeks are red and puffy and her eyes are the same. The hair around her face is slightly damp from the tears and is matted against her skin. She looks like a little girl again. Like my little girl. She sniffs up the tears and I tell her to take a deep breath. She finally calms down and I look at her and ask her what's going on.

'There's a boy at school, Andy Moss, he's in my year. He's the best looking boy and everyone wants to be his friend. He's on the football team and everything. I thought he liked me, Mum. He acted like he did so I asked him out. Jessica said I should. But he doesn't and now he's going out with Sarah Middleton.'

'I'm sorry. I know how it can feel. Love is a tricky business, but trust me it's going to be alright. There'll be other boys who do want to go out with you. Lots of boys. Trust me, your father's going to have a field day keeping them all away.'

I look at Alice and she finally smiles, before stifling a laugh.

'I doubt it.'

'Look at me,' I say, lifting her face up so her eyes are on me. 'Over the next ten years there's going to be so many boys in your life. It's going to happen. Some will last and some won't, but eventually you'll find the one, and none of this will matter. I know it hurts now and it will probably hurt for the next week or two, but you'll move on. That's what happens.'

'Is that what happened to you? Is that how you met Dad?'

'Something like that.'

'And do you still love Dad the same as you did then? When you first met him?'

'Of course, love. Your father and I are fine.'

'Because you argue a lot.'

'We do, but that's because we love each other a lot. Sometimes it's easier to fight with the people closest to us, just like you do with Josh and Daisy.'

'So, you and Dad are alright?'

'Of course, love, and you will be too.'

'Thanks, Mum,' says Alice, before she gives me a hug.

Hugging Alice makes me so happy. I'm so relieved her problems are just with boys. She's only fourteen and I know over the next few years we're going to have quite a few boy problems and maybe even girl problems with Josh, but that's OK because it's normal. I was worried she was being bullied or worse. I keep track of all her online things. I have access to her social media accounts and even her texts. I try and keep out of her business, but as her mother, I can't sit back and do nothing. I monitor her Instagram and Snapchat pages because I'm a concerned parent. It's such a different age now. When I was fourteen, the only thing my mother had to worry about was whether I was listening to albums with swear words in them. Nowadays a few naughty words are the least of our worries with the whole internet awaiting them.

Alice and I eventually make it downstairs and she helps lay the table for dinner. Josh and Daisy finish their homework and Pete comes home on time, before we sit down to eat. After this morning and my coffee with Mark, I'm feeling good again. I'm feeling ready because what I said to Alice was right. Pete and I have been arguing a lot, but it's because we love each other a lot, and I'm sure that once we talk, really talk, our love will shine through and everything will be alright.

Twenty

Dinner goes well. Alice perked up after our chat and Josh and Daisy gave us the latest on their lives. Daisy's rehearsing twice a week for her play and she's loving every minute of it. She's been so good since she started acting I'm worried what she's going to do after it's done. Josh is on the school football team now, as well as his regular Sunday team, and it's all he talks about. He wants to be a footballer when he grows up. It's good to see him so happy and enthused by something, but we have to keep reminding him he needs to study hard too because not everyone makes it playing football. It's always such bittersweet joy with children because behind every beautiful painted door there's always a shitty hallway with a dodgy rug ready to trip them up. I'm always encouraging them to follow their dreams, believe in themselves, but with the caveat that they need a good education in case they fail.

We get everything tidied up, get the kids to bed, until it's just Pete and me. I open a bottle a wine and we sit down in the living room. Since coming home from work, I've noticed something's definitely wrong with Pete. He's been absent, quiet, and I can tell there's something on his mind. I know that whatever it is he won't talk about it because he's Pete. Cold hearted Englishman to the end. He didn't used to be this way, but as he's aged, he's become more and more like his own father. The irony is that when we were younger, he'd rant for hours about how his father annoyed him and how he'd never be like him. Perhaps turning into our parents is something none of us can help.

'You alright?' I say, taking a sip of wine.

'Fine,' mumbles Pete.

'I know you're lying.'

'Sorry?'

'I know something's on your mind. I can tell.'

'How?'

'Because I've been married to you for seventeen years, Pete, and despite what you might think, you still have the same expression on your face now when something's bothering you as you did from the day we met.'

'Oh,' says Pete. 'You always were rather good at that sort of thing.'

'What sort of thing?'

'People. You're good with people.'

'I think it's called being a woman,' I say, laughing to try and lighten the mood. 'There's something I need to talk to you about, actually.'

I look across the sofa at Pete, my husband, and I know this is the time to talk about everything. For so long I've felt as though my life was stuck, that I was plodding along, trapped in the life we created. I've wanted more for so long and finally I feel as though it's about to happen. I know Pete and I have grown apart, but we love each other and there's nothing we can't fix with a bit of love, commitment, and hard work. Pete looks at me and he still has the same expression on his face. He's worried, but hopefully my news will help.

'Go on,' says Pete, taking a big gulp of his wine.

'Alison's asked me to go back to work full-time, and I really want to do it. I know it's going to be difficult with us, the kids, the house, and everything else, but I think it will be good for me. For us.' I'm so excited I can't help myself. The words keep falling out of my mouth, tumbling like building blocks. 'I know we haven't been at our best for a while now and I'm not saying who's to blame because it's the both of us. I know I haven't been the easiest person to live with recently, but I think this is going to change everything. I'm going to be happier, I think the kids will be fine and hopefully being around them less will mean that when I am I have more patience. I think we've let things fall apart, but we can be amazing again, I know we can. I was thinking, I'd love a holiday. A proper family holiday abroad. You, me, the kids, on a beach somewhere hot. Time away together to enjoy life because you've been working too hard, Pete, you have, and I want us to be better, all of us. I want us to feel like we did years ago, the same love, and the same…'

'Please stop,' says Pete quietly.

'Sorry?'

'I said please stop.'

'Sorry, I'm just excited. This is a chance for us to hit the reset button. You and me, we can be happy again. Unless that's not what you want?'

I look at Pete, a sudden wobble of nervousness sitting in my stomach making me feel sick. I was so excited to share my news and I really thought he'd be excited too. Why isn't he excited? Why doesn't he want us to be happy again?

'Of course it's what I want,' says Pete, finally looking at me. He reaches across and holds my hands in his. 'It's what I've always wanted.'

'Then what's the problem? Why is there this wedge between us you won't let us fix? For months and months you've been distant and I've tried to talk to you, but you won't. I want us to be happy, but the only way we can move on is if you're with me. If you talk to me and tell me what's going on.'

'There's something,' says Pete, taking a deep breath, his face changing and he looks afraid. 'Something I need to tell you, Rosie. I've wanted to tell you for so long because it's eating me up inside. It's killing me because I want what you just said. I want us to be happy again, but we won't be unless we get over this first.'

He's holding my hands and I'm holding his and I'm scared. I'm scared because happiness feels so close, but he has something to say and I have no idea what it is. I'm sure whatever it is we can get past it. It's Pete. I love him and he loves me. All you need is love.

Pete takes another deep breath and I see his eyes beginning to fill with tears. His normal sparkling blue eyes are glassy and red and his face looks older and puffier. He hasn't been sleeping well or eating and he's been working too hard. He needs a rest, a holiday. We all do.

'I don't know how to tell you this, or what to say, so I'm just going to say it. But first I have to say how much I love you, Rosie. You mean the world to me and you're right, things haven't been great with us for a long time, and it's more my fault I know that, but it's no excuse. I'm so sorry for what I did…'

'For what, Pete. What did you do?'

'I slept with someone else, Rosie. It was just one night. A mistake. I'd been drinking and I wasn't thinking straight. I'm so sorry.'

Pete stops talking and I'm numb. Completely numb. I didn't even hear some of the words at the end because of the piercing ringing sound in my head. Pete slept with someone else. My Pete. My husband. I can't believe it and it doesn't seem at all real. How can it be? For weeks or months he's kept this secret from me. While I went about my day taking care of the kids, making lunches, dinners, and making sure Pete's shirts were ironed for work, he was sitting on this the whole time. The night he slept with another woman. I feel sick and the room is spinning. How could he have done this? No matter what problems we were having, no matter how bad our relationship, to have sex with someone else, to break our marriage vows is beyond my comprehension. I didn't think he was capable. It's Pete. So very English, uptight, civil, and so very sensible. He doesn't have it in him to have an affair. I can't even begin to imagine him with someone else. Who was it? When did it happen? Where did it happen?

'Rosie, please say something? I know what I did was awful, the worst thing in the world, but I love you and I want us to be happy again. I'll do anything to make you happy, just say it and I'll do it.'

I come back to reality. I'm still feeling light headed and my mind is fuzzy and doesn't feel like my own. I realise I'm still holding Pete's hands and I pull away quickly. Those hands that touched another woman's body. Did he enjoy it? More than with me?

'Who?'

'Sorry?'

'Who was she?'

'Does it matter?'

'Yes it matters, Pete. Who did you sleep with?'

My brain is in a fluid state as I feel a sudden coherence. A clarity of thought and it's all anger and jealousy and hatred. How could he do this to me? To us? To the kids?

'Someone at work. One of the paralegals.'

'Which one? What's her name?'

'What difference does it make? Can we move on from this? Let's talk about us.'

'I want to know which one it was, Pete.'

My voice is hardening like water slowly turning to ice. I need to know which one it was. I'm going over the options in my mind because I've met them all. They've met me and the kids too probably. Louise Faulkner, 37, married, tall, slim but with a large nose and no breasts. Claire Graham, 27, short, large breasts, posh, but I'm sure she has a boyfriend. Then lastly, I get to Sarah Wakefield, 29, from Leeds, definitely the most attractive, medium build, nice breasts - bigger than mine anyway, wears a bit too much makeup, but has a bum and legs I'd die for. The line-up is clear in mind and yet I still don't know which one it might be.

'It was Claire.'

'Fuck, Pete. I can't believe this. Doesn't she have a boyfriend?'

'Did, yes, not anymore.'

'Oh, so you can keep fucking her? What was it, Pete, the posh voice? One of your own,' I say, standing up, pacing around the room.

My mood is fluctuating constantly between anger, disbelief, and sadness. Without warning I'm crying, pacing the room with tears streaming down my face.

'Rosie, please, let me explain. It wasn't like that.'

'Explain what, Pete? You cheated on me. You shagged someone else. Fucking Claire. Was she even worth it?'

'Rosie, please keep your voice down, we don't want to wake the kids.'

'So now you care about the kids. Where was that when you were shoving your dick inside Claire?'

'Rosie, please,' says Pete, standing up. 'I know you're angry and you have every right to be, but can we discuss this properly?'

'Properly?' I shout, before I lower my voice. 'I'm sorry. You have sex with someone else and you expect me to "discuss it properly"? What would you like, Pete, a list of reasons why I'm angry and a simple five step plan and a written affidavit as to when I'm going to stop fucking hating you? Would that make you happy?'

I can't stop the tears that keep coming out of my eyes, one after another, falling down my face and onto the floor. The wooden floors we refinished after we moved in. I remember the weekend we did it. I read all about it and we hired the proper tools and we did it ourselves. The kids stayed with his parents and Pete and I did it together. We sat on the sofa eating takeaway pizza from the box in our old clothes, me in a pair of overalls, and Pete in a pair of faded cords. We had sex on the sofa that night because the kids were all gone and we could. Every place in this house has memories like that. Every piece of furniture, photo, piece of art or decoration has a memory attached to it because that's what happens when you have a family, you create memories. But now this is one of those memories. The night Pete told me he slept with someone else. The night that changed everything.

Pete walks towards me and tries to touch me, to hold me, but I push him away.

'Don't fucking touch me.'

'Rosie, please,' says Pete, tears swimming around his eyes. 'It meant nothing. One night of madness. Of stupidity. We can't throw everything we have away because of one mistake.'

'And is that what you were thinking when Claire asked you to have sex with her?'

'It wasn't like that.'

'Then please tell me how it was, Pete, because I'd love to know.'

'I was drunk.'

'When was this?'

'Months ago. Two months ago. I was working late with Claire, we went for a drink…'

'One thing led to another and your cock was suddenly in her mouth?'

'I don't remember making a conscious decision. It just sort of happened.'

'Where did it just sort of happen?'

'At the office.'

'Fucking hell, Pete. You shagged Claire at work. That's just fucking brilliant.'

'We got dressed and I came home.'

'Wait. That was the night you came home at midnight, smelling like a brewery and you told me it was Edward's birthday drinks.'

'Yes.'

'I can't believe this.'

'I'm sorry, Rosie, really, truly, it's the worst thing I've ever done and will ever do, but you have to forgive me.'

'Do I?' I say, feeling so angry.

The tears are drying up and all I want now is to be left alone. I want Pete gone.

'Rosie, please.'

He tries to walk towards me and put a hand on me, but I bat him away.

'I think you should sleep somewhere else tonight.'

'On the sofa?'

'No, Pete, somewhere else outside of this house.'

'But where will I go?'

'To be honest, I don't really care. I just want you gone.'

'But what about the kids? What will you tell them?'

'I'll say you left early for work.'

'You really want me to leave?' says Pete, looking at me, his face broken.

'Yes,' I say quietly, looking away from him. 'Just pack a bag and go.'

'Right, yes, of course. Whatever you want.'

Pete stands for a moment, the room is silent and heavy with emotion, before he walks out and I hear him going upstairs. As soon as he's gone, something inside of me shatters and I fall onto the sofa, the tears coming stronger and stronger than before. I can't help them and my body is shaking in sadness and pain. My husband slept with someone else and no matter what happens for the rest of my life, for the rest of our lives, that's something I can't change, that I won't be able to forget. I don't know if I'll be able to forgive him or whether our marriage is over, but right now the only thing I can think about is the kids. I've spent every second of every day trying to protect them from the world, from all the nasty people, the terrible things out there, but now it's something inside that's going to get them. This might break our family and tear it apart. I don't know because the future seems so far away right now, but if it does then we will have failed our children and that's something I never thought Pete or I would do.

I eventually hear Pete walking down the stairs, a bag hitting against the wall. He stops in the hallway, while I'm sniffing up as many tears as I can. I don't want him to see me like this.

'I'm off,' says Pete, poking his head around the door.

I don't say anything. I can't. There are no words to say and nothing can change what's been done. I let Pete leave the house in silence, before I sink back into the sofa, tears hurting my eyes, and a headache throbbing deep in my skull. I thought tonight was going to be the night when we'd start again, get back on track, when life would start to take shape and become something solid we could build on. Tonight was supposed to be a fresh start. Pete and Rosie. Rosie and Pete. Instead I lie on the sofa, crying myself to sleep, and Pete is gone. Our marriage in tatters, my life in a place I never imagined, while upstairs our three beautiful children sleep snug in their beds, completely unaware that their selfish father has changed their lives forever.

Twenty-One

North London, 1996

I've had a couple of one night stands before and the one thing they've all had in common was a slightly embarrassing morning after. You wake up, hungover, next to a practical stranger with the vague notion that something happened. You aren't quite sure what. I know it's awful and something I've never set out to do, but at university it happens. It happened last night. But this one is different. When I opened my eyes this morning and looked across at the man next to me, I remembered everything and I wasn't hungover. I smiled to myself because I know we had an amazing night. A life changing night.

Pete's still sleeping, front down, his face turned towards me, his hair sprawled upwards onto the pillow. He looks happy and even more handsome in the cold light of morning. I'm not wearing a watch and the curtains are drawn so I'm not sure what time it is. I stretch up slightly, trying to be quiet so I don't wake up Pete, and I look around the room for a clock. Luckily, he has a digital alarm clock on his nightstand. It's says 8:41 in bright red numbers. I'm not hungover, but my mouth is dry and I really need a wee. I look for my clothes and surprisingly, they're folded neatly on a chair. I don't remember doing that last night.

I draw back the duvet ever so slightly and slowly get out of bed as quietly as I can. The cold air outside hits me and instantly makes me shiver. It's freezing. I get dressed and walk, tip-toeing, out of his room. I close the door softly and look along the landing. Nothing seems familiar and last night I didn't use the bathroom, so I'm not sure where it is. Luckily, the house is quiet and no one else is either awake or home. I walk along the landing until I come to the only open door and walk inside, locking the door behind me.

The bathroom is amazingly clean considering this an all-male student house. It's cleaner than my house. Lauren, Aimee and I have a cleaning rota, but we never stick to it and to be honest, we're all quite messy. The bathroom is especially bad. It's full of bottles of shampoo, conditioner, facial creams, moisturisers, and makeup. The towels are usually hung up to dry, but always retain a certain dampness due to the coldness of the house. The radiator in the bathroom is on the blink and doesn't ever get hot. We've complained to the landlord, but he doesn't care and we don't have a leg to stand on so we just get cold. This bathroom is clean and organised and there's nothing on the shelves except toothbrushes, a cup for water, and a few cans of deodorant. They even have a little wooden shelving unit that has towels on and a can of air freshener. They're living like kings.

I go for a wee, wash my hands, then look in the mirror. I look awful. Whereas I looked at Pete this morning and thought he looked even better than last night, he's going to think the opposite of me. Unfortunately, I left home without my emergency morning kit. I usually bring supplies for this eventuality or if I happen to end up sleeping at a friend's, but I wasn't planning much and so my handbag is basically empty. I have some lipstick, chewing gum, and a small bottle of perfume that's almost empty. I wash my face with water, brush my teeth with some toothpaste on my finger, chew chewing gum, put on some lipstick, and spray myself with the perfume. I run my fingers through my hair, which to be honest, doesn't help much but it's better than nothing, before I open the door and walk out onto the landing and immediately into Pete.

'Oh, hi, hello, good morning, I was just,' I mumble.

Pete looks gorgeous in a white t-shirt and a pair of boxer briefs. He must be freezing.

'I need a quick wee. Then I'll be back in.'

'Right,' I say with a slightly uncomfortable smile.

Pete rushes past me and into the bathroom, while I walk back into his room and sit down on the bed. I suppose the one thing I haven't really considered is whether Pete still feels the same this morning. Last night we both said how much we liked each other and he seemed so genuine, but that was then and this is now. Maybe now he won't feel the same. Perhaps he can't wait to get rid of me, out of the door as quickly as he can before breakfast. Irrational, paranoid thoughts start swirling through my mind. Maybe he has a girlfriend. Perhaps last night was all just an act so he could get me into bed. I stand up and start looking around the room for any signs of a significant other. His desk, like everything else, is neat and tidy. There's a computer, a CD player, a few books, and a framed photo. In the photo there's Pete with what I assume is his mum, dad, sister, and a dog, a brown cocker spaniel. They're in the country, smiling, looking happy and full of money. They're all so brilliantly white and healthy looking, so pure, wholesome, and so very English in their wax jackets. Even the dog looks superior to other dogs and definitely better than Rex, the mutt we picked up from the dog shelter when I was little and had bladder problems. This is who I'm dealing with. It makes me instantly on edge because I'm nothing like this. My family are nothing like his and I'm not sure I can compete. Browsing around the room there's countless law books, a small television, and a few more photos, but no signs of a girlfriend.

I hear the door to the bathroom open and footsteps on the landing. I sit down on the bed, suddenly nervous. It's silly because last night was amazing, one of the best nights of my life, and I know Pete and I had something. Had something - the words fizzle out like a dud firework that won't light. The sort Dad used in our garden when I was growing up, with Mum shouting at him to stay back because he was going to get his face blown off. I imagine Pete's fireworks nights were nothing like ours. His were probably orchestrated affairs, proper big displays, while they sat in the Land Rover, sipping hot chocolate, and oohing and aahing at the cracks in the sky. Mine were about cheap hot dogs and cans of Coke in the back garden, while Dad got out the old biscuit tin with maybe five fireworks inside that would barely light up our garden. We'd stand around in the cold making figure eight shapes with sparklers, while inside Rex howled in a puddle of his own pee.

'Sorry, I was desperate,' says Pete, walking back into the room, closing the door behind him. 'And sorry it's so bloody cold. This house is always freezing. I'm sure someone died here.'

'It's fine, ours isn't much better.'

Pete gets back under the duvet and puts his hands

behind his head. His biceps flex slightly. He has muscles. Actual muscles cultivated from exercise. My last boyfriend, Alex, was tall, but skinny, and had no muscles because you don't get muscles playing guitar, drinking beer, taking drugs, and smoking cigarettes. Pete used to row and he still probably plays squash or has friendly games of rugby and no doubt belongs to a gym. I went to the university gym once. It was the tour during fresher's week and I haven't been back since.

'So, what shall we do today?' he says.

He sounds even posher than he did last night.

'Sorry?'

'Do you have plans? I thought we could do something. Sorry, am I getting ahead of myself?'

'No, no, it's fine. No plans. Oh wait, let me check my diary,' I say, pretend-rifling through my handbag, picking up a pretend diary and skimming through the non-existent pages. 'No, nothing on the agenda today.'

Pete laughs.

'Then how about you come back to bed because it's still very early.'

'And what makes you think I'm still tired?'

'Who said anything about sleep?' says Pete, and this time it's me who's giggling.

I get undressed and hop quickly back under the duvet and cuddle into Pete. In a moment, we're talking easily and it feels just like it did last night and all the silly doubts I had are gone and replaced with a steady confidence that this is something special. Something different. We have sex again and it isn't awkward or difficult and it feels as though it's something we've done a hundred times before. With Pete everything is so comfortable and familiar and nothing feels strained or as if we're trying too hard. I haven't felt like this before. With Alex I was always on guard, always trying to be something because he was a wannabe rock star and I was trying to be that too. Every weekend with him was going to gigs, listening to him play, hanging out with the same too cool crowd that all looked, dressed, and acted the same. I was never just me around Alex because I don't think just me was what he really wanted. But with Pete, I find myself being the me I am when I'm alone, when no one's watching, and it's the most honest, true version of myself. He doesn't crave anything other than the truth, to know the real me, warts and all, and we talk all morning. He gets up, makes us tea, coffee, and toast, and comes rattling back to bed, sliding in next to me and we eat together, the crumbs falling onto the cracked plate between us.

We don't get out of bed until after lunch, by which time the sun is shining and we take a walk. We walk to a nearby pub and have a late lunch and a drink, but it feels ever so grown up and different from how things were with Alex. That would have been beer and crisps, smoking cigarettes, maybe a game of pool, while dissecting the naff songs from the jukebox. It would have been posturing, we'd have called friends, and had a big one because that's what he did. Always a big one with Alex. Pete and I talk, drink wine, and it feels so natural, so right.

At the end of the day, it's almost dark, and he walks me back to my house in Wood Green. Right up to the front door like a perfect gentleman.

'Want to come in for a cuppa?' I say, realising as I'm saying it how common I sound compared to him. He's probably never uttered the word, 'cuppa' in his entire life.

'I'd love to. I don't want this day to end, but I have to get back. I have studying to do.'

'No, it's fine. Today's been wonderful.'

'It has and maybe if you're free, we could do something tomorrow?'

'Let me check my diary,' I say, about to get out my imaginary diary again.

Pete laughs, puts both hands behind me, and pulls me closer.

'I'll take that as a yes.'

'It's a definite yes.'

'Good,' says Pete, before he kisses me again, his lips pressed firmly but gently against mine and I don't want it to stop.

It's getting cold as the sun disappears behind the houses. I watch him walk away, out of our front garden, and along the pavement. He turns once, smiles and waves, making me feel giddy again before he's finally out of sight. For the first time today I'm alone and I sort of sink into myself. I can't believe what's just happened. Last night I went out for a bit of a laugh with Lauren, but the idea of meeting anyone, especially someone special, was the furthest thing from my mind. The next few years are supposed to be about me and my career and not a man, but I didn't know the man was going to be Pete because with him, I feel like I can have it all. I can be with him, while still having my career, and maybe I'm lost in some sort of idealistic love bubble after the day we've had, but I really feel like he might be *the one*. It sounds silly just thinking it, but it's there, in my brain, and as I turn the key in the front door, I can't help but smile the biggest smile. I'm coming home a different person than when I left and the future is something that frightens me less because I'm sure I won't be facing it alone.

Twenty-Two

I open my eyes as the sound of something like thunder jolts me awake. I quickly realise it isn't thunder, but Josh and Daisy coming down the stairs. For a split second, I'm not sure why I'm on the sofa, but it floods me in a second and all the memories from last night come back in a terrifying mess, fragmented and jumbled up like the world's most depressing jigsaw puzzle. But then the ending hits me, succinct and clear, forcing me to sit upright. Pete slept with someone else. My husband cheated on me. This is when I feel the pain in my head, the throbbing headache, no doubt caused by all the crying and the feelings that are still locked inside me trying to force their way out.

'What are you doing, Mummy?' says Daisy, suddenly standing in the doorway.

Behind her Josh stands looking at me too, his eyes as usual this time of the morning, barely open.

'Just sitting on the sofa,' I say, trying to my best to act normal. To not give anything away.

'Where's Dad?' says Josh.

Where's Pete? I have no idea where he ended up last night. A hotel I'd imagine. He's probably getting ready for work about now.

'He had to leave early for work,' I say, standing up. 'Right, breakfast!'

'Are you sure you're alright?' says Daisy curiously.

'Because you look weird.'

'Fine, love, just a bad night's sleep,' I say, walking quickly from the living room to the kitchen. If I keep moving and get the kids ready for school, I'll be able to keep myself together and not give anything away. That's the key, just keep moving. If I stop for a moment and think about it, it will crush me and I'll crumble. 'OK, who wants what?'

'Cereal or something,' mumbles Josh, sitting down at the table.

Josh isn't a morning person. He can barely function for the first hour he's awake. He's definitely going to be a coffee lover when he's older. Daisy is far more awake and talkative.

'I was thinking about porridge, but then I remembered those eggs you made last week. You know the ones with the potato waffles, Mummy?'

'Poached?' I say, rifling through the fridge, hoping we have some eggs.

'Yes! Poached eggs on potato waffles with bacon!' says Daisy excitedly.

'I'll have that too,' says Josh.

'Is Alice awake?' I ask, finding eggs, bacon, and looking through the freezer for potato waffles. I know we have some in here. If only the freezer wasn't so full.

'Dunno,' says Josh.

'No,' says Daisy. 'Do you want me to wake her up?'

'Yes please, but be nice,' I say, but Daisy's already off, running up the stairs, her feet heavy on the landing. I find the box of potato waffles, flick the switch for the grill, fill the kettle with water, and turn it on. I'm getting plates ready, getting the saucepan on for the poached eggs, unwrapping the bacon, and I'm not thinking about Pete or last night. Or Claire, let's not forget about Claire.

I hear Daisy waking up Alice then Alice telling Daisy to leave her alone. Josh is sitting at the table with his handheld device and he's playing a game of something. I switch the radio on and start listening to the morning show on Radio 2. I'm keeping active, moving, cooking, listening, then Daisy comes back downstairs and plonks herself next to Josh.

'She's awake,' says Daisy.

'Thank you. Now what day is it today?'

'Wednesday,' says Daisy.

'Right, so you have P.E. and Josh you have football practice after school, right?'

Josh doesn't answer me. His mind and hearing are lost to a video game world.

'Mum's talking to you,' says Daisy, nudging Josh with her elbow.

'What? Sorry?' says Josh.

'Today's football practice, right?' I say again.

'Yeah, think so,' says Josh.

'Do you have your kit ready? Boots and everything?'

'Dunno,' mumbles Josh.

'Make sure you check before we leave for school,' I say, sliding bacon into the pan, which immediately starts sizzling. The potato waffles are under the grill, the water for the eggs is heating up, and the kettle is boiling. I need a cup of coffee before my headache gets any worse. 'And Daisy make sure you have your P.E. kit please.'

'Rodger dodger, Captain!' says Daisy in a funny accent, which I think is supposed to be American. I look across at her and smile. She puts her hand to the side of her head and does a military salute.

'Love you guys,' I say, trying to keep everything inside.

'Love you,' Josh and Daisy say in unison.

I get breakfast ready, drink coffee, and Alice eventually comes down in time to eat. She isn't the brightest, liveliest person in the morning either, but she's already in her school uniform and ready to go. I eat one piece of toast while the kids scoff down their breakfasts because it's all I can stomach before getting the kids out of the door and to school. I manage to avoid Mark at the school gates, which is such a relief because I can't imagine seeing him today.

I pull into the driveway when I get back from the school run, and head indoors. It's a cold, blustery day, the sky is slate grey, and the clouds are low and heavy. It will probably rain later. As soon as I open the front door I know he's here. I can feel him in the house. His shoes are against the side and his coat is hanging over the bottom of the stairs. He knows this drives me mad. I've asked him countless times to please hang it up properly with all the other coats. I'm not sure I'm ready to see him yet. I haven't had time to properly digest, analyse, and really understand how I feel about all of this. I don't have time though because I hear the kettle boil then I see Pete, standing in the doorway to the kitchen, looking sad and apologetic and lost like a naughty puppy returned home after running away.

'Tea?' he says weakly.

'Shouldn't you be at work?'

'I couldn't go in today, Rosie. I had to see you. I didn't sleep all night.'

'And you think I did?'

I grab his coat and hang it up properly before I walk through into the kitchen and sit down at the table. Pete makes us both a cup of a tea even though I didn't ask for one. The problem is that my world has been turned upside down and I don't know what I want at the moment and that includes tea.

'I'm so sorry,' says Pete, sitting opposite me. 'You know me, Rosie, and what I did was a one-off, a terrible mistake, a lapse in judgement, but it won't ever happen again.'

'But how can I trust you? You've broken our wedding vows, Pete, and no matter how much I want to believe you, how can I trust you after this?'

I look at Pete, my husband, and for a moment I feel sorry for him because he's right about one thing, it isn't him and I know it was a mistake. Can we end our marriage because of one mistake? Everyone deserves a second chance, surely? I didn't do anything with Mark, but I felt something and I didn't tell Pete about him. I still haven't. I didn't do anything physical, but mentally I did and maybe that's worse. What Pete did was one night and he didn't love her or have feelings for her, it was just sex. A shag. But me, I had coffee with Mark a few times a week, I went into London with him for the day, and I have feelings for him. I feel something for him that's more than just friends. Surely when it comes to cheating and breaking vows, I'm just as guilty as Pete. How can I judge him so harshly when I'm as much to blame?

'I know I broke our vows, Rosie, and I ruined everything. It's why I've been so distant because I couldn't comprehend what I did and I felt so awful. It's also why I had to tell you because I couldn't live with myself if I didn't. But I'm here now and I'm telling you, it won't ever happen again and I want everything you said last night. I want to hit the reset button and start over. I want it more than anything in the world.'

I'm drinking my tea and I'm listening to him and I know it makes sense what he's saying, but something is wrong. With us. With our marriage. It's more than just his cheating and my feelings for Mark. Why did those things happen? I know things between Pete and myself haven't been great, but I'm sure lots of couples with three kids and stressful jobs have the same problems without cheating. We cheat because we want something different. Because we're bored of what we already have. Pete made a mistake, but it was a mistake he chose to make and every time I met Mark, I knew what I was doing. I pretended I was shocked by Mark's confession he had feelings for me, but was I really? Was I shocked or just afraid of how I might feel about him? Pete isn't the sort of man to cheat, but surely the fact he did says something awful about our marriage. About us. Our marriage became so bad that even Pete felt the need to sleep with someone else. And I, for all my thoughts about myself and the life I want, for all the wonderful memories, and even with the kids, still thought about being with another man. Doesn't that mean our marriage is broken and that maybe it's beyond repair? The only thing I know at the moment is that I'm not sure about anything. About Pete, Mark, or myself.

'I think you should move out,' I say coldly and quietly. 'We need some time apart, Pete, to figure out what's going on here.'

'No, Rosie, you don't mean that. You're just in shock or something.'

'We need time to figure this out. I need time.'

'But how is being apart going to help and what will we tell the children?'

'The truth,' I say, finally looking directly at him. 'That we're having problems and we need some time apart. They'll understand.'

And for the first time since all of this happened, tears start leaking out and down his face. Pete's falling apart in front of me and there's nothing I can do, or at least want to do, to help him. Yesterday I was ready to start over, to rebuild our marriage, to be happy again, but today all of that is gone because of what he did. We can't forget it happened and move on because if we do that, if we brush it under the carpet, at some point in the future it's going to come up again and what then? We have to deal with this now. We can't stick a plaster on it and hope it gets better because this isn't a little gash, it's a giant gaping wound and it's bleeding all over the place.

'You can't do this, Rosie, you can't. Why are you giving up on us so easily?'

'I'm not giving up on us, Pete. Don't you see, I'm trying to fix this properly. If we don't take the right amount of time now to really figure this out, then we're never going to be happy. It will always be there, slowly breaking us down until eventually it will destroy us and maybe we'll be too old or too scared to start again and we'll both end up miserable. Is that what you want?'

'Of course not, but do you think me moving out is going to help?'

'The only thing I know is I need some space and maybe you do too. We both need to figure out what went wrong with us and why you did what you did…'

'It was a mistake, Rosie, I was drunk.'

'And you believe that, do you? That it was just a mistake?'

'It was,' says Pete, trying to keep himself together rubbing the tears away.

'And what if I told you, I've been having coffee with another man, a parent, and that we've become really close. Would that change your mind?'

'Sorry?' says Pete, looking confused.

Now's the time to tell him everything. I have to. He has to know everything because otherwise there's no chance of us working. I tell him all about Mark from the day I met him until yesterday. I don't hold back and I tell him all the details including my feelings about him. It feels good, so freeing, to finally admit everything and get it all out in the open. For the first time in a long time, Pete and I are talking and telling the truth.

'So, you're in love with this man?' says Pete, dumbfounded.

'That's not what I said. I said I have feelings for him. I don't know what these feelings are, but we're in such a bad place, and he was there for me, and I enjoy spending time with him. He gets me and I understand him, and we connected. I don't know what it is, but don't you see? Between you cheating and Mark and I, our marriage is in real trouble, Pete, and I think we both need some time apart to get our heads round it.'

Pete stands up suddenly. His face that was so full of

fear and anxiety is suddenly angry and annoyed.

'I don't believe this,' says Pete. 'All this time I was feeling awful about what I did and you were having an emotional affair with another man.'

'And that's why we need a break,' I say, standing up too, my voice getting louder. 'To see if we really want to fix this or not.'

'What do you mean "or not"? Surely, we either want to fix it or we don't. How hard is that to figure out? Do I want to fix it? Yes, of course. We've been married for seventeen years, you don't throw that away on a whim. What other choice is there?'

'There's always a choice,' I say, realising what I'm saying and it terrifies me, but what if there is another choice? What if Pete and I are over? What then? I can't imagine my life without him, but you can't just stay with someone because it's convenient or because it used to work. You stay married because you love that person and they make you happy. If either of those two things are compromised, you have to look at it again, you have to ask the difficult questions. If not you're only going to end up old and sad and full of regrets and I can't do that. I can't lie on my death bed and think about all the what ifs and regret my life. It's too precious and too short to spend being unhappy. I know Pete would trudge on because that's him, stiff upper lip and all that, keep calm and carry on, that's Pete in a nutshell and I don't know if that's a good thing or not. Maybe people were happier in those days, before we had so many choices. But I'm forty and I'm at this crossroads in my life and I need a moment to reflect. I need a second to pause and really think about what I want the next forty years to be like. Is that so wrong?

'And I suppose I have no choice in the matter,' says Pete, his voice cutting me to shreds.

'It isn't like that. I want to get this right, Pete. Make sure we make the right choice.'

'But that's the thing, Rosie. I know what I want. I know where I belong.'

'And so did I yesterday. Things change.'

There's a pause and neither of us seems sure what to say. It's deafeningly quiet for a minute until Pete says,

'I'll get some things together then.'

'Where will you go?'

'My parents. They'll be devastated, but like you said about the kids, they'll understand.'

'I'm sorry,' I say, as he turns and begins walking out of the kitchen.

'Me too,' says Pete. 'Me too.'

I sit down at the kitchen table and immediately start crying again. It's incredible I have any tears left after last night, but I do and they keep coming. I know I'm making the right decision, but it's so hard and difficult to accept. I know I could take the easy way out and just try to move on. Accept we both did something wrong, book a two week holiday to Tenerife and just soldier on. That's the English way, isn't it? I know what I'm doing is making life more difficult for everyone and the thought of telling the kids is terrifying and heart breaking, but I'm tired of plodding along, of accepting life without questioning what I'm doing, and I know this is going to be hard, but in the long run, I think it's for the best.

Some friends of my parents, Sandra and Rodney

Bishop, got divorced last year. They've been unhappy for as long as I've known them, and longer if you ask Dad. They stayed together for their kids, trying to keep up appearances, but as soon as the last child left home, they got divorced. They're both in their early sixties now and it's almost too late for them to really start again. They could have been divorced twenty years ago, in their early forties, and given themselves the chance to be happy. I can't be Sandra and Rodney. I don't want to wake up at sixty and think, fuck, what have I been doing for the last twenty years?

Eventually Pete comes plodding down the stairs carrying a suitcase. The suitcase we last used during that week in Cornwall two years ago. I bought it especially, but it's only been used the once. I never imagined that the next time would be for this.

'I'm off then,' says Pete, standing by the front door.

I walk up to him, not sure what to say or what to do. He's leaving our house.

'Thank you.'

'For what?'

'For doing this. You didn't have to.'

'And yet I did,' says Pete. 'How long?'

'How long what?'

'How long until you know? How long until I can come home?'

'I don't know, Pete.'

He looks sad and forlorn. He looks broken and it breaks my heart to do this, but we both did things that made this happen. He slept with Claire and I have a relationship with Mark. We're here now because of the choices we made.

'Bye then,' he says.

'Bye, Pete.'

He turns to leave, but I can't let him go without a final goodbye. I grab him and wrap my arms around him. I bury my face deep into his shoulder and let the tears go. He's holding me, and our bodies are shuddering together, trembling in anticipation at the future. At the possibility of a life without each other. Eventually we let go and after one more look, one more goodbye, he leaves. I sit on the sofa and cry because I don't know what else to do until eventually I pull the blanket we keep over the back of the sofa on top of me and go to sleep. My eyes are heavy and so very sore and it feels good to finally close them. To let myself go.

Twenty-Three

When I get to her room, Mum's sitting up staring into space. I put the magazines I've brought on the table next to her bed and swap the flowers for the fresh ones I got on the way over. When I walk in she looks at me, not a flicker of recognition or change in her facial expression, but she looks at me. She's aware of my presence in the room, which is more than some days when she doesn't even move. She arches her neck slightly and lets out a low groan, a mumble. It isn't a word, but a sound and I like to think it means something.

'Hi, Mum,' I say, leaning down and giving her a kiss on the head.

I sit down in the chair, reach across and hold her hand. I can feel every bone through her sallow skin. I give it the gentlest of squeezes, a small reminder I'm here and I'll always be here until the end. I'm afraid that when she finally goes it will be in the night, in the dark, all by herself in this strange room. Alone at the very end. I hope it isn't like that and I can be here, holding her hand, stroking her hair, and telling her it's alright. Maybe it doesn't matter to her, I don't know, but it matters to me.

'I won't ask how you are because I already know the answer to that one. It's shit, I know, but you're still here, Mum. The kids are all doing great. Alice had a crush on a boy at school and it was hard on her because he didn't feel the same, but on the plus side it really brought us together. It was nice to feel like her mum again. Like we're on the same side for once.'

I remember when I was about Alice's age, maybe a year older, I had the same sort of problem. I liked a boy. I went to an all girls' school, but I used to see him on my walk home. He went to the nearby boys' school and he was the most handsome boy I'd ever seen. I used to blush horribly as soon as I saw him. My friends encouraged me to talk to him, poking me, prodding me, but I was too afraid, too nervous. Eventually one day I plucked up the courage and said hello. It was the hardest thing I'd ever done in my life and it felt monumental at the time. However, as it turned out, Glenn Thompson might have been the most handsome boy in the world, but he was also arrogant, annoying, and not very nice. I was crushed. I talked to Mum about it because she knew something was going on and I told her everything. She hugged me tight and told me I was amazing and when it came to men, I should never accept second best. The Glenn Thompsons of this world didn't deserve someone like me. I felt so grateful to have a mother who made me believe I could do anything and be anything. She empowered me with a determination and self-respect that gave me the confidence to become the woman I am today.

'Daisy's in the school nativity play and she's doing so well, Mum. I wish you could see her. It's changed her. She's such an incredible little girl. Josh still has dreams of playing for Tottenham, but he's ten so why not dream big? If you can't do it then, when can you? Although we're trying to keep his feet on the ground and make sure he keeps working hard at school.'

I'm starting to well up because I have to tell Mum about Pete and me. I know it's silly because she doesn't know what's going on, but I still feel like I've let her down. She loved Pete so much. When I first brought him home, she was instantly smitten and so proud because I'd found a man who was strong, intelligent, funny, a real gentleman, who adored me and encouraged me to follow my dreams. She loved us because we lived our life and did things she had only dreamed about. She loved our whole family, especially the kids, with such a passion that telling her about Pete moving out feels like a huge failure. I know she wouldn't have approved. I wish I could talk to her about it. I wish she could give me advice and tell me what to do just like she did when I was young.

'I have some news, Mum. It's not good news I'm afraid. Pete and I are having a trial separation. I don't know how long it's going to last or what's going to happen when it's over, but I wanted to tell you. I know you loved Pete and thought we were so good together and we were, but people change. Situations change, Mum, and I know I always said I wanted a marriage like yours that stood the test of time, but we aren't you and Dad. I wish we were, but we're not. I hope we can still work things out, but if we can't it won't be because of the example you and Dad gave us. I always envied your marriage because it was so strong, so full of love, and Pete and I used to have that, we did, but sometimes things happen and you have to change. I hope you understand.'

I stop for a moment and look at Mum, at the mangled wreckage of her body, wondering if she understands any of this. I know she can't respond, but can she hear me? Can she comprehend what I'm saying? Maybe it's best if she doesn't because I know this would break her heart.

Tonight I'm going to tell the kids. I think it's going to be one of the hardest things I've ever had to do. It's been two days since Pete moved out, and I've told them he's busy at work, which isn't that hard to believe, but Alice is getting suspicious so I'm going to tell them. Actually, we're going to tell them. Pete's coming over for dinner and we're going to give them the news together. It's heart breaking just thinking about it. I don't know how I'm going to keep myself together in front of them. I know I need to be strong, but I don't know if I have it in me. Pete and I have barely spoken and seeing him is going to be hard enough, but telling our beautiful children that their mummy and daddy are having a break is going to be by far the most difficult part of the evening.

'So, that's it, Mum. I'm sorry we couldn't knuckle down and get on with it, but I really think this is best. I wish you could talk to me,' I say, holding her hand again. 'I wish you could say something.'

But she doesn't. She sits in her bed, looking at nothing, her face blank, expressionless, until a girl comes in and says it's time to give her some food. It's my cue to leave so I give Mum a kiss on the head and get my handbag. As I'm walking out I can feel the tears again. So many tears. It's normal to feel emotional leaving Mum because I never know if it's going to be the last time I see her, but today it's not just for her. It's for all of us. For me, Pete, and especially the kids.

Outside it's a bright, clear day, and as I start the car,

the radio coming on at the same time, I take a deep breath. I rang Alison yesterday and accepted the job offer. I'm starting back full-time in two weeks. This is my ray of sunshine. I'm holding onto this positive because amongst all the negativity in my life at the moment, this is something I'm excited about. I'm arranging for the kids to stay at the after-school club four days a week, and Alison said I can leave early on Fridays. Life is going to be so different once I'm working again and it's all coming at once, but perhaps amongst all this upheaval, we can all find something to hold onto, to be positive about, and maybe we'll come out the other side better for it.

If you saw us sitting at the table, you'd probably think we were a normal family. I used to love watching the television show, Outnumbered, and I'd say, 'That's us'. Two parents with three young kids living in south London. We were just like them and I loved that. It gave me comfort because their life was always stressful and difficult, but it was laced with a humour, a pathos, that made our life seem so normal, so acceptable. This is what I'm thinking about now as we're sitting at the table together, eating our dinner like the most normal family in the world. Pete at the head of the table, a solicitor, handsome, and so very English. Me at the other end, about to return to her career after a break to raise a family. The children, all adorable and perfect in their own way. All of us sitting around the dining table in our south London home, the very epitome of the middle-class dream, the BBC sitcom family that's dysfunctional, but it works and it's far more interesting because of it. Our imperfections are what make us so perfect. From the outside looking in, you wouldn't know what was happening and what was about to happen. You'd think it was just another night in suburbia. Let the hilarity commence.

'I've been moved from the wing to centre forward,' says Josh to Pete. 'Manager reckons I should bag a few more goals.'

Since Pete got back, Josh has been going on non-stop about football. I don't think Pete or I realised just how much Josh would miss him. Sometimes Josh seems like such a typical little boy, almost indestructible, and independent, but it's easy to forget he's only ten and still needs his father. It's making this whole thing even more difficult.

'Is that right,' says Pete, putting a mouthful of steak in his mouth.

'We've got a match on Friday, can you make it?' says Josh, looking desperately at Pete.

'Of course, son. I'll be there.'

'Yes!' says Josh, picking up a chip with his fingers, plopping it in a puddle of ketchup then into his smiling mouth.

'The play's going really well,' says Daisy, not to be outdone by her brother.

'Right, yes, the big performance. When is it again?'

'Oh, Daddy, I already told you like a million times.'

'Sorry, love,' says Pete.

'December 15th. It's a Friday night.'

'December 15th, got it,' says Pete, adding it onto his phone. 'And how are you, Alice?'

'Fine,' says Alice, looking across at Pete then at me. She knows something's going on. It's funny, she's only four years older than Josh, but she's so much further along in life. Whilst Josh and Daisy are just happy Pete's home, they can't detect the tension in the room or the fact Pete and I have barely said a word to each other all night, but Alice has. She knows something's amiss. As soon as we've all finished eating, it's going to be time. My heart is beating so hard inside my chest because the last thing any parent wants to do is break their children's hearts. I can't bear it.

'Done. Want a game of FIFA?' says Josh to Pete. 'I'll be Tottenham and you can be Man U. I'll set it up.'

'Calm down, Daisy isn't finished yet,' I say to Josh, who looks up at the ceiling and huffs in disappointment.

'Done,' says Daisy quickly.

'Now?' says Josh, half getting up.

I look across at Pete and he looks at me. I know what he's thinking. This is all your fault. I didn't want any part of it. If it was up to me, I'd still be living at home and we wouldn't have to be doing this. For a moment, I think about not doing it, letting the kids get on, and renegotiating my deal with Pete. Because what are we doing? I'm so confused and in limbo that I'm not even sure what I'm trying to achieve. Why are we putting our children through this when we aren't even sure ourselves of what we're trying to accomplish? Maybe Pete could sleep on the sofa until we get through this. But then I remember he slept with someone else. He had sex with another woman and lied to me about it. This is not OK. Our marriage is not OK and maybe in the long run, it's better to have our children know the truth than to hide it them from it. Maybe honesty and openness is always better and if Pete and I had been more honest with each other, we wouldn't be here now.

'Sorry, Josh, your father and I need to talk to you all about something,' I say.

Josh sits down with a heavy sigh and Pete looks uncomfortable.

'What's going on?' says Alice, looking worried.

'Should I?' I say to Pete, who shrugs his shoulders like a petulant teenager. He obviously wants no part of this. 'So, kids, firstly I'd like to say that your father and I both love you very much. This isn't about you it's about us…'

'Oh my God, you're breaking up!' says Alice.

'What?' says Daisy.

Josh suddenly starts paying attention.

'No, love, we're not breaking up, are we?' I say, looking across at Pete for support.

'No, we aren't breaking up,' says Pete, his voice hollow and deadpan.

'Then what are you talking about?' says Alice.

I take a deep breath because I can't even imagine the words coming out of my mouth, but I've gone this far and I have to continue. Despite the damage it's going to cause there's no going back. As tipping points go, I know this is a significant one.

'Your father and I are having some problems and we've decided to spend some time apart,' I say, my voice wobbling slightly as I look at the kids, trying to gauge a reaction.

'I don't understand,' says Daisy.

'It means Dad's moving out,' says Alice, coldly.

'No it doesn't,' says Daisy. 'Daddy lives here. That's stupid.'

Poor Daisy is breaking my heart.

'No, love, she's right. Daddy's moving out for a little bit,' I say.

I look around the table, at my children, and I don't know what they're thinking or what they're going to say next. All I know is that this is awful and I want it to be over. I want now to be in two weeks when my job's starting and all the crying, all the talks and all the explanations have been done. I want to be at the point when we're all moving on.

'But he can't,' says Daisy, tears stinging her beautiful eyes. 'Daddy lives here with us.'

'I know,' I say. 'It's just for a little bit until we can work things out.'

The table is quiet, except for the sniffles from Daisy. Pete isn't saying anything. Josh and Alice looked shocked as if they don't know what to say either.

'But I don't understand,' says Daisy. 'You always tell us to talk about things and use our words.'

'We have, we are,' I say, trying to hold back my own tears. 'Isn't that right, Pete?'

Everyone looks across at Pete. For a moment he doesn't say anything. He looks, as he's looked since he arrived, shell shocked.

'Of course we have,' says Pete eventually, looking at Daisy. 'We're doing everything we can to fix this.'

'Who's fault is it?' asks Alice, her voice sharp and cold.

'It's no one's fault,' I say. 'Sometimes people just drift apart and you have to talk about it and decide what's best. How to move forward.'

'I think it's stupid,' says Josh, finally saying something,

tears in his eyes too.

Josh is clenching his fists together and I can tell he's desperately trying not to cry like his little sister. Be strong and maybe it will keep us together.

'Me too!' says Daisy.

'I know this is a lot to take on board, but we're doing our best,' I say, realising how weak and pathetic my voice sounds. I'm trying to convince my kids of something I'm not even sure I believe myself.

Alice stands up, pushing her chair back behind her, her face angry and sad all at once.

'Are you doing your best?!' she shouts at us.

'Alice,' I say, but she doesn't want to hear it and she storms out of the room and upstairs to her room. We all wait for the noise and then it comes, like a shotgun, making Daisy jump slightly in her seat. Alice's bedroom door being slammed shut.

Pete, Daisy, Josh, and I sit around the table. It's uncomfortable and I want it to be over.

'We both love you very much,' is all I can say to the kids.

'So much,' says Pete, echoing my words.

'Then don't move out!' shouts Josh, getting up like his sister and running out of the room.

'Daisy, need a hug?' I say, offering her my arms, hoping she says yes because at least then I'll feel like I'm helping at least one of my children.

She looks at me, then away.

'No. I want Daddy to stay,' says Daisy, then she gets up and walks out too, leaving Pete and I alone.

I'm numb with grief. How did this happen? How did

Pete and I come to this? Breaking up our family and for what? It's ridiculous and I'm so angry at Pete for making this our reality. I never imagined in a million years, even when Pete and I were at our lowest, that this would happen. How could it? I've never felt this sad and heartbroken in my entire life. Telling the kids we've failed is worse than the failure itself. I feel like a magician who's spent the last fourteen years tricking them that magic is real, that life is wonderful, but now suddenly I'm revealing myself and telling them it's all a lie. Sorry kids but everything you thought was solid and reliable in this otherwise difficult and unpredictable life is gone.

'That was hard,' I say, tears filling my eyes, and looking towards Pete for some comfort.

I don't know what I'm expecting from him. I'm hoping he feels the same as me. I'm hoping he feels the same sadness, the same regret, and understands how I'm feeling.

'Well,' says Pete, standing up looking angry. 'You wanted this. This was your choice, not mine.'

I'm flabbergasted and I'm trying to comprehend what he said and how to respond when he walks out. Like my children, he's left the room and left me alone. I hear him walk up the stairs after our children and I finally let the tears go. I can't believe he's blaming me for this. He's the one who slept with someone else. I understand he's angry about me asking him to leave, but it's his fault not mine. I didn't want this to happen. I was the one who came to him and said I wanted to start again, hit the reset button, and make our marriage work. I was the one trying to fix us before I found out what he did. I'm suddenly so angry at him again because he has no right to make me feel bad. No right at all.

I start cleaning up dinner. I'm throwing things in the dishwasher loudly, crashing plate against plate and rattling the cutlery into the drawers. I'm so mad and frustrated by all of this because it's not what I wanted. None of it. Seeing Mum today was so hard because I've let her down, I've let the kids down, and I've let myself down. I feel it so pointedly, so acutely, and if there's one thing in life I can't stand, perhaps more than anything else, it's the feeling of complete failure and this is worse because although I've failed, it wasn't caused by my weaknesses, or my shortcomings, but Pete's. He's the one who tore this family apart, but for some reason, it's me who's taking responsibility for it. Perhaps this is another part of being a mother. Pete can't tell the kids what he really did and neither can I, so it's up to me to protect them by taking their pain and absorbing it myself. And I do because I love them all so much and it's better to feel my own pain than to feel theirs. It's better to suffer myself than to let them suffer because this is what being a proper parent, a real mother, is about.

It's almost midnight when I make it upstairs to bed. Alone. It's so hard sleeping by myself after all these years. I've had the occasional night alone here and there and it was quite nice to have the whole bed and not have to listen to Pete snoring. It felt like a bit of a treat. But now it just feels awful and lonely. As usual I go upstairs and check on the kids. I kiss Daisy and Josh goodnight. As usual Daisy is lying straight in her bed, arms down by her side. She hasn't moved a muscle and her bed sheets and duvet are intact. My little girl. I watch her sleep for a moment, so perfect, like a doll. I love her so much and I'm worried this is going to set her back again. She doesn't deserve this.

I walk into Josh's room and he's almost the exact opposite of Daisy. He's sprawled across his bed sideways. The duvet is half on the floor and there's mess everywhere. This is Josh. It used to drive me crazy how messy he was, but I've come to accept it and realise it's just who he is. I kiss him on the head too, before I walk downstairs and into Alice's room. My big girl. She's so tall now her feet almost touch the end of her bed when she lays straight. Today though she's curled up on her side, the duvet pulled tight up to her chin. I sit and watch her sleeping for a moment. She's such a big girl and it's hard to imagine but in four years she could be leaving home for university. Gone. I stroke her hair and give her a kiss before I close the door and walk into my own bedroom. Sleeping alone is strange and I don't like it. I want Pete back, but not the version of him he is now. When he left tonight it was awkward and he felt like a stranger. It's so hard to see a way back to the way we were, in the same way it's hard to imagine the kids being younger again, but I have to believe it's possible. I need hope, if not for me, at least for the kids because surely every child in the world is entitled to that. A little bit of hope.

Twenty-Four

Wandsworth, London, 2010

Daisy's screaming in her room. I couldn't bear the noise so I closed the door and I'm sitting on the sofa, my hands over my ears. It's been like this for days and I'm starting to crack. I never had this with Alice or Josh. The constant crying. The screaming. What's the matter with her and what's the matter with me? I'm not coping. I don't understand what's going on and why she can't just go to sleep. When Alice was six months old she was sleeping through the night and taking two naps a day. Josh was the same. But Daisy won't sleep through the night and she naps maybe once a day. Some days she barely sleeps at all. I feel like the worst mother in the world.

The last six months have been so difficult. I haven't been working at all because I'm still on leave and so I feel completely closed off to the world. Alice is at school and Josh is at nursery in the mornings. The idea with Josh is that it gives me time to bond with Daisy, but I'm not feeling it. I don't know what's wrong with me. Every day I wake up in the hope it will get better. I tell myself it's going to be a good day and I start off hopeful and optimistic, determined to finally bond with my daughter, but I don't and every day I'm getting more worried about her. About us.

I tried taking her to a local mummy and baby class. The leaflet said it was a unique bonding opportunity. A chance for new mums to get together and socialise as well as spend invaluable time with their little ones in a caring, nurturing, fun environment. It wasn't. While the other mums looked so happy and full of joy, I spent most of the time trying to stop Daisy from crying. I went twice and couldn't go again because I felt sorry for all the other parents. I was embarrassed because here I was, already a mother of two, and obviously not coping with my third. I'm exhausted, and my nipples are so sore from all the breastfeeding because despite her lack of sleep, she's hungrier than Alice or Josh, and I'm sure she's extra hard on purpose. I'm at my breaking point and I don't know what to do about it.

'There, there, come on,' I say, picking Daisy up from her crib. She's been crying for half an hour. I was hoping she'd fall asleep, but she hasn't and I can't listen to her crying anymore. 'What's the matter? What do you need?'

I look down at my baby. At her beautiful face because she is beautiful, there's no doubt about it, but it's scrunched up and she's still crying. I try rocking her backwards and forwards, backwards and forwards, singing to her, humming, and she's still crying and before long so am I.

'Come on, Daisy, please be quiet. Go to sleep, Daisy. Please. Mummy needs you to go to sleep. Rock a bye baby. Please go to sleep.'

I can't help but cry and the more I do the more she does. Eventually I lie her down in the crib again, turn off the light, and leave the room. I hear her crying louder and louder, but I can't cope. I can't help her and she obviously doesn't want me. I go downstairs and sit on the sofa again.

This time I turn the television on loudly so I can't hear her crying. I feel horrible and I'm crying, hugging myself, while watching This Morning. I'm not really watching the show because how can I focus on anything they're talking about while my daughter is distraught in her room, staring up at the ceiling, her evil mum having left her alone? I'm trying to block her out and hoping she falls asleep. I'm hoping she's quiet so I can lie here and not have to think about her for a moment. I need to escape, to be somewhere else.

'I'm sorry. Sorry, my darling baby girl. I'm so sorry,' I whisper to myself.

Thirty minutes later and I can't take it anymore. I can't do this. I need help. We need help. I pick up my phone and call Pete. I'm so exhausted and stressed from all the crying I can barely hold the phone. My hands are shaking and my voice when it comes doesn't sound like my own.

'Pete, I'm sorry, I can't do this,' I sob into the phone. 'I can't do this. Sorry.'

'Rosie, what's the matter?'

'It's Daisy, she won't stop crying. She won't stop and I can't help her. I'm sorry.'

'I'm coming home now. Just sit tight. I'll be home soon.'

'OK.'

'It's going to be alright. I promise,' says Pete, his voice strong and soothing.

'OK.'

'Love you.'

'Love you,' I mumble into the phone then Pete is gone, but he's coming home. He's coming to save me.

I sink into the sofa with relief. I don't know why it's

all too much, but it is and I feel awful. How can I feel this way about my own daughter? I love her so much, but I don't feel the same connection with her as I did with Alice and Josh. I don't feel the same bond and it breaks my heart to admit that right now, but at this moment, I don't feel like her mother. I don't want to be her mother. It's the worst thought I've ever had and it kills me to think it, but I can't help it. The pain is reaching inside of me, scooping out my insides until I feel physically sick. Until I want everything gone. I can't help the thoughts that are rattling like trains through my mind. Daisy is still crying and I sink further into the sofa, wrapping myself in the blanket, hoping that Pete comes home soon. Hoping my husband comes to rescue us.

I don't hear Pete come home or open the front door because the next thing I know I open my eyes and Pete is stood at the doorway holding Daisy.

'Oh God, I'm so sorry,' I say, sitting up.

'Rosie, it's fine,' says Pete ever so calmly. 'We're fine, aren't we, Daisy?'

Daisy looks at her father and looks so happy, like a different child.

'But I'm a mess, Pete. I don't know what's going on with me. I'm so sorry.'

'I'll tell you what. It's a lovely day outside, let's take a walk to the cafe around the corner. How about that, Daisy?' says Pete and Daisy giggles. 'We'll get a coffee and some cake and everything will be alright, won't it?'

Daisy giggles again.

I get myself off the sofa and hug Pete and my baby girl. I embrace them both and I'm about to start crying again when Pete tells me to get a coat while he puts Daisy in the buggy.

Pete's right, it is a gorgeous day outside. It's a bit chilly, but the sun is bright and clear, and it feels good to get some fresh air. Sometimes when you're a parent you can feel trapped in your own home, confined by the walls and everything between them, but getting outside feels like a different world. I feel different too. Pete pushes the buggy and Daisy seems to be the happiest little girl in all the world. It's only a ten minute walk to the cafe, but by the time we arrive, Daisy is fast asleep. She looks so peaceful and adorable it makes me wonder how in a million years I could have been so wrong, so impatient with her. Why couldn't I handle her on my own? She's hugging her fluffy baby kangaroo, Kanga, close to her and she looks perfect.

The cafe is a little place on the corner. It's quiet except for a few mums who are talking in their workout clothes while their perfect little kids sit and eat healthy snacks. I admire them so much because they make it all seem so easy, but I know it isn't. How do they keep it all together and still have time for yoga or Pilates or whatever class they go to at the gym? How do they keep their houses so clean, their husbands so happy, and keep their own sanity, while still cooking their kids a wonderfully healthy meal from a proper cook book in their bespoke kitchens? More importantly, why can't I do it too? Why aren't I good enough at this?

I sit outside with the buggy, while Pete goes inside and gets us coffee. Just watching him makes me think how lucky I am. He's waiting to be served and looks so handsome in his suit. He's kind and good and a wonderful father. I needed him today and he rushed home as fast as he could to be here for me. That's love. That's what good husbands do. These other women might look like they have perfect lives, and maybe they do, but perhaps they don't have a Pete. Maybe they have to keep it together because they have no one else to rely on. I have Pete and looking down at Daisy, I realise how lucky we all are that we have each other because we all fail sometimes. We all make mistakes, but family means putting everything aside for each other.

'Here you go,' says Pete, gently putting my latte down on the table.

He also puts down a large white plate with a delicious-looking slice of cake on it. He pops back inside and gets his coffee, before sitting down too.

'Thank you,' I say, trying to keep the tears at bay.

I'm so brittle that any act of kindness, large or small, is enough to break me down and bring the tears. I cried at Neighbours the other day.

'You're welcome,' says Pete with a smile. 'I called the doctors' and made you an appointment.'

'What for?'

'Rosie, you aren't coping. This isn't you. You're normally so strong, so independent, and full of life, but recently you've been drowning and I can't watch it and not do anything.'

'You think something's wrong with me?'

'Don't you?'

I look at Pete and I know he's right. Of course there's something wrong with me. I questioned whether I wanted my own daughter. I'm drowning and luckily I have Pete trying to save me. I have a husband who won't let me go.

'Thank you,' I say quietly.

Pete smiles and we both take sips of our coffee. I suppose I knew I needed to see or talk to someone, but it's hard to admit you can't be a mother. It's the one thing we're meant to be good at as women. I never felt this way with Alice or Josh so I thought it would go away. I'm a woman. I can do anything and get through anything, but the reality is that I can't. I need help. Today I needed help.

'Sorry it's taken me so long to do something. I've been so busy at work and you've always been so strong, Rosie. I just didn't think you needed me.'

'I always need you. It might not seem that way sometimes, but I'll always need you.'

'Always?' says Pete with a gorgeous smile.

'Of course, always,' I say, and we both smile at each other. 'You know I thought about smoking again. I almost bought a packet the other day.'

'But you didn't, right?'

'No I didn't, but I wanted to.'

'Then I'm glad I'm here. I'm taking next week off too, no arguments. I'm here to help you.'

Pete's being so lovely that I start crying again. I can't help myself.

'Sorry,' I sniff, trying to compose myself.

'It's OK. I want to help you get through this.'

'I know,' I say, taking a sip of my coffee and it feels good. Warm and smooth it helps relax me. 'Now what's going on with this cake?'

Pete laughs and looks across at me.

'I'm glad you can still make me laugh. It's for you. It's a double chocolate cake with chocolate something inside. It sounded like she said, her gash, but I'm pretty sure she meant ganache.'

This time I'm laughing and it feels good. So good I almost start crying again.

'Gash or no ganache, it looks divine. Thank you.'

Pete and I sit and drink our coffee and I eat the cake, which is delicious, as the warm sun moves slowly overhead. We sit like this for an hour. Pete gets another coffee, while Daisy sleeps and I feel for the first time in months, a calmness. I feel like a huge weight has been lifted off my shoulders. I feel a bit like an addict, hiding others from my problem, trying to cope, while inside I've been a mess, slowly falling apart, crumbling into smaller and smaller pieces. Having a child, especially a young one, should be such a happy time and it was with the others, but this has been a nightmare and finally I'm going to get help. Daisy is going to get the mum she deserves. I don't think I've ever loved Pete more than at this moment. We go through life and sometimes we take each other for granted. It's easy to do that when you're married, when life's so busy, it's easy to not take a moment to appreciate each other, but then something like this happens and it brings you back again. It makes you stop and maybe all these years together would have made Pete complacent or numb to my pain, but it didn't and when I needed him, really needed him, he was here for me. I won't forget this because maybe, one day, he'll need me and I'll be here for him. That much I can promise. That much I know.

Twenty-Five

Standing at the front door of my father's house with the kids isn't just sad and gut wrenching, but it's one of the lowest points of my life. The kids haven't handled Pete moving out well and today I have to tell my father and brother that my marriage is falling apart. I've never felt like more of a failure than I do right now.

It's being made worse by how the kids have been since Friday when we told them our news. The past two days have been awful. After Pete left, I tried talking to them individually before bed, but they weren't interested. I tried again yesterday, but none of them want to talk about it. Alice is doing her best, 'I'm a teenager and I don't care about anything' routine. After the business with the boy at school, I was hoping I'd broken through with her, but she's back to stubborn, glib Alice again. Josh is taking it harder than expected. I've always thought of him as a typical devil may care boy, but he's really taking this to heart. I've been leaving him alone to play FIFA. Daisy isn't talking to me. Every time I try and say something to her, she puts her hand up and walks away. I'm dead to her. So, we're standing on the doorstep waiting for Dad to answer, and no one is speaking.

The door eventually opens and my father is stood there.

'There you all are, come here,' he says smiling, opening his arms and embracing all my children. This was a lot easier when they were younger, and today it's made even harder by the fact they're all annoyed and angry. 'What's going on? Why the unhappy faces?'

Alice, Josh, and Daisy struggle free from Dad and walk into the house. James, Sarah, and Lilly, are already here. Lilly is thirteen and so her and Alice are as thick as thieves. As soon as Alice walks in she's off upstairs with Lilly under a cloud of secrecy.

I made a promise to myself I wouldn't cry today. I've cried so much over the last few weeks and days, but today I'm done. I can't keep breaking down and especially not in front of my family. It's time I accepted what's happening and dealt with it rather than crying about it. It isn't helping the kids and it isn't helping me. I need to start moving on and perhaps trying to imagine a life without Pete. As ridiculous as it sounds, even to me, it's a possibility and I need to be strong through this for the kids and to make the right decision.

'What's going on?' says Dad looking confused. 'Where's Pete?'

'Let's go inside and I'll tell you everything,' I say, making Dad look even more worried.

I follow Dad through into the living room where James and Sarah are sitting down having a cup of tea. The kids are all off upstairs doing goodness knows what. I say hello to my brother and his wife, while Dad puts the kettle on and makes me a cup of tea. One must always have a cup of tea as soon as you walk through the door - is the family motto. I make small talk with James and Sarah. I ask about Lilly. She's an only child and goes to a local private school. They decided they were having just one child and would give her everything. The problem is that every time they get together, Alice comes home telling me about all the things Lilly has and why can't she have them too. It's hard for children to grasp that having only one child and having three is significantly different. There's been talk of Alice going abroad with them next year. Alice is desperate to go and James said it won't cost us a penny, which is all fine and good, but she's my girl and I'd like to take her on holiday myself.

'Here you go, love,' says Dad, handing me a cup of tea.

I take a sip before realising that everyone is looking at me, waiting for me to tell them what's going on. Why are my children acting so strangely and where's Pete?

'Right, so, this is difficult to say, but Pete and I have been having problems for a while now. It's not been good and so we're taking some time off,' I say, before adding the death knell to the whole thing. 'We're having a sort of trial separation.'

I manage to get the whole thing out without tears.

'Oh, love,' says Dad, walking across and giving me a hug. 'I'm sorry. I had no idea things were that bad.'

'Yes, well, I guess neither did I, but here we are.'

'Did something happen?' says James, asking the obvious question.

I can't tell my family about Pete's affair because if we do work things out and stay together, they'll never be able to look at him the same way again. Despite my anger at Pete and what he did, I'm trying to think about what's best for everyone and I'd hate for the kids to somehow find out their father slept with someone else. No matter what happens, he's their dad and I don't want anything to get in the way of that.

'No, nothing happened, just us not spending enough time together. Drifting apart and losing touch with each other. It happened so slowly I don't think we saw it coming until one day we both woke up and realised our marriage wasn't working anymore.'

'I'm sorry that must be awful,' says Sarah, looking genuinely shocked and emotional.

I've always loved Sarah. She's such a kind, caring person. My brother did well with her. I told him the day I met her that he was punching well above his weight and he agreed straight away. Sarah's incredibly smart and could be making all sorts of money in the City, but she works for a non-profit, raising money and awareness of childhood poverty in the United Kingdom. She does all sorts to help underprivileged children including running last year's London marathon (in under four hours). She's tall, slim, attractive, well spoken, and it would be easy not to like her because she's so bloody perfect, but she's unbearably lovely.

'It is what it is,' I say, trying to keep this Question Time session strictly to the facts.

'If there's anything we can do, please just shout,' says Sarah. 'We'd love to have Alice stay for a few days if it would help.'

'Thank you that's very kind. I'm sure she would jump at the chance,' I say, knowing full well that Alice would move in with them permanently if she had her way.

'How are the kids taking it?' says Dad, looking pensive and worried.

'Oh, you know, not well, but it's early days and we're

working on it. Pete and I both want what's best for the kids.'

'Of course you do,' says Sarah.

'Is it a temporary break or more permanent?' says James.

'Honestly, I don't know. I hope temporary.'

We sit and drink our tea and my family ask more questions and offer more support. By the time we're finished, I've somehow agreed for Alice to spend most of Christmas with James and Sarah, and Dad's offered to babysit Josh and Daisy whenever he can so Pete and I can work through this. I'm literally going to be on my own. It's lovely to have the support of my family, but I can't help feeling as I'm sitting here that I need to handle this my way. This is my mess and my life and I need to sort it out myself. I love my family dearly and since Mum, I think we've all become closer and our relationships have changed, but I still feel the same need I've always felt to take care of things myself. I've always been independent and strong willed and I hope that doesn't change. I think getting married, I didn't take care of my own needs as much as I should, and perhaps this is part of the reason why we're in this position. I stopped being so independent and started relying on Pete. I stopped questioning what I was doing with my life and accepted the way it was and I became lazy and soft. It's my own fault, I realise that, but now it's time for me to change. I need to find myself again. Rediscover who I am and what I want from life.

I find the kids upstairs. Alice and Lilly are in my old bedroom. They're watching YouTube videos together. They love watching videos other teenage girls put up about their life, their friends, likes, loves, and what it's like living in

California or Australia. The world is such a small place now and they have complete access to the homes of children all over the world. It puts my brief spell as pen pal to Dimitar Ivanov during the mid-eighties to shame. I learnt very little about Bulgarian life and culture as the only thing he wanted to write about was his infatuation with Star Wars. I think he wanted an American pen pal with an intimate understanding of Jedis and Ewoks, not a teenage girl from Woking, who'd seen none of the Star Wars films and quite liked My Little Pony. As soon as I walk in the talking and giggling stops and Lilly pauses the video.

'What do you want?' says Alice with all the attitude of one of those American girls you see on TV. Her soft southern English accent suddenly has a hint of valley girl about it and it isn't endearing.

'I'm just making sure you're alright,' I say, feeling both of their eyes on me.

'We're fine. You can leave now,' says Alice coldly.

I detect a slight uncomfortableness from Lilly, who I know doesn't talk to her parents like that. Normally I'd tell Alice off and march her downstairs and give her a good talking to, but I'm trying to be understanding. After all, it isn't her fault her parents are separated. It isn't her fault the whole world she relied on and built her life on has suddenly been ripped from underneath her. As much as I'm trying to be more independent and strong, I'm also trying to be understanding for my kids. We fucked up and they shouldn't have to pay for it.

I leave the room and let them get on with their videos. I stand outside for a moment and listen to them. Lilly asks if she's alright and Alice gives a very good impression of a girl who's totally fine. It's strange having them sitting in my old bedroom. The bedroom I used to sit in with my friends and plot our futures. It doesn't feel that long ago, although saying that it also feels like hundreds of years ago too. I find Josh and Daisy in the dining room and they aren't saying much, especially once I walk in and it goes silent. Luckily, Dad is soon on hand, and he gets them both helping in the kitchen. Dad's making his famous roast beef and Yorkshire puddings and they are fabulous. Josh and Daisy are reluctant at first, but Dad has a way of getting through to them and before long they're all having fun in the kitchen. I hear laughs for the first time in days and it warms my heart.

'Wine?' says James, holding a bottle of something red.

'Just a glass or the whole bottle?' I say.

'Hilarious. I'll get you a glass and we can talk in the garden.'

'Wait, what? We're talking? I didn't know the wine came with conditions,' I say and James laughs, before he walks off and comes back moments later with two glasses of wine.

Dad's garden hasn't changed since we were kids. The same patch of green grass, the same flowers, the same dilapidated shed that hasn't yet fallen, and the same apple tree at the bottom of the garden. James and I stroll down to the apple tree where the bird bath sits, a small puddle of yellowing water at the bottom.

'So, tell me the truth,' says James. 'Are you alright?'

I look at my little brother and smile.

'Of course I'm not alright. My marriage might be over, but what can I do? I have the kids to think about.'

'I know, but don't forget to take care of yourself. This

is important. If you need anything just call me. We're here for you and the kids.'

'Thanks, little brother,' I say, playfully punching him on the arm.

'Because I haven't forgotten about Stuart Winchmore, you know.'

'My year ten boyfriend, Stuart Winchmore?'

'He broke your heart, Rosie. You told me you wanted to die and so what did I do?'

'You got your big mate, Andy Mulligan to rough him up a bit.'

'Exactly,' says James, winking at me, and I can't help but laugh.

'Thanks, but I don't think Andy Mulligan is the answer this time.'

'Just keep it in mind. Andy and I are friends on Facebook.'

'I will,' I say, smiling. 'And how's things with you? Perfect as usual?'

'Annoyingly so I'm afraid,' says Pete and I laugh.

'That's good, really. No matter how shit my life gets, I'll be OK as long as I know your life is perfect.'

'Then I'd better do my best to keep it that way.'

'You always were an annoying little shit.'

'Sorry.'

'No, don't apologise, just be happy. That's all I want too,' I say, before pausing for a moment and taking a sip of my wine. 'I'm starting back to work full-time.'

'Blimey that's a big change. Excited?'

'Yes, I am, actually. I think I need this.'

'Then let's toast to that,' says James, raising his glass

in the air. 'To change.'

'To change,' I say, before we clink our glasses together.

The drive home is the same as the drive there. None of the kids are talking to me, although it's late and they're tired so they sit in silence. I get everyone to bed, have a couple of glasses of wine in front of the television, before I go to bed myself. It's been a long day and I'm exhausted physically and emotionally. I'm in bed and about to turn off my bedside light when I get a text. I look across at my phone and it's from Mark.

Meet for coffee tomorrow? I'd love to see you. Need to talk x

As soon as I see it, my heart leaps in my chest and I'm immediately sucked into a whirlpool of doubt and confusion. Can I meet him for a coffee after everything that's happened? Is it the worst idea in the world? My brain is giving me a no, this is a terrible idea, but my heart wants to see him. I need to talk and I love talking to Mark. But he likes me more than he should and I like him more than I should and Pete and I are separated and…I could go on and on, but I don't. I pick up my phone and type a quick reply.

Usual place. 9am?

I send the text and another one comes back quickly.

Thank you x

Instead of going to sleep, I spend the next hour lying here going through a hundred different Mark scenarios in my mind. Do I tell him about Pete and our trial separation? Do I tell him about Pete cheating on me? What do I say if he tells me he likes me again? Eventually I fall asleep, but even that is short lived as I wake up soon after with Daisy standing in my doorway in floods of tears.

'What's up?' I say, getting out of bed and scooping her up in my arms.

'I had a nightmare,' she says, her whole body shivering in fear and sadness.

I don't say anything else. I put Daisy in bed next to me and we go to sleep together, her little body tucked up close to mine. It's all she needed and as it turns out, it's all I need too.

Twenty-Six

I'm on my way to meet Mark for a coffee. I haven't seen him since he told me he had feelings for me. I'm not going to lie, I'm feeling a bit awkward because despite what's happened between us, he has no idea what's been happening with me.

It's a truly gorgeous day. For early December, it's not that cold and the sun is shining brightly overhead. It's hard not to feel a sense of optimism on a day like today. But when your husband is living at his parents' house, your children are upset and won't talk to you, and you're off to have coffee with a man who recently confessed he likes you, it's almost impossible to feel anything but sadness. I'm trying to put a positive spin on it. It's my new thing. I'm trying to be like the old me again. I'm trying to remember how I was back then, before we had kids and my life changed forever because I'm sure I was optimistic and excited about life. I want to feel that excitement again. I need to feel the ripple of adrenalin rushing through my body at the possibility of something life changing. I want to feel like I'm alive and that anything is possible. Perhaps it's something as hackneyed as a midlife crisis, I don't know, but now I'm here, now my life is already so changed, there's no way I'm going back to how it was before. Life is scary, but I think that's good. Scary means change and change is positive.

I take a deep breath before I walk into Caffe Nero.

Our Caffe Nero. Mark's already sitting down waiting for me. He stands up and smiles as soon as he sees me and God he looks handsome today. I know I shouldn't be thinking about this, but it's nice to see every positive and to try - in the words of Monty Python - to look on the bright side of life. And Mark's Colin Firth-esque good looks are something positive, if not a little distracting.

'I'm glad you came,' says Mark, leaning in and giving me a kiss on the cheek, the hand firmly on my waist. I wish my waist wasn't quite so fatty and spongy. I can feel his hand sink into me and it makes me shudder. I haven't seen a photo of his wife, but I imagine she was incredibly beautiful, probably tall, blonde, and without a hint of fat on her perfect little waist.

'Of course,' I say sitting down, hanging my handbag on my chair. 'Coffee? It's definitely my turn.'

'I'd love one.'

'The usual?'

'Please,' says Mark with a smile.

I walk over and order our coffee. I can't help but notice Mark looking at me while I'm ordering. I wish I could understand what he sees in me. He's so handsome, funny, intelligent, a great father, and I'm sure he could have his pick of women far more attractive than me, but he can't keep his eyes off me. I'm not imagining things. I get my latte and Mark's flat white, and head back to the table. I sit down with a smile. There's a moment of slight awkwardness before Mark starts talking.

'I'm sorry, Rosie. I shouldn't have said what I said the last time we were here. You're a married woman and I should have kept my feelings to myself.'

'It's fine,' I find myself saying, and my cheeks flush. 'Really.'

'No Rosie, it isn't. The truth is, since I moved here, with the new job and trying to survive with the kids, it's been hard. Seeing you every day and having coffee together, I think my feelings became confused and I crossed a line, but I need your friendship. I don't know what I'd do without it. So, I promise, from now on, strictly mates and that's it.'

I'm almost on the verge of tears again because he's being so nice and I'm feeling so low and rotten about everything. I want to tell him about Pete, but I'm worried it will confuse things between us. I'm such an emotional wreck at the moment, it's hard to know up from down or right from wrong. I decide to tell him because I need to talk and he's right about one thing, I value his friendship above everything else.

'And it won't, Mark. I promise. It's just...life's hard and it doesn't always go to plan. Since I saw you last something's happened with me and I want to be honest with you too.' I look at Mark and he gives me a look to continue. 'Pete and I have split up. I mean it's a trial separation, but I don't know how it's going to work out. We've been having problems, we've both been unhappy, and I think it's been coming for a while now.'

'I'm sorry, it must be so difficult.'

'It is, but we're working through it.'

'I hope I had nothing to do with it?' says Mark cautiously.

'I think in a way you did. Not in a bad way, but you made me realise I needed to try and save my marriage,' I say, before pausing. I'm trying to be honest, but I'm also trying to choose my words carefully. 'When you said what you did, it made me realise I felt something for you too. It woke me up and maybe it's why I reacted the way I did. I knew I felt the same as you or at least similar and I went home and decided to save my marriage.'

'And what happened?'

This is it. Time to tell him everything. I haven't told anyone else because I'm too afraid it will get back to the kids or it will ruin relationships if Pete and I do manage to fix our marriage. But Mark isn't in any other part of my life and I trust him.

'I talked to Pete, tried to get everything out in the open, and he confessed he'd slept with someone else.'

Hearing the words out loud, telling them to someone else, I get the same sick feeling in my stomach again. The same feeling I had the night Pete told me.

'Rosie, that's awful, I'm so sorry.'

'I was shocked, still am. I asked Pete to move out while we figure this whole mess out.'

'And what are you going to do?'

'Honestly, I have no idea,' I say, wondering if Mark thinks this gives him a chance. I'm far too fragile and confused to comprehend what this means for me and Mark. 'But right now I need a friend. I need you to be my friend.'

'Of course,' says Mark with a smile. 'Right, I think before we say anything else we need cake. Something big and chocolatey.'

'Thank you,' I say, smiling back. 'For everything.'

Mark smiles at me again, that same gorgeous smile, before he walks off to get us some cake. I sit for a moment and stare out of the window at the world. It feels like such a different place from the one I used to inhabit. I remember feeling as though the world was enormous and that everything in it was possible. I remember sitting in cafes when I was younger and being so excited about life. About all the things I could do and achieve. Now looking out of the window at the same London, I can't help but feel that the world is still out there, the same opportunities, the same chances to be happy are there, but it's me that's changed and not for the better. But another part of me, the part that's determined to be happy again, feels as though I've reached a tipping point in my life and because of that anything is possible. It's far more complicated than it was, far more difficult to imagine a way forward where I'm completely happy and have everything I want, but it's not impossible and it's this small fragment of hope that keeps me going. Hope is all you need.

Mark comes back with the largest slice of cake I've ever seen. I think he asked them to cut an extra special piece just for me. A special, your-husband-cheated-on-you-so-here's-some-chocolate-cake-to-make-up-for-it slice of cake. I talk some more about my marriage and about how the kids are coping with everything before I change the subject and ask Mark about his life. It feels good to know that everyone in the world has their own 'stuff'. Mark's wife died and that's far worse than my problems with Pete. I say this to Mark and he says it's all relative. Yes, he lost his wife and it's been incredibly difficult, but there are people in the world who are starving or trying to survive in war torn countries. He says his kids don't have a mother, but they have a father who loves them enough for two parents, a lovely house, great friends and family, and their lives, despite them being so young, are full of hope. That word again. Hope.

By the time Mark and I get up to leave, almost three hours have passed and I'm glad I gave him a second chance. I didn't know if this was a good idea, but we're leaving as friends. We've told each other the truth, how we feel, and it's liberating and honestly, it's lovely to feel needed, to feel wanted, and yes to feel attractive to somebody else. When Pete told me about the night he slept with someone else, I felt hurt in so many ways that it's impossible to describe them all, but one thing I felt so strongly afterwards was a complete lack of self-worth. I must be so unattractive because even my husband felt the need to have sex with someone else. It made me lose any sense of myself as a sexual being, of being someone that anyone would find attractive. But here's Mark and he's gorgeous and I know he thinks I'm beautiful and it feels good. It gives me hope that whatever happens with Pete, I'm not lost, I'm not alone, and that one day, someone else might want me as much as Pete used to.

Twenty-Seven

'We're going to be late!' I shout up the stairs.

It's Monday morning and it's my first day back at work. I'm trying to get the kids moving and out of the door before I head off. As usual no one is ready and I'm resorting to screaming at the top of my voice. Before it only mattered if they were late, but now I have to think of myself too. I have a reason to be out of the door on time and it feels good.

I woke up at five o'clock this morning and got myself ready. It felt strange putting on makeup and slipping into my new work dress - I finally went shopping at the weekend while Pete spent time with the kids and I bought some new work clothes. I'm excited, nervous, and worried about the kids. They've had so much upheaval in their lives the past few weeks and now this. Alice is doing her best to keep it together and she's even started talking to me again. I think she realises I'm not the bad guy in all of this and is old enough to understand. Josh is slowly getting back to normal. He's playing football and complaining when I tell him he needs to stop playing FIFA. It's Daisy I'm worried about. With Pete gone, she's gone back to her old self again. When she started acting she made so much progress and changed for the better, but since Pete left she's gone backwards. The spark she had has been diffused and it's like she's gone into herself. I've tried talking to her, Pete's tried, but nothing is getting through. Alice is spending this weekend with Lilly, Josh is going to be with Pete, and I'm hoping to spend some quality time with Daisy. I need her to be alright.

'Leaving in five minutes!' I shout.

Alice finally comes walking down the stairs, shoving books and folders into her backpack.

'Just because you have to work now, we shouldn't have to leave earlier,' mumbles Alice.

'It's fifteen minutes,' I say, taking one last look at myself in the hallway mirror. Not too bad. I'm so nervous. I don't know why, I've done this job before and I've been working part-time for the last fourteen years, but for some reason this feels huge. It feels like my first day at a new school.

'Fifteen minutes I could have spent in bed.'

'Oh, stop being such a grump,' I say, leaning across and giving Alice a kiss on the cheek. I wouldn't say she loves it, but she doesn't stop me.

'This is so early!' says Josh, finally coming down too.

'It's fifteen minutes earlier!' I say again. 'Where's Daisy?'

'In her bedroom,' says Josh, sitting down on the floor and putting his school shoes on. He needs some new ones because they're scuffed from all the lunchtime football and there's nearly a hole in the front of one of them. For some reason this feels important because it's something I can control. I can make sure my son has a proper pair of school shoes. I make a mental note to buy him a pair at the weekend.

'Come on, Daisy!' I shout up the stairs again.

We all wait at the bottom of the stairs for Daisy. I'm

starting to get nervous because I don't want this to become a big drama. Not today. I'm on tenterhooks as it is, I'm not sure I can cope with Daisy having a breakdown too. Luckily, after a few moments, Daisy comes plodding down the stairs, her face a picture of annoyance and frustration.

'There's my beautiful girl, all ready?' I say, attempting happy. Attempting positive.

'I'm not beautiful,' says Daisy.

'But you are. So beautiful.'

Daisy doesn't say anything, but looks at me with disdain before she grabs her shoes, backpack, and sits on the bottom of the stairs. I feel awful for going back to work full-time. It's too soon. My kids need me at home and for a moment I think about calling Alison and telling her I've changed my mind. Now just isn't the time. I need to be at home with my family. They need me. But I don't make the call. I don't because I know we can't go back. There's no going back now. Only forwards. Daisy gets ready and we all leave the house. I know it's difficult for them, but change is hard, for all of us.

I drop the kids off at school, trying my best to hold back the tears, then I head off to work. I have time to get a quick coffee at the train station before I start. It's a new chapter in my life and it reminds me of the day I walked into the building for the first time. I was twenty-one years old and it felt like I was entering a different world. This was what I wanted to do. The publishing industry felt so glamourous and exciting. I'd wanted this since before university so to finally have a job at one of the biggest publishing houses in London was almost too much. I was overwhelmed, but quickly settled in, made friends, and it became my life. Standing here again, the feeling is different, but the buzz of adrenalin and excitement is still there. The desire to make this my life is still strong.

'There she is,' says Alison, greeting me at reception. 'Ready?'

'As I'll ever be.'

'Nice dress.'

'Thanks. I thought it was about time I started over.'

'You're never too old to start over,' says Alison with a knowing smile.

I admire Alison because she's one of those women who have done it all and have it all, while making it look ridiculously easy. She started a few years before me and has been working full-time ever since. Her husband is an investment banker and they have one child, a boy named Rufus, and she's made it all work. She loves her job and she's good at it. She also somehow still finds time to go to the gym and she looks stunning. You wouldn't know she was nearly fifty.

'This is your office,' says Alison, showing me a small office with a window facing Euston Road. It's only a small space, but it's mine.

'It's perfect,' I say, looking down at an almost empty desk. There's a computer, but nothing else. It's a clean slate.

'I'll let you get settled then pop in for a chat,' says Alison.

'Right,' I say, putting my handbag down on my chair.

'It's good to have you back, Rosie.'

'It's good to be back,' I say and I mean it. I really mean it.

Alison walks off towards her office, while I get used

to my new surroundings. I turn the computer on, put my coffee down on the desk, and look out of the window. It's cold out and so the window has some condensation on it, but I can see cars on the Euston Road, people everywhere on their way to work, and the BT Tower in the distance. Across the road there's a couple of great pubs, a restaurant, and cafes where I'll be having lunch, drinks, and creating a new life. I'm itching to get started.

'Morning,' says Georgie, popping her head around the door.

Today she's looking beautiful in a long Nordic print jumper, black leggings, and boots.

'Morning,' I say smiling.

'I hear we have you back full-time.'

'You heard right. How's the novel going?'

'Really well. I mean it's super hard because I'm busy all the time, but I'm loving it. It's so cathartic and almost spiritual to get all of these thoughts and experiences out, you know.'

'So when you get the huge advance will you be leaving us?'

'Oh God no. I love working here. I can do both if I need to. Sleep when you're dead, right?'

'Exactly,' I say, and it's hard not to be enthused by Georgie. She glows every day. I'm hoping some of that enthusiasm rubs off on me. Georgie is a living, breathing version of something I want to be more like. I realise I don't have her energy and time, I have three kids, and fifteen years on her, but that drive and desire to do something extraordinary is inside all of us if we want to grasp it and not let go. I know it's still inside of me, I just have to find it.

I arrange the few photos I brought with me on my desk. There's pictures of my family, which are nothing like the photo shoot, adventure photos that Georgie has on her desk, but they make me happy. Alice, Josh, Daisy, Pete, and me at various times of our lives. Fragments, moments in time, captured forever, smiling, and happy. I wonder if we'll ever feel like that again?

I walk into Alison's office where she's sitting behind her desk and there's a young girl sitting across from her. I've never seen this girl before, but that doesn't mean much as there's quite often new graduates starting every year in a variety of positions. She looks young. She might even be on work experience.

'Ah, Rosie, there you are,' says Alison. 'This is, Molly, she just started. She's going to be your editorial assistant.'

'Hello, it's so nice to finally meet you, I've heard lots,' says Molly, standing up.

Like most of the girls who start here, Molly is well spoken and dressed impeccably. She must be fresh out of university because she looks about eighteen, but is probably more like twenty-two. She's dressed in a black skirt, a white shirt, and a grey cardigan over the top. Her dark hair is tied back, and she has on a pair of fashionable glasses.

'All good I hope,' I say, shaking her by the hand.

'Of course,' says Molly with a smile.

'Right, we have the morning meeting in ten minutes, but I suggest you two take the rest of the morning to get to know each other. There's that lovely cake shop around the corner. Pop there, have a coffee and a chat. Remember my motto Rosie?'

'Relationships are everything,' I say, remembering the

day she said that to me for the first time and she's right, relationships are everything.

The morning meeting takes about half an hour. We have one every Monday and our big editorial meeting is on Thursday. Molly and I walk across to the cake shop, get a coffee and eat some cake. I'm not sure why - perhaps due to the large percentage of female employees - but publishing always seems to include cake. I get a large piece of coffee cake and Molly gets a honey and lemon drizzle cake. We sit down by the window and I instantly love her. Molly is funny, bright, confident, ambitious, and for someone so young, she's done a lot and knows so much.

Molly Barton grew up in Nottingham before going to university in Bristol. She had a gap year before university and travelled the world. At university, she was editor of the literary magazine, she worked summers at another publisher in London, and fiction is her life. She's read just about every book you can imagine and even many I haven't. Her knowledge of literature is amazing for someone so young. She has a blog and a YouTube channel with interviews and book reviews. She's charming, great company, and I know we're going to get along wonderfully. She reminds me a lot of myself at her age, only she's done all the things I wanted to do and is so much more ready for life than I was. I feel like at twenty-one, I was still a child, still learning, growing up, not ready for life outside of education, but doing my best and keeping afloat. I hadn't travelled the world, I wasn't editor on the university magazine, and I hadn't read quite so widely. Molly is the me I wish I was at twenty-one. I'm glad we get to work together and hopefully I can help her grow.

The rest of the morning and afternoon goes by so

quickly I can't believe it when I look at my computer screen and it says five o'clock. It's been such a wonderful day and I've barely thought about Pete or the kids once. I've been so busy I ended up having lunch at my desk with Molly. She went out and grabbed us both a couple of sandwiches from Pret A Manger and we worked all afternoon. I haven't been this happy in a long time.

'It's time to pack up and head off home,' I say to Molly.

'I'm going to stay on for a bit and read through these manuscripts,' says Molly.

I'm standing by her desk, which is clean, and without any decoration or photos.

'Don't stay too long,' I say with a smile.

'I promise,' says Molly. 'And, Rosie, thanks for today.'

'What for?'

'For being so nice and making me feel so welcome. I was so nervous this morning, but now I'm just excited to get going.'

'That's good to hear, but make sure you don't neglect your social life. All work and no play.'

'Don't worry, the girls I share a house with won't let that happen.'

'Where do you live, exactly?'

'Islington. There's four of us, two of the girls I know from uni and the other is a friend of a friend. It can get a bit crazy, but it's fun and there's always something going on.'

'Sounds brilliant,' I say, feeling rather wistful, and knowing I have to go home, get the kids, make dinner, get the kids in bed, and by the time I sit down it will be nine o'clock and I'll be exhausted and ready for bed myself.

'Can't complain,' says Molly.

'Night then. See you tomorrow.'

'Night,' says Molly, before she gets back to her manuscript.

To be fair, most of the other employees are still here and I'm first out of the door. I know it's going to get harder the more work we take on, and I'm going to have to stay late sometimes, but today I'm leaving on time. I say goodnight to Georgie and Alison, before I make my way outside. It's dark and cold so I wrap my scarf around my neck and pull my woollen hat over my head. I start walking towards the tube station when my mobile phone starts ringing in my pocket. I take it out and answer without looking at the caller.

'Hello?'

'Rosie,' says Dad.

'Dad, everything OK?' There's a pause and in this moment, I know that everything is not OK. I stop walking. 'Dad?'

'It's your mother, Rosie. I think you'd better come.'

My heart stops beating for a moment and a pain engulfs my stomach. I knew this moment would come, it has been coming for years, but now it's here I'm not ready. I thought I wanted the day to come so Mum wouldn't have to lie in that bed anymore not knowing what's going on, not really living. But now the day is here - and today of all days when I'm so happy - I don't want it after all. I don't want to say goodbye to my mother.

'I'm coming,' is all I say, before I flag down a black cab and head home.

Twenty-Eight

In 1986 we went on holiday to Cornwall. I was ten years old and James was seven. I remember it so vividly because it was one of those moments in your childhood that even then I knew was significant. Before Cornwall we'd been camping a few times, taken short breaks to Brighton, Wales, and one to Birmingham to visit some of Dad's family, but this was our first proper holiday. We rented a cottage near the beach and we were there for a full seven days. It was during the summer and for that week we had nothing but sunshine. I remember Dad getting sunburnt on the second day after he fell asleep on the beach. We didn't know back then. People didn't worry about things like UV rays and climate change. It was the 80s. Madonna was number one in the charts, mobile phones were a thing of the future, and my parents didn't pack sunscreen for a week in Cornwall. Evidently Dad did pack lots of white vests though because he's wearing one in every photo.

We stayed in a small cottage just outside Newquay. We drove there in our brown Ford Cortina. We stopped twice on the way to use toilets and eat sandwiches. I remember stopping at a service station so my parents could get tea, while James and I played arcade games. It all felt so exciting and new. We were still in England, but this was a different England. It felt more tropical, more exciting, and Mum and Dad were different too. Back home, Dad worked hard and Mum was always so busy cleaning, cooking, and taking care of us. Sometimes I think she'd forget to just be herself, but on holiday everyone was so relaxed and happy, that it felt for the first time in my life as though we weren't just parents and children, but a family; four people who wanted to spend time together.

The cottage only had two bedrooms so James and I had to sleep on a bunk bed, which we loved, although I had the bottom bunk so James spent most of the time bouncing up and down trying to crush me. It was the first time we'd stayed somewhere else that wasn't a tent or the floor of a relative's house. I knew then I wanted to travel. It might sound silly because we were only going from Woking to Cornwall, but I got the travel bug. I loved feeling so far from home, not knowing where I was, and having so many new places to explore. We spent most of the week in and around Newquay, but we took a couple of day trips to St Ives and Land's End. On one of the last days, Dad took James to play pitch and putt golf, while I spent the morning with Mum. They had the car so we walked from the cottage to the beach and spent the day there. It was a glorious day and the sea was packed full of people.

'This is the life,' said Mum, leaning back on her striped deckchair.

'Yeah it is,' I said, lying on my towel next to her. 'No boys, just us.'

'That's right,' said Mum. 'I'll tell you what, I'll get us both one of those big ice creams in a minute. The ones with a double cone and we'll get two flakes!'

The sand on the beach was nothing like I'd felt before. I'd been to Brighton, but that's just pebbles. This felt like something you'd see on beaches abroad. Bright yellow and soft between my toes. After a minute, Mum and I got up and we walked over to the ice cream van that was always parked next to the beach.

'What flavours would you like?' said Mum.

'Strawberry and chocolate!'

The ice cream man made a huge double ice cream, popped two flakes in the top, and passed it to me. Mum got the same and we made our way back to the beach. It was hot and the ice cream was melting. We had to eat them quickly before they started running down our hands.

'I'm so happy,' I said to Mum.

'Me too, love,' said Mum with a huge smile.

I'll always remember Mum that way. She was young then, just thirty-two years old. Eight years younger than I am now. I always looked up to her because she really was the best mum. So dedicated, patient, warm, funny, and the only thing she cared about was making sure we were happy. She gave everything to us and even though I've tried to do the same with my own children, I've also tried to have a career, tried to fulfil my own wishes and desires because I'm not as selfless as my own mother was. Sitting with her on that beach on that hot summer's day, I'd never been happier in my life. We were so close and I could tell her anything. I wanted to share my life with her because she meant the world to me. Mum made me want to be a better person, to do more, to be the very best I could be. She didn't travel much, but she always encouraged me to dream, to go on adventures, and she was never happier than when we were young. I remember looking up at her on that beach, the sun catching the side of her face, and thinking how beautiful she was. Because Mum was beautiful.

On my graduation day as I walked across the stage to get my certificate, I searched my parents out in the crowd. They were both so happy, Mum had tears rolling down her cheeks, and Dad sat with his arm around her, drying his own eyes with his other hand. Afterwards, when Mum and I were alone in the pub, she leaned across and said to me, 'I'm so proud of you, Rosie. Not just because you're a graduate, but because you're everything I ever wished for myself. You're living the life I couldn't have and watching you do it is like living it myself.'

She never really spoke about her own wishes, her own dreams, but in that moment as she looked at me, I realised she hadn't achieved everything she ever wanted to, but it didn't matter to her as long as I achieved them for her. It's one of the reasons why I've always been so hard on myself and why I have this need to keep pushing myself to do things because I don't want to let her down. She was then and still is today, everything to me. She's my inspiration.

Twenty-Nine

Pete's with the kids, while I go to see Mum. Perhaps for the last time. As I'm driving, all I can think to myself is, I hope she isn't gone yet. I want to be there when she dies. I want to hold her hand, let her know she isn't alone. I'm thinking about the woman on the beach, thirty-two years old, she didn't know she wouldn't have forever. She didn't know she'd die like this and that the last ten years of her life would be a living nightmare. She laughed, loved, and she was happy. We both were. We didn't know the happiness wouldn't last forever because we never imagined it would stop. At least I didn't.

When I arrive at the home, Dad's already there waiting for me outside the room. The doctors are in with her and we have to wait outside.

'Hi, love,' says Dad, giving me a hug, wrapping his arms around me.

'What's going on?'

'She's not well, Rosie. You know she's had that chest infection for a while now, but it's worse and there's nothing they can do now but make sure she's comfortable. Her body's shutting down, love. She's near the end.'

'Is she awake?'

'Barely.'

'Is James on the way?'

'He should be here soon. It's time to say goodbye. Are

you ready?'

'I'll never be ready for that, Dad.'

'I know,' says Dad, tears sitting uncomfortably his eyes.

I feel awful for Dad because for so long he tried to take care of Mum. He wanted to keep her at home. He stopped working, stopped his life to be there for her. In sickness and in health never meant as much as it did for Dad. For years, he managed to look after her, but eventually it became too much. Mum became too much. I remember the day that broke him like it was yesterday. He rang me in a panic. Mum had been having more and more manic episodes and her mental state had declined badly. She was on different drugs and medicines to try and keep her stable, but because of the ever-changing nature of the disease, sometimes they would make her worse or do nothing, and her paranoia became dangerous. On the day he rang, Mum had been trying to escape the house all morning. She was convinced Dad was trying to hurt her. Dad rang me, tears in his voice.

'I need you to come,' he said.

'What's up, Dad?'

'I'm sitting on your mother trying to stop her from escaping. I can't do this anymore, love, it's tearing me apart.'

I went over and found Mum in the living room, Dad blocking the door. She was grunting and groaning and pacing up and down. Dad was a wreck and I could see in his eyes that although he wanted to do his best, he wanted to take care of his wife, he couldn't. This was beyond him.

'It's OK, Dad, I'm here now,' I said walking in behind him.

'I'm sorry,' said Dad, visibly shaken, with tears drowning his eyes. 'I tried my best.'

'I know, Dad, it's alright. You're amazing. What you've done is amazing.'

'I'm sorry,' said Dad again, looking at his wife, at my mother. 'I'm sorry.'

Once the doctors have finished with Mum, they tell us we can go in. Dad and I sit down next to Mum's bed. She's lying there, barely a skeleton of the woman she was even a year ago. Her body has been whittled down by the disease and now she's almost unrecognisable. She's breathing erratically, sometimes heavy then barely at all. The doctor said the infection has spread and her body is shutting down because it doesn't have the energy to fight it. It could take days, it could take hours, they don't know. I'm praying for hours.

'On the way over I was thinking about our holiday to Cornwall. Do you remember, Dad? Nineteen-eighty-six.'

'Yes, love. Such a wonderful holiday.'

'It was the first time I remember feeling excited about travel and going to new places. It made me feel a lot closer to you and especially Mum. I spent a lot of time with her on that holiday. It sounds silly because I was ten, but we really bonded there.'

'It was your mum's idea to go there. She'd been there when she was little with her parents and she'd always wanted to go back. Do you remember the night we went to that restaurant and James threw up in the fireplace?'

'Vaguely.'

'It was our last night so we wanted to go somewhere special. We found a lovely restaurant in town, and James being James, eyes always too big for his belly, wanted the mixed grill. I said I'd get it for him on the condition he ate the whole thing.'

'And did he?'

'He did, but when we were leaving, he said he wasn't feeling well and the next moment he turned round and threw up all over their fireplace. Right in the middle of the restaurant.'

'Oh my God,' I say laughing. 'I don't remember that.'

'I don't think I'll ever forget it,' says Dad wistfully.

'We had such a great time growing up. James and I were so lucky to have you and Mum. You gave us everything,' I say, feeling overwhelmed with emotion. I reach across and hold Mum's hand, while Dad reaches across and holds my other hand.

We sit like this for a while until James eventually turns up.

'Sorry, I was working in Kent and it took me ages to get here,' says James, walking in and giving us both a hug.

Dad fills James in on what's been going on, while I nip out to get us something to eat and some coffee because it might be a long night. I ring Alison and apologise profusely. It's my first week back at work and I'm already taking days off. She says it's fine and to come back when I'm ready, which is lovely and makes me feel even more thankful I agreed to go back to work.

Before Dad rang, I was having such a wonderful day, being back at work and feeling like a part of it again. I felt a spark inside of me that I haven't felt for a long time. Meeting Molly and talking with Georgie, and sitting in the meeting and discussing projects, I really felt alive and I'm so glad I'm working again. I love my children more than anything, but the truth is they don't need me as much as they used to. It's difficult to accept our children are growing up and becoming more independent, but they are and as they do, it's giving me the freedom to work again and to start thinking about myself. As they move on and embrace the world away from me, I can embrace it too and it feels good. I'm glad I kept my toe in all these years, working part-time, because now going back isn't as difficult as it would have been. I know other parents, other mums, who gave up work completely and now ten years later, they have no idea what to do with themselves. They feel lost and despite having degrees and in some cases previous careers, now they're desperately trying to find something to do outside of their families.

I return with coffee and fish and chips because it was the first thing I could find. James, Dad, and I sit next to Mum, eating fish and chips from our laps, talking and sharing stories.

'Dad was telling me about the mixed grill vomit incident in Newquay,' I say to James.

'Oh Christ, I remember that,' says James laughing. 'Although I blame them. Who buys an eight-year-old boy a full mixed grill and makes them finish the whole thing.'

'You wanted to do it,' says Dad.

'I also wanted to be an astronaut, a pirate, and get a top of the line BMX, none of which I was allowed, but two pounds of meat, go on then, son,' says James and we all laugh.

Mum makes a low growling sound, her breathing becoming more and more erratic and noticeably fainter. We all stop giggling at our childhood stories and look towards her. It's nice to look back and remember, but it gives us a sharp reminder why we're here. We stop eating and talking for a moment before we carry on, Mum still breathing, still with us.

'You probably don't remember this James because I think I was about seven or eight, so you'd have been five or six. We went camping in Wales. We were staying at this campsite and one night Mum and Dad spent the night drinking with our campsite neighbours. We were in the tent trying to sleep when Mum came back absolutely wasted and she threw up everywhere. All over her sleeping bag. Remember, Dad?'

Dad laughs.

'They had some homemade wine,' says Dad. 'Lethal stuff and your mum being your mum drank way too much. She spent the whole next day asleep. She was a right mess.'

'And what did we do?' says James.

'I took you two fishing while she slept it off. James, you were crying your eyes out.'

'Why?' says James.

'You hated it when we got drunk and with your mum throwing up, it was all too much for you.'

'Ah you poor little thing,' I say, rubbing his back.

The nurse comes in and checks on Mum every hour and it's almost nine o'clock when I call home and talk to Pete. I tell him what's going on and check on the kids. Alice is still awake and I talk to her for a bit before I get back to the room.

We sit with Mum until gone midnight. The people at the home are lovely and bring us tea and let us stay as long as we need to. The nurse comes for the last time at just after one in the morning. Mum's heart rate is almost non-existent and we all sit together, holding her hands, and watching her slowly drift away. It feels strangely anticlimactic given how dramatic the disease has been at times. I think back to when she was fine, right at the beginning, when it was just the occasional tic or involuntary movement, to the full blown mental episodes when we had to pin her down to the floor. Now she's leaving us without speaking for the last two years, her body barely a shell of the person who's somewhere inside. It's a strange feeling because Mum, my real Mum, died a long time ago, but as she breathes her last breath, as her life finally ends, I feel a deep pain inside of me and I think it's the whole pain of the last ten years that's been so hard to rationalise.

It's nearly two o'clock in the morning when the doctor officially announces she's dead. That my Mum, my children's grandmother, is gone. We all cry and hug each other, leaning on and supporting each other as best we can, but despite the pain and sadness, we also know it's a good thing. She had no life. Dad didn't have much of one either, and now we can all finally start moving on. It seems to be something of a recurring theme at the moment. Everything is changing and a part of me knows we have to adapt and embrace it, but sometimes, on days like today, I want to stop the world for a moment. I need time to reflect on the past and think about the future. I need to start learning how to enjoy the moment without worrying about everything else because it's one of the hardest things in life, to just enjoy the moment. It's hard because when you have three children, when your husband is living at his parents' house, when your mother just died, when you feel so old and past it sometimes, when you're tired, it's hard to smell the roses. It's hard to embrace the moment and far easier to be wistful about the past and optimistic about the future. But I'm not living in the past or the future, I'm living in the now and this is what I need to do. I need to find ways to enjoy this as it is, with all its imperfections, because this is my life and after what happened with Mum, we never know how long we're going to get.

Dad, James, and I stand next to Mum's bed and take one last look at her. It isn't her, I know. It isn't the woman who sat with me on that Cornish beach eating double ice cream. And yet it is. She's my mum, the woman who raised me, loved me, and gave me everything. The body is still now, gaunt, and broken, barely a bump in the sheets. It's so terribly sad to see her like this and I can't help the tears that fall from my face and onto her. I lean down one last time and give her a kiss. Her skin feels strange and alien, not like the smooth, soft skin I kissed as a child. I say my last goodbyes to Mum and then we leave. For the very last time, we walk out of the home where Mum died.

It's almost three in the morning when I finally get home, walking in the door, trying to be quiet. There was a time in my life when I used to sneak in at this time drunk, trying not to wake my parents up, but now it's my children. Pete is standing in the doorway to the living room.

'You're still up?' I say, walking towards him.

'I wanted to wait for you. How are you?'

'She died, Pete. Mum died,' is all I can say before I'm crying and Pete has his arms around me and he's pulling me into his body. I can't stop the tears and Pete just holds me.

I'm so tired and without asking, Pete takes me upstairs

and puts me to bed. I don't fight it or say anything, but let him undress me and tuck me in. I feel him give me a kiss on the head, before I close my eyes. It's been a long day and despite still having so many thoughts flying around my mind, trying their best to keep me awake, I can't and I'm soon sound asleep. The last thought I have is of Mum, not the old, sick Mum, but my real mum; young and laughing her beautiful laugh, then nothing but darkness.

Thirty

The first thing I hear in the morning is the sound of the kids, which is confusing because I have no idea what time it is and how long I've slept for. My head feels heavy and my eyes are still bloated and red from all the tears. I slowly get up and look across at my alarm clock on the side. It's just after eleven o'clock on a Tuesday morning so I'm even more confused. Why aren't the kids at school and where's Pete?

I get up and after putting on my pyjamas, I slowly make my way downstairs. I can hear everyone in the living room and when I walk in, I find Alice, Josh, Daisy, and Pete all together watching television. They're watching Wanted Down Under, the show I sometimes watch on my own, dreaming about a new life in Australia.

'Oh, morning,' says Pete, getting up as soon as I walk in. 'How are you?'

'Fine, confused, why aren't you all at school?'

'Dad told us what happened with Grandma and said we could have the day off,' says Alice.

'I thought today should be a family day,' says Pete. 'I hope it's OK.'

'Yes, of course, but what about your work?'

'I called in sick. This is more important.'

'I'm sorry Grandma died,' says Daisy, walking over and wrapping her arms around me, burying her face into my chest.

'Thank you,' I say, feeling her warm little body against mine.

'Me too,' says Alice, joining in with the hug, then Josh follows. My children are all hugging me and it feels nice and comforting and when I look down, Pete's on the sofa smiling.

'Well you might as well get in here too,' I say to Pete.

'Come on, Dad,' says Daisy.

Pete gets up, slightly gingerly at first, but puts his arms around us all, until the whole family is together as one, and I know Mum would have loved this and it does feel good to be together again. Almost as if we're sort of back to normal.

After we're done hugging, the kids get back to the show and fill me in on what's going on, while Pete goes into the kitchen to make breakfast. He comes back a moment later, popping his head round the door.

'I'm going to Sainsbury's Local. You're almost out of bread, milk, and I'll get some more breakfast stuff,' says Pete with a smile.

'I'm not that hungry,' I say.

'You have to eat. I'll be back in a minute.'

Pete leaves, the front door closing with the same slam - the knocker hitting the door and making that familiar sound, while I settle on the sofa with the kids. It feels strange to think that Mum is gone. No more visits to the home. No more worrying about her, about what's happened to her. It's over now and it feels surreal. I am sad, but I'm also relieved because she suffered for so long. I've often thought how much better it would have been if she'd had a short sickness then died. It might have been sadder in the short term, but with Huntington's it was like losing her in stages, each stage chipping away at me. I feel cheated in so many ways because I lost the last ten years of her life because she wasn't herself and even now I can't really feel the sort of sadness I should feel at the loss of a parent. The whole thing has drained me physically and emotionally and maybe it's a part of why my marriage has fallen apart.

Pete returns from the shop with bacon, sausages, croissants, fruit, bread, milk, and eggs. He spends half an hour in the kitchen before he calls us in to eat. When we walk in, I'm surprised to see the table full of food. Pete never did this while we were married. He used to make breakfast when we first lived together, when it was just us, but as the years have gone on, he's done less.

'Breakfast, well brunch, I suppose, is ready,' says Pete.

'This looks amazing,' I say, sitting down at the table. 'I didn't know you could cook.'

I look at Pete and he looks momentarily abashed before he regains his composure.

'I suppose it's been a while.'

'Looks lush, Dad,' says Alice, sitting down.

I look across and Josh already has three croissants on his plate.

'Why don't you put at least one of those back,' I say to Josh.

'Fine,' says Josh.

'Right everyone, tuck in,' says Pete.

And we do. It's wonderful to be around the dinner table again, talking, laughing, eating and being a family. It's one of the things I've missed most about Pete not living here. The evening meals have become so depressing I've started letting the kids eat in the living room in front of the television. The nightly meal around the table is something I never imagined would die, but it has, and so quickly. Sitting here together, the day Mum died, it seems ridiculous to be in this position. I suppose the one big thing about death is that it helps you put things into perspective. Why am I being so stubborn about Pete? Yes, he made a mistake and did something awful, but I have feelings for another man. Pete's was just one night, mine has been happening over weeks and weeks. I haven't done anything physical, but the emotions are there, the thoughts are there, and so why am I putting my family through this? Why am I forcing Pete to live at his parents' and making my children so unhappy? He's been so wonderful the last twenty-four hours. I don't know what I would have done without him. And now, sitting here, with Mum looming large in my mind, it seems ridiculous he isn't here with us. I was so angry about his one night of stupidity, but at some point you have to move on. At some point you draw a line under it and start again. You have to.

We all finish eating, and as it turns out, I was a lot hungrier than I thought. Pete was right, I needed to eat. As soon as we're done we make plans to go for a walk - something we haven't done for so long. It's a beautiful day and Wandsworth Common is close by. While the kids are upstairs getting ready, and Pete and I are tidying up, I decide to talk to him.

'Thanks for everything.'

'Not a problem,' says Pete. 'It's your Mum, Rosie.'

'I know, but with everything that's happened recently…'

Pete stops putting plates in the dishwasher and looks

at me.

'Rosie, you're my wife, and I love you. I'd do anything for you,' says Pete, and in this moment, right now, I want him back. Fuck everything that's happened, he's my husband, and I need him. I'll get over the affair, in time, and it will be fine. We'll be fine.

'Move back in,' I say suddenly.

'Really? You mean it?'

'Yes, Pete, I mean it. I'm still angry about what you did and it's going to take time to get back to how we were, but if we don't start it's never going to happen, is it?'

'Thank you,' says Pete, standing in front of me.

'Let's just see how it goes. I want this to work.'

'Me too. More than anything. I've missed you so much, Rosie,' says Pete, and he has tears in his eyes and it shows me how much this means to him.

This time it's going to be different. I'm working now and I think I'm going to be happier because of that and it will reflect in our marriage. I think all the problems we were having were because we got lazy. It's easy to do. You stop putting in 100% and before you know it, things start to slip, cracks start to appear, and if you aren't careful it can break apart. Maybe everything that's happened is a good thing because it's woken us up. People say that things happen for a reason and this is a perfect example of that. Pete and I used to be happy, we used to have a brilliant marriage, we were happy, but we got complacent, made a few bad choices and it unravelled. But now we have the chance to put it right. We have a second chance at happiness and we have to give it our best shot.

'I've missed you too, and I don't mean the last couple

of years you, but the old you, the old us. I want to get that back again.'

'Me too,' says Pete, smiling like I haven't seen him smile in a long time. 'I promise I'll do whatever I can to make it work.'

'Ready,' says Alice, walking into the kitchen, closely followed by Josh and Daisy.

'Before we go, we have some news,' I say with a smile, taking hold of Pete's hand and turning towards the kids. 'Your father's moving back in again.'

'Yes!' Josh shouts.

'Really?' says Alice, who looks like she might burst into tears.

'Yes, really,' says Pete.

Daisy runs over and throws her arms around us both.

'I'm so happy,' says Daisy. 'Thank you! Thank you! Thank you!'

It's hard not to be moved by this. I think I've cried enough over the past day and so I smile instead. This is a fresh start for all of us. It's a chance to get it right this time and I know Mum would have wanted this.

We all get ready, before we leave and start walking towards the park. It's only a five minute walk until we're there, the soft grass beneath our feet. The sun is shining brightly in the sky today. It's December so there's still a chill in the air, but walking along next to Pete, the kids in front of us, feeling the warm sun on my face makes me happy and I can't help feeling Mum's spirit is in there somewhere. As we're walking, I start thinking about how lucky I am. I realise how much I've complained of late, and I realise all pain, all unhappiness is relative, and it was a very real unhappiness, but when I look at my family and think of where I live, the career I have, I am so lucky. Maybe my life's not perfect, but perhaps that doesn't really exist. This is good though and maybe it's because of Mum dying, but it really does feel like a fresh start, a new day, and perhaps the beginning of something wonderful.

Thirty-One

Watergate Bay, Cornwall, 2015

The cottage is about a half mile from the beach. It isn't the same cottage I stayed at with Mum and Dad when I was little, but it reminds me of it so much. I've wanted to do this holiday for years because I have such fond memories of my time here, and I want to share it with my own children. We also haven't been on holiday for so long and to be honest, things with Pete aren't the best right now.

I don't know what it is or what's changed, but something isn't right in our relationship. We discussed moving into the new house for a long time because we knew it would mean a much higher mortgage, but we decided we could just about afford it if Pete did a bit of overtime. But I don't think we realised what this would do to our marriage. It's always easy in hindsight, but I'm starting to doubt whether moving house was right for us. Especially as we were happy enough in the old place. The schools weren't quite as good and the new house is bigger and shinier and nearer to Pete's work, but is it worth hardly ever seeing my husband? Is it worth struggling financially? Looking back, I don't think it's been worth it, but now we're here, in our little holiday cottage, I'm hoping this makes up for it. I'm hoping this week gives us back enough of us to keep going for another twelve months. Here's to hoping.

We've unpacked our bags, put away the shopping we brought, and the kids are itching to get to the beach. It's summer and although it isn't Mediterranean hot, it's warm and certainly warm enough for an afternoon at the beach.

'Come on, we're ready!' bellows Alice from downstairs.

It's nice and slightly ironic that for once the children are downstairs shouting at me to get ready. I'm upstairs putting on the new swimsuit I bought especially for this holiday. I spent ages trying to find the right bikini. It isn't easy when you don't have a beach-ready body like all the adverts of the women they use to show us how wonderful the bikinis are. And yes, they are wonderful on the models, but when I was in the changing room trying them on, the mirrors judging every square inch of my body, I felt horrible. Why do bits of my body sag down and why do certain parts, no matter what diet I do or how much exercise I do, never change? I'm sure none of the models have had three kids. But as I'm standing in the bedroom in our cottage, looking at myself in the mirror, I don't think I look too bad. The lighting is darker here and that helps. Pete comes walking in, ready to get into his shorts. He stops and looks at me.

'What do you think?' I say, turning to him.

'You look very sexy.'

'Really?'

'Yes, really. Why do you always think you look terrible?'

'Because I'm a woman,' I say, trying to be light hearted and funny, but Pete doesn't laugh.

'You shouldn't always think the worst,' says Pete, before he opens his suitcase and starts getting undressed.

Do I always think the worst? I don't think I'm like that, but maybe it's how I've become. I don't know. I used to be a more positive person I'm sure, but perhaps over time I have become more negative. Always look on the bright side of life, Rosie Willis.

'Sorry if I do that,' I say. Pete's changing from his jeans into his shorts and pulling on a t-shirt. He's officially in holiday mode. 'I don't mean to be.'

'It's fine,' says Pete, noncommittally. 'Let's just have a good week.'

'Yes, let's,' I say, skipping across and giving him a kiss on the lips. 'Let's just have a really nice time. And maybe when the kids are asleep later -'

'You'll fall asleep watching TV with a glass of wine in your hand?' says Pete, smiling, his hands around my waist, touching the soft spongy flesh just above my bikini bottoms. I should have gone for an all in one.

Hilarious. Like you're Mr Up All Night. It's you who's usually asleep first.'

'Some of us have to get to work early,' says Pete, a slight niggle in his voice. A tetchiness that's become more prevalent in his voice the last six months.

This is how so many arguments start and I'm not going to fall into the same trap today. This holiday is going to be wonderful and it's going to help us get over this blip because that's all it is, a blip. Pete's been working too hard, Daisy's becoming more difficult and it's driving a wedge between us. I'm not going to let it though. This place has such fond memories for me, it's where I remember being so happy with my own family and I want to replicate that with my own children and Pete. This is an important place and nothing is going to ruin this week.

'OK, ready?' I say brightly.

'Ready,' says Pete, not quite so cheerfully, although to be fair he did do all the driving and is probably quite tired. I can see he's trying though.

We go outside and start the walk to the beach in high spirits. The kids are all very excited and rightly so. Alice is twelve, Josh is eight, and Daisy is five. These are great ages for a holiday like this and the poor things haven't had too many holidays over the years. I'm not sure what's happened because before we had kids, Pete and I travelled quite a bit and we both seemed to love it. But with the cost of moving house, the cost of having three kids, living in London, the stress of Pete's hectic work schedule, and just general laziness I suppose, the years have gone by and we've only been on a few holidays. But while our friends have been popping off to Spain, Portugal, Greece, and other warmer climes on a regular basis, we've hardly gone anywhere and so for the kids, this holiday is a big deal.

The three kids are walking ahead of us down the country lane, while Pete and I lag behind, carrying all the stuff we need for the beach. It's only a ten minute walk, but already I'm dreading the walk back (uphill). We could have driven, and it's such a nice day, but when you have towels, beach toys, buckets, spades, changes of clothes, sunscreen, water, food, and books to read, this half mile feels a lot longer. We eventually reach the beach and as soon as we do, the kids are running off towards the sea.

'You still need sunscreen!' I shout after them but it's too late, they can't hear me.

'This alright?' says Pete, looking down at the small

patch of beach we're standing on.

It's just after lunch and the beach is busy with families, couples, and there's topless girls lying on towels showing off their perky young breasts. There's no chance of me going topless and showing my breastfed, ravaged, middle-aged boobs.

'Fine,' I say, putting down the towels and the rest of our stuff.

The kids are already splashing around in the sea, while Pete and I get settled. I take off my clothes to reveal the bikini beneath - and the amazing amount of very white, spongy skin. I feel like a floury white bap compared to most of these skinny, brown girls around me. To be fair, there are also quite a few overweight mums squeezed into bikinis, sitting on deckchairs while their kids build sandcastles and dig holes. I'm not the worst bikini offender here, but seeing the young girls with their lithe bodies does make me feel awful about myself. I see Pete sneakily checking out a few of the topless ones nearby and I can't blame him. I wish he'd check me out in the same way from time to time.

'This is nice,' says Pete when we're finally settled down, lying on our towels, while our kids are running around and splashing in the surf. I hope they come back soon though so I can put sunscreen on them before they all get burnt.

'It's gorgeous, just like I remember it,' I say with a smile.

A part of the reason why I wanted to come on this holiday was to reconnect with Pete. I also want to spend some quality time with the kids when I'm not shouting at them to get ready, clean their rooms, and to be more relaxed about everything. It soon becomes apparent as we sit here together while our children are off playing that Pete and I don't have anything to say to each other. This is a problem when one of you is gone so much, you lose that connection, the thing that drew you to them in the first place. When Pete and I got together, we used to talk for hours about everything. We never ran out of things to say to each other and Pete was so funny and interesting. He was interested in me and would listen intently to every word I said. But now we have nothing to say to each other. After five minutes of silence, Pete starts playing on his phone and I get out my book. Reconnecting with Pete will have to wait for another day.

The kids eventually come back after about thirty minutes because they're hungry, cold, and need a quick rest before they hit the sea again.

'This is wicked,' says Josh when I cover him in a towel.

'We need to get you dry and put on some sunscreen before you get burnt,' I say, passing a towel to Pete so he can dry off Daisy.

'Wicked,' says Josh again, looking across at a row of bare breasts just along the beach.

The boy is ten and already interested in breasts! We have no chance. We get the kids dry and give them snacks while we apply sunscreen. They all complain and wiggle around, but after a few minutes they're all coated and off again, running full tilt towards the sea.

'It's nice to see them so happy,' I say.

'Yes, it is.'

'You'd better lotion me up too,' I say, passing him the

sunscreen. 'I don't want to get burnt.'

'Righto,' says Pete, squeezing some lotion onto his hands, before he starts rubbing it on my shoulders and back. It feels nice.

'Although there's no chance of me going topless so don't worry.'

'I wasn't worried.'

'What does that mean?'

'Nothing.'

'Maybe I was going to get them out. What would you think then?'

'It wouldn't bother me.'

'Even though mine aren't all young and perky like the girls over there?'

'I hadn't noticed.'

'Oh, Pete, I saw you looking. Of course you noticed and why wouldn't you? They all look far better than mine.'

'Not true,' lies Pete. 'Yours are perfect.'

'I appreciate the lies, but I know mine aren't what they once were.'

'They're fine for me,' says Pete, finishing up with the sunscreen.

'Do you want some on?'

'No, I'm fine. I put some on my face earlier,' says Pete, before he gets back to his phone.

I think about trying to start a conversation, but decide against it and start reading my book again. Within twenty minutes, Pete's asleep, and I decide to get up and play with the kids. They're all down by the water and I bring along a frisbee and try to get them interested. Soon we're all playing frisbee together, the cold sea water splashing against my feet and legs, the sun shining, and I'm so happy. Being a parent on holiday is so different from regular life and I can see now why the holiday here as a child was so important to me because it lets us be us without all the mundane routine of normal life. We need to do this more. We need to be on holiday more and at home less. This is what will save our marriage and save our family. I haven't had this much fun with the kids for such a long time. I hope that as the week goes on, Pete starts to relax too and remember who he really is and who we are. I know he's under such stress at work and being off for a week only adds to that stress, but he needs to learn how to switch off and remember that life is more than work. He also has a family and wife that need him.

As the week goes on, we all start to relax more and get in the holiday spirit. Even Pete stops checking his phone every five minutes. On the second to last day, Pete takes Josh to play mini golf, while I take the girls into town for lunch and a bit of shopping. This is their choice and Daisy wants to get a souvenir. She saved up ten pounds and is itching to spend it. Alice wants to get something too, so we're off shopping and I'm very excited to spend time with my girls.

Newquay isn't that big of a town, but there's a plethora of shops the girls can look in. I love a bit of shopping, but after looking in about ten souvenir shops for Daisy, who is looking for something 'special' I'm in need of a coffee and some lunch. Alice is determined to buy something surf related. She says she loves the surf culture - I think it might just be the surf boys actually - and wants something to bring back to London that reminds her of it. The kids all had surf lessons yesterday and got on well. Daisy found it a bit difficult only being five, but enjoyed some boogie boarding, while Alice and Josh both managed to stand up on their first real wave. I think it was the highlight of the holiday for them. Especially Alice, who I think had a crush on their instructor, Ollie, who was a very handsome eighteen-year-old with long blond hair and rippling abs. With eight-year-old Josh ogling boobs all week, and now twelve-year-old Alice having a crush on her surf teacher, I'm starting to get worried about the next few years.

I persuade the girls to take a break from shopping so we can have lunch. We find a Prezzo and I end up having a glass of Prosecco and the girls are happy with pizza.

'I love hanging out with just you two,' I say, as we tuck into our food.

'This is the best,' says Daisy.

'It's sick,' says Alice, who appears to have picked this word up from Ollie.

'Is that right?' I say. 'It's sick, is it?'

'Yeah, sick,' says Alice. 'Any chance we could try surfing again?'

'Maybe we could hire a board tomorrow. It's our last day.'

'I don't want to go home,' says Daisy. 'I want to stay on holiday for always.'

'Me too,' says Alice.

'Me three, but unless Daddy goes back to work and earns more money we won't be able to afford to come back next year.'

'My friend, Jenny, her family are going to Spain,' says Alice. 'Could we go to Spain?'

'Maybe next year,' I say.

'I want to come back here,' says Daisy, before taking a huge chunk out of her pizza slice.

'We'll see,' I say, drinking Prosecco and feeling so warm and happy.

The rest of the afternoon goes by with more shopping - another coffee for me - until eventually the girls get what they want. Daisy gets a snow globe and a t-shirt that says, 'I love Newquay', on the front. Alice gets a surf t-shirt and a necklace, and we all get matching friendship bracelets. It's a fun afternoon and when we eventually get back it's almost time for dinner. The boys are back from mini golf and we decide to get fish and chips and eat at home because everyone is so tired. We have one more day then it's back to our normal life in London. Back to cooking, cleaning, and being boring old parents again. I wish there was a way we could be like this all the time. We're all so relaxed and happy. Daisy has barely had a tantrum all week. Pete and I haven't exactly recaptured our old selves again, but as the week's gone on and he's relaxed, it's been better. We're starting to remember what we loved about each other again without the constant distractions of work, life, and television.

The last day in Newquay and we're heading down to the beach. It's quite windy and Pete bought a kite on the way and the kids are excited to try and fly it. I'm bringing my book because I've almost finished it and I'm determined to get it done before we leave. I have a pretty decent tan too. I remember the first day here, I felt awful stripping down to my bikini, my body like a mushy block of cold cut meat from a can, pale and anaemic, squeezed into a bikini. But now, six days later, I have colour and I know my body isn't any different, but I don't care. I'm OK with how I am. I've relaxed into the week and now I'm lying here, watching my children and Pete trying to fly a kite and I couldn't be happier. I know my life isn't perfect, my marriage isn't perfect, but this holiday has given me hope we can put it right. Like Pete and the kids trying to fly the kite - which isn't going well - we have to keep trying. We're a family and even though today, this is the best of us, I know that in the weeks and months ahead, we're going to have bad times and low points, but if we keep working hard and being patient, we can fly - I would say like the kite, but it doesn't really get off the ground and eventually they all get bored and the kids start playing in the water. Pete comes back and lies down next to me.

'Better luck next time,' I say.

'It was the kite. Next time we'll buy a proper one.'

'Next time? There's going to be another holiday soon?'

'I hope so,' says Pete with a smile.

'Me too,' I say, reaching out a hand and holding his.

'You know, it's the last night.'

'I know.'

'And we haven't really made full use of the bed,' says Pete with a grin.

'I know.'

'And I was thinking…'

I look across at Pete and smile.

'I know,' I say, and Pete smiles back.

We lie on the sand, our faces turned up to the sun, while our children run and frolic in the sea. I finish my book and Pete takes a short nap, before the afternoon turns to early evening and we head back to the cottage. Pete heads out in the car and buys dinner, while I get the kids cleaned off and ready to eat. By the time Pete gets back, we're all starving and we don't even use plates, but sit at the table eating from the paper. Pete went all out and bought three pieces of fish, two battered sausages, a pineapple fritter, pickled onions, and a mountain of chips. We squeeze a big dollop of tomato ketchup onto the paper, and the kids have cans of drink, while Pete and I open a bottle of wine. It's a fitting last night and the kids go to bed early because they're all so tired from being at the beach all day.

Pete and I are tired too, but it's the last night and we made a promise. Our skin feels so different after a week on holiday. We're both tanned, our skin is softer, and smells of the beach and sunscreen. Lying in bed together, and having sex here, it feels different and new. It feels more like the sex we used to have that was passionate and intense, and so unlike the sex we've had recently which has become boring and routine. Holiday sex with Pete reminds me how much I still fancy him and when we make the effort, how much he still fancies me. It reminds me for a moment of our time in Thailand. I had to convince Pete to take this holiday, but now we have, I hope we don't go back to how we were before. I know it'd be easy to slot back into life and forget this ever happened and how we felt, but I hope we don't. I love this feeling.

Afterwards we take showers, and clamber back into bed, both exhausted, and we fall asleep in each other's arms, something we haven't done in years and it really does feel like a tipping point. We were having some problems, our marriage had become stale, but we're Rosie and Pete and we'll always be together and I know it won't always be like this, but just knowing it's possible, will keep us together forever. I've never been more certain of anything in my entire life.

Thirty-Two

I'm in Wahaca on Charlotte Street having lunch with Lauren. It's been a week since Mum died and I'm back at work. It's been a tough week and I still have the funeral to come, but with the support of my family and friends, it's been bearable. I haven't seen Lauren in ages so we decided to catch up over lunch. For once, I have so much to talk about.

'I'm sorry about your mum,' says Lauren. 'You must feel a bit relieved though.'

'I am,' I say, browsing the menu.

It's been a busy morning at work and I really could use something to take the edge off so I order a Margarita with our food. Lauren looks amazing as usual, but there's something different about her. Something has changed. I can sense it. I remember when we lived together at university, our periods quickly got in sync and we always had a close bond and could tell when something was off with the other one without saying a word.

'I want to hear everything about what's been going on,' says Lauren. 'Don't hold back.'

I tell her everything. I tell her all about Pete and his one night stand, about Mark, about our marriage problems, and how Pete is back in the house again.

'Wow, Rozza, I can't believe Pete cheated on you. He never seemed like the sort.'

'I was as shocked as you.'

'But you're giving him a second chance?'

'I sort of feel like I have to. I mean, I'm not entirely innocent…'

'Wait. I don't think having coffee with a man and thinking he's a bit fit is the same as sleeping with someone.'

'Yes, I know, and I'm not saying it is, but I'm not blameless. It takes two to make a marriage work and we both let things slip. I haven't been happy for a long time and I didn't do anything to change it. Pete wasn't happy either and yes, he made a terrible mistake, but he's apologised and I know it won't happen again.'

'So you think you're going to be alright?'

'I don't know. Maybe. Maybe not. It's hard to know, but he's really trying and I want us to be happy again, for us and for the kids. That's the thing too, Lauren, we have kids to think about.'

'I know,' says Lauren, and she definitely has a look.

'OK, spit it out.'

'What?'

'Something's going on with you. I knew it the minute you sat down, but right then you had a look. Something's on your mind.'

'I wasn't sure about this until the other day so it's really new.'

'Is it about Dave? Have you broken up?'

'No, it's not Dave. I mean, he's involved, but…'

'What is it then?'

'I'm pregnant,' says Lauren suddenly.

'What? But I thought…'

'It was an accident,' says Lauren, her face loaded with

uncertainty which is so unlike her.

'What are you going to do?'

'I'm not totally sure, but I think I'm going to keep it,' says Lauren, a small smile on her face.

'For what it's worth, I think you'll be an amazing mum.'

'Thanks, but for the moment, mum's the word - maybe not mum - but you know, keep it quiet.'

'Of course,' I say, as our waitress comes over, bringing us our drinks and a ton of food. Lauren said she was hungry and now I know why. 'But if you need anything, need to talk or just want someone to vent to, you know where I am.'

We start tucking into our food and I'm thinking about tonight. It's Daisy's play and I know she's feeling nervous and I'm anxious for her. I'm sure she's going to be amazing because she's been working so hard and since Pete moved back in again, she's been a lot more settled and focused. All the kids have been happier since he moved back in, although it hasn't been easy and the initial excitement I felt has been replaced with more doubt and worry. What if it doesn't work out? Can I really truly trust him? I know he said he wouldn't do it again, and he probably won't, but he broke that promise once, so what's to say he won't again?

'I'm thinking about going on holiday,' I say. 'I think a complete break will do us all the world of good.'

'Sounds like a good idea. Dave and I are thinking about taking a few trips. You know, before I get too massive and pregnant. I think they call it a babymoon.'

'Babymoon? I've never heard of that before.'

'Yeah, it's a honeymoon before you have a baby. We

still have the best part of nine months, so we can fit in two or three holidays before then.'

'Two or three? Gosh you're so lucky, Lauren, I'd give anything for just one.'

'Then make it happen. If you weren't happy before, you can't go back to how it was, you have to change. You're working now, you have the money, make it happen.'

'I am, we will,' I say semi-triumphantly. 'Pete's in a very giving place right now, so I think it's a good time a to float the idea.'

'There you go. Girl power!' says Lauren, holding up her water to clink with my Margarita.

'Girl power!'

'I was never the biggest Spice Girls fan, but you have to love girl power.'

'Such optimistic times in the nineties. It feels like such a long time ago now.'

'It was, Rozza. Twenty years ago.'

'Don't say that please, it's depressing.'

'Sorry, but it's like I was saying to Dave the other day, decisions matter now. It's not like in our twenties when we could do anything and start again. If we choose to have this baby, this is it. We either have this one or have none.'

'Is Dave excited to be a dad?'

'Yeah, he can't wait the soppy sod. It was always me holding back.'

'This is it then. You're going to be a mum and I'm going to make it work with Pete. Decisions have been made.'

'It's not the carefree nineties anymore and this isn't Kansas, Toto.'

'Definitely not,' I say, taking a sip of my Margarita.

'And please, don't call me Toto.'

She's right, it isn't the nineties anymore and we aren't in our twenties. Life was much simpler then and decisions didn't feel so huge and overwhelming. Pete and I are both at that age when we can't waste years and years going down the wrong path. If we stay together and break up again in ten years, that's ten years closer to death, ten years of not creating something new, and ten years of not being happy. But we've been together for so long and we have three kids, we're married, you don't give up on that. Even after what Pete did, I still love him and I still want us to be happy again because we can be. I'm sure of it. Sitting here with Lauren and having lunch, listening to her talking about becoming a mother, I honestly don't know if things with Pete will work out. I hope they do and I'm going to give it my best shot, we both are, but you never know, do you?

I remember something Mum once said to me. I was about to leave home and head off to university. I was eighteen and Mum was obviously upset her first child was leaving home - albeit only moving less than an hour away by car - but before she said goodbye, she said this to me, 'Rosie, I'm so proud of you. Your life is going to be full and exciting and there will be many ups and downs, but remember this: Life isn't about celebrating the highs or commiserating the lows, it's about not getting complacent when things are going well and not giving up when they aren't. Remember that and you'll be fine.' Mum was right. Maybe Pete and I were complacent when things were going well, but now it's our chance to follow her advice and not give up when things aren't going well. It's time to dig in and make us work.

Daisy is being very quiet in the back of the car. It's early evening and we're driving her to school for her nativity play. Pete's driving, Alice and Josh are in the back with Daisy and Dad. Dad drove up this afternoon and is staying with us tonight. I think after everything with Mum, he needed this. We all need this. It's dark out and there's a chill in the air. It's almost Christmas so there's lights up everywhere, trees are sparkling in windows, and there's an air of excitement and nostalgia filling the car. I remember performing in my own school nativity play aged seven. I was so nervous, but seeing my parents in the audience helped. I also only had one line, 'Look a shiny star!' is all I had to say. Daisy is the lead actress and has lots of lines. I look in the mirror and see her mumbling something to herself. She's probably going through the lines in her head. I can't put into words how proud I am of her. All of those days when she was having a hard time, the arguments, the fights, tears, and heartache, all of it means nothing compared to this. This feeling is worth all of it.

'Break a leg, darling,' says Pete to Daisy.

'You're going to be amazing,' says Alice.

'Proud of you, sis,' says Josh.

'Your Grandma would have been so proud of you,' says Dad, a huge smile on his face.

'Thank you,' says Daisy, suddenly looking so young.

We're at the stage door and she has to go inside by herself and get ready. Other parents are dropping off their children too.

'Go ahead, give me a moment,' I say to Pete, Dad, and the kids, who wander off towards the front of the school. 'OK, ready?'

'Yep,' says Daisy.

'You're going to be brilliant and I'm so proud of you. Prouder than I've ever been in my entire life. You know, my mum, Grandma, she always gave me the best advice and calmed me down when I was feeling worried or nervous. Are you nervous?'

'A little bit.'

'Then do this. If at any point during the play you feel scared, worried, nervous, or just need something, find me in the crowd and look at me. Pretend it's just us running lines at home. Everyone else is gone and it's just you and me on the sofa. OK?'

'OK,' says Daisy, and I'm almost crying I'm so overwhelmed with love for her.

'Now go and break a leg,' I say, giving her a kiss on the top of her head, before she disappears inside and I join the rest of my family.

The atmosphere inside the school hall is electric. They've done an amazing job putting up Christmas decorations and the whole place looks so festive. They've set up rows and rows of chairs and all the parents and kids are sitting down in anticipation. At the moment they're playing Christmas carols over the speakers while we wait. There's children running around and teachers looking flustered as last minute preparations are underway. I'm sitting between Alice and Josh and Pete's on the other side of Alice next to Dad. After ten minutes of waiting the lights finally go down, the curtain goes up, and standing in the middle of the stage all by herself is Daisy. My little baby girl.

'I can't believe this is happening,' says Daisy, her voice

loud and clear. 'Me, pregnant? How can it be?'

'What's that, dear?' says a boy, presumably Joe, walking onto the stage.

'Oh, nothing,' says Daisy, getting a giggle from the audience.

She looks confident and she's delivering her lines perfectly.

'Are you sure because I'm sure I heard you say preg…'

'No, no, no, you must have misheard me,' says Daisy, getting another laugh. Daisy walks to the front of the stage and looks out at the audience, the spotlight just on her. She looks around and then says to us, 'Shall I tell him?'

'Yes!' the audience say back in unison.

'Alright, fine, but he isn't going to like it,' says Daisy, getting another big laugh.

Miss Hollingshead was right, Daisy is a natural. I'm amazed at how good she is. I knew hearing her lines at home that she could do it, but doing it like this in front of an audience is something special.

The rest of the play is brilliant and it's clear - to me at least - that Daisy is the star of the show. The little boy playing Joe forgets a few lines and there are moments when Daisy has to rescue him. She, on the other hand, delivers all her lines perfectly and when it's all over, the audience as one stands and applauds. Alice and Josh are both clapping, whistling, looking amazed and keep saying how brilliant she was, and even Pete has tears in his eyes. When I look at Dad, he's crying, and it's about to set me off too. Luckily, Pete pre-emptively brought tissues and he passes them to me. Our little girl has done herself and us very proud.

As soon as we see her afterwards, the whole family engulfs her and gives her kisses and hugs.

'How did I do?' says Daisy.

'Oh, Daisy, you were amazing,' I say.

'I can't believe how good you were,' says Josh to his little sister. 'I mean, really good.'

'Thanks,' says Daisy, revelling in being a star for the day.

'So proud,' says Dad, hugging his granddaughter to within an inch of her life.

Miss Hollingshead walks over and gives Daisy a big bouquet of flowers. We thank her for all the hard work and dedication and for helping Daisy find something she truly loves. Miss Hollingshead tells us how amazing Daisy is and how it was a pleasure working with her. We really need to get Daisy enrolled in drama classes.

We leave the play and as promised, we head out to get pizza, and we let the kids order dessert too. It's Pizza Express so at least Pete, Dad, and I can enjoy it too. Dad and I have a glass of Prosecco, but Pete is driving so he sticks to coffee. The kids go crazy and order loads of food and for once, Pete and I let them. Pete's being more relaxed and we're both trying hard to make everything seem like normal again, even though it obviously isn't. Every night getting into bed, the tension and uncertainty is still there. We aren't having sex right now because it still feels too soon, but how long do we wait? And how long before it becomes a problem? I don't know if I'm ready or if he is yet. All I know is that right now, sitting around the table with my family, eating pizza, drinking Prosecco, talking and celebrating Daisy's big night, I want it to be OK. I want everything to be back to normal again and for all of us to be really, truly happy.

'A toast,' says Pete, raising his cup of coffee in the air. 'To Daisy and her amazing debut performance.'

'To Daisy!' we all say together and looking down at Daisy and her huge bouquet of flowers, she looks so proud of herself and after everything we've been through with her, it makes me so happy.

We eventually get home past ten o'clock and all the children are tired. Pete carries Daisy upstairs and puts her to bed. Josh and Alice stumble upstairs and I tuck them both in giving them kisses. Dad has Alice's room so she's sleeping on Josh's floor on the blow-up bed. Dad's tired too and says goodnight, before Pete and I head off to bed ourselves.

It's become the part of the day I dread and I don't know why. Coming to bed with Pete is still uncomfortable and I wish I knew where we were physically. Today though after talking with Lauren, watching Daisy, and thinking about the future and where I want us to be, I know I need to do something. Just lying in bed night after night not knowing how the other one is feeling isn't working and it's going to tear us apart.

'That's one tired little girl,' says Pete, walking into our bedroom behind me and closing the door.

'She was amazing though.'

'She was,' says Pete, standing in front of me.

Luckily, I've had two glasses of Prosecco so I'm feeling a little bit more daring than I would normally. I reach across and pull Pete's arms around me and pull him close until our faces are almost touching. I look at him for a second and he seems a bit unsure, but I start kissing him, grabbing at his body, and before long we fall on the bed and all that uncertainty is gone. It's been such a long time since we've had sex, it feels strange at first, but we soon remember what we're doing and it's good. It blows away all the cobwebs and uncertainty, and when we finally lie still on the bed in each other's arms, hot and sweaty, both done, I can't help but laugh.

'What are you laughing at?' says Pete.

'I don't know. I think it's more relief than laughter.'

'I know what you mean,' says Pete, sitting up and resting his head on his hand, his bicep bulging slightly beneath. 'I didn't know what you were thinking about this, about us. I know we're back together, but not really. It didn't feel like we were.'

'Too much walking on eggshells.'

'Exactly. So, are we done with the eggshells?'

'I hope so. If we're going to make this work, Pete, we need to be honest with each other.'

'All I want is for us to be happy.'

'Me too,' I say, and Pete leans across and kisses me.

Pete and I eventually fall asleep after we've had a really good chat about everything. We both say everything we want to say and we both agree that from now on, we're going to be open, honest, and we're not going to be complacent again. This is our marriage and it's going to be forever. It has to be. After everything that's happened, with Mum, the kids, Mark, Pete, and with me, I close my eyes with a new sense of hope. Life is what we make it and as I learnt from what happened with Mum, we never know what's around the corner, so we must embrace it, all of it, and never stop trying to find happiness.

Two years later

Thirty-Three

As I open my eyes, I'm still not properly awake, but I hear the kids downstairs. It's hard to tell if they're having fun or arguing. Since Alice turned sixteen, she's really matured, and she's suddenly so much more pleasant to be around. I think the realisation that she's growing up and won't be living at home forever is starting to sink in. Josh, on the other hand, is now a teenager and spends most of his time grunting and growling in his room. Daisy has changed the most though. Since she started drama classes she's grown so much. She's nine now and such a beautiful little soul.

I rub my eyes and sit up a bit. I have no idea what time it is, so I reach across and grab my phone. I can't believe it's almost ten o'clock. I must have been so tired last night. It's a Saturday morning in April and the sun is shining in through the window, warm against my face and it feels nice.

I have a text from Lauren.

How did you do this 3 times? Been up with Alfie half the night. Knackered. Looking forward to tonight, Rozza X

This makes me smile. It's been so nice to watch Lauren become a mum. It's brought us a lot closer together. I type a quick reply.

See you tonight...if you're still awake! x

I slowly sit up properly and check my emails and as usual there's quite a few. I'm busy these days and there's always something to be done. Being commissioning editor at a big publishing house in London, means I always have emails to answer and manuscripts to read, but I've never been happier in my work.

Tonight, I'm meeting up with Lauren and Aimee for one last big night out before Aimee finally leaves for Australia. She's emigrating with her husband, Gordon and their two girls. She's talked about it for years, but it's finally happening and I must say, I'm a tiny bit jealous. Still, maybe it will finally give me that push to get on a plane and visit her.

I can't be bothered to get up yet. I still can't decide if the kids are arguing or having fun, and I'm too relaxed and happy to get caught up in that. I text downstairs instead.

I'm awake. Fancy bringing me a coffee in bed? Maybe some toast?

I know it's a bit cheeky, but sometimes we must think of ourselves and I really could do with another thirty minutes in bed before I face the day. A reply quickly pings back.

Morning. I'll be up soon with coffee and toast. Anything else madam needs?

I smile to myself and reply.

Just you x

I put my phone down for a moment and stretch up towards the ceiling. Today's going to be busy with Daisy going to her friend Jessica's house later. Jessica and Daisy go to the same drama class and they're now BFFs and spend all their time together. Jessica lives in nearby Putney and her family are lovely, and perhaps because Jessica is an only child, they don't mind Daisy spending a lot of her time over there. Alice is going to Lilly's for the night. James and Sarah are brilliant with Alice and she loves spending time with them. We're going to watch Josh play football this afternoon, before he spends the night with Pete.

I hear footsteps on the landing then the door opens.

'Your coffee and toast,' says Mark, walking into the room. 'Where would you like it?'

'On my lap's fine, thank you,' I say, before he places the tray down and gives me a kiss.

'Good morning, beautiful.'

'Good morning, handsome,' I say. 'So, what's happening downstairs? Fun or fight?'

'I think a bit of both. I'm keeping out of it.'

'Good idea,' I say, taking a sip of coffee. 'Mmmm just what I needed.'

'That's all you need?'

'I didn't say that, did I? Although with all the kids gone tonight, you might have to wait.'

'If there's nothing else you can say about me, I'm patient. I waited a long time for you, I can wait a few hours for a bit of nooky.'

'Nooky? Who are you, a sitcom character from the eighties?'

'Hilarious,' says Mark, giving me another kiss. 'Right, I'll be downstairs. If they realise I'm gone there'll be chaos.'

'Thank you.'

'What for?'

'For having patience,' I say, before Mark walks out, leaving me to finish and my coffee and toast in silence.

Pete and I really tried to make our marriage work. We tried for so long, but ultimately, we weren't happy. The first six months after he moved back in were good and we both made a real effort, but once we were alright again, the complacency started to kick in and all the old issues came back. I think it took us too long to realise we'd drifted apart and wanted different things from life. Pete moved out a year ago and it was hard on the kids, but we've remained friends and he sees them every weekend. Pete and I are in a good place, he's dating someone new and she's lovely. I'm not just saying that to keep things good between us. Sally is genuinely lovely and we've become sort of friends. I would never have imagined that a few years ago, but here we are.

My relationship with Mark started soon after Pete moved out. I think he was always there in the back of my mind and we remained friends throughout everything. When things with Pete began to fall apart, Mark was there as a friend and he waited for me. If the truth be told, once I started dating Mark, it was clear how right he was for me. Mark and I just click. Being with him made me realise how far off track Pete and I had gone. Pete and I used to be so good. When we first got together wanted the same things, but as the years went on, as life changed and got in the way, we weren't the same and our relationship wasn't the same. I think we realised a year ago we didn't want to wake up in twenty years and think, what if? We both realised that as much as we wanted it to work, our marriage was over and it was painful to admit, but now, a year later, I think we're all a lot happier. Mark's kids and mine get on well, and we're still trying to work out how we might eventually live together with so many bodies.

Pete's living in a flat nearby while I'm in the house with the kids. He's been so good about everything and I think we're better friends now than we've ever been. He's happy with Sally, I'm happy with Mark, and all our children are happier because of it. What's it called? Blended families? This is us. And it works.

I eventually get up, get dressed, and head downstairs. Mark's kids are staying with his parents this weekend, so it's just my mob. Daisy and Josh are in the living room watching television. Alice is in the kitchen making a snack, and Mark is reading the paper on the dining room table. This is my family.

'Morning kids,' I say, popping my head in the living room.

'She rises!' says Josh sarcastically.

'Love you too,' I say, before I walk into the kitchen. I give Mark an absent kiss on the cheek as I walk past him. 'What are you making?' I say to Alice.

'Sandwich. I'm starving,' says Alice. 'Have you forgotten I'm going to Lilly's today?'

'No I haven't. We'll drop you off on the way to the football match.'

'And I'm going to Jessica's,' says Daisy walking into the room.

'No I haven't forgotten that either.'

'My match is at two,' says Josh. 'But we need to get there early, like one, so I can get ready and warm up.'

'Already the plan,' I say, clicking the kettle on.

Josh and Daisy sit down at the table next to Mark, while Alice finishes making her sandwich and sits down too. They talk and ask Mark questions about this and that and it's incredible to me how resilient and open to change children are. One of our biggest worries about breaking up was how the children would handle it, and it's been Pete and mine's biggest concern over the last year, but they've been brilliant. It makes me love them more than I already did because they love us so much, so unconditionally, that even when we fuck up they let us off the hook. It was the same when they were little. I'd have bad days and have no patience for them and I'd shout at them for the silliest, most trivial things, but they'd forget in no time and I was forgiven. I've tried to use this same sort of attitude on myself. It took me a while, but I've forgiven myself for failing with Pete. It was one of the hardest parts about getting divorced, accepting we failed. But the kids did and they still love us, still have time for us both, and it's that attitude that's helped me through this. They were even amazing when I finally introduced them to Mark. I was so worried they wouldn't like him, but they've been nothing but supportive. It's enough to melt even the coldest, most cynical of hearts. Children really are just the most wonderful little people.

We eventually leave the house, all of us bundling into the car. We have to drop Daisy off first, Alice second, then we're going to watch Josh playing football. Pete's meeting us at the football pitch and Josh is going home with him for the night. I drop the girls off with kisses and promises to behave and have fun, before we head to the playing fields with Josh.

'Hi there,' says Pete, shaking Mark's hand and giving me a kiss on the cheek.

We're standing on the side of the pitch. It's a glorious day and despite the recent rain, the pitch is looking good. Josh is warming up with his teammates on the other side of the pitch. Pete and I try to come to as many games as we can. Today we're both here, which is a bit of a treat for Josh.

I hope he has a good game. He still wants to be a professional footballer, but I'm glad he's doing well at school too. I think he's starting to realise the importance of having a backup plan.

'How's everything?' I say to Pete.

'Good, good, yes. I have some news actually,' says Pete, slightly uncomfortably. 'Sally and I are moving in together.'

'That's great news,' I say and really mean it.

'Well done,' says Mark.

'We think it's time. We're both renting at the moment, but we're going to buy somewhere together,' says Pete. 'But we're staying nearby. I want to be here for the kids.'

'Good, that's good. I wouldn't want it any other way,' I say.

There's a moment's silence before Mark offers to get in the coffees from the park cafe. I'm so glad parks all seem to have decent cafes these days. It makes coming to football matches so much more appealing. As soon as Mark's gone, Pete turns to me.

'Are you really OK with it?'

'Yes, of course, why wouldn't I be?'

'I don't know,' says Pete. 'I suppose it's still a bit weird, this, us, you and me. I'm still adjusting.'

'But that's life though right? Aren't we always adjusting?'

'I suppose so.'

'Pete, honestly, when it comes to us, I hope we're always OK because you know what?'

'What?'

'There will always be an us. Whether it was the love

we had or the life we have now, and even with Mark and Sally, in some ways it will always be about us.'

I smile at Pete and he smiles back at me, the sun shining against the side of his face. I look across and see Mark walking back with three coffees and I couldn't be happier with him. I look at Josh warming up, my little baby boy, so grown up, and I think about the girls. Sometimes life doesn't go to plan and we're forced to make choices that perhaps we don't want to make. Sometimes we're happy and sometimes we're sad, but life just goes on. We can't stop the tick tick tick of time and maybe that's the most beautiful thing about it all. We can't go backwards, only forwards and that means we make mistakes and have to deal with the consequences. We make plans that don't work out and then we're forced to make new ones. We meet people who change our lives, some for the better and some for the worse, but if there's one thing I've learnt through all of this, it's this: Going back in time and fixing things wouldn't make life better because no matter what you fix, what you change, you'll never be completely happy unless you learn to enjoy every day as if it might be your last. Sometimes I look at my kids and I think I'm going to burst with love and when I see Mark look at me a certain way across the room, as if I'm the only person in the world, it gives me goosebumps and makes me realise how lucky I am to be loved and wanted so much by one person. Life is a continual journey and every day we make decisions that affect our lives and change their course, but thinking too much about the past and worrying too much about the future won't make any of it worthwhile. No, the way to be happy, the way to really enjoy life is to live now and enjoy today. Life is extraordinary, it is, and it's the small moments that really matter. That make it extraordinary.

Josh runs out on the pitch, sees us, smiles and waves. I wave back at him, my son, and I take a sip of my coffee on this most wonderful of days.

Thirty-Four

Primrose Hill, 1996

It's the day after all the hullabaloo of graduation and Pete and I are heading up to Primrose Hill with a picnic and a bottle of champagne. After celebrating with our friends and family yesterday, today is time for our own little celebration. Today it's just about us.

'Come on, slow coach,' I say to Pete, who's walking up behind me.

'Who's carrying all the stuff?'

'Who insisted because guess what, a silly little girl can't possibly carry her own bottle of champagne up a small hill by herself?'

'Why can you never accept a small gesture of kindness without a glib remark like that?'

'Because I'm a feminist. I'm a strong, independent woman, who doesn't need a man to take care of her,' I say reaching the top of Primrose Hill and turning around. The view is incredible. All of London is stretched out before me and it feels like it's the whole world. I feel like the whole world is at my feet. I suppose graduating university makes us feel a bit like that.

'Is this the same strong, independent feminist who threw a fit the other morning because I didn't make her eggs the way she likes them? The same one who rang me to take care of, and I quote, "a huge spider" the other day?'

'Fine, whatever. I'm a modern feminist,' I say, sitting down.

Pete sits down next to me, dumping the backpack full of food next to him. He takes out the blanket and lays it down. We unpack the food, open the champagne, and settle in to enjoy the rest of the afternoon. It's mid-afternoon and it's such a bright, sunny day. It's the sort of day that makes me feel so alive and as if anything is possible.

I'm starting work on Monday at a publishing house and to be honest, I'm terrified. It's going to be my first proper job and I really want it to go well. Pete's starting work too, while he continues his studies. He's got a long road ahead of him before he's a fully qualified solicitor. My career path is a little easier and simpler than his. I'm starting off as an assistant, but hopefully over the next few years I can work my way up to editor then commissioning editor, and who knows where I'll end up. The important thing is that I love what I do and I'm happy at work. Pete and I are also moving in together in a few weeks. We have a flat lined up, but we need to wait until the end of month until the current tenants move out. We're so lucky because we got some help from Pete's family and the flat is gorgeous. I can't wait to live with Pete. Life's moving so quickly and I'm trying my best to grab every moment and hang onto it before it's gone.

'This is the life. Just messing about in boats,' says Pete, sitting down next to me.

'I don't want to be the bearer of bad news, but this isn't a boat, Pete.'

'I know that. It's from The Wind in The Willows. It

was my favourite book growing up.'

'I'm still learning so much about you,' I say, cuddling into him and taking a sip of champagne.

'What was your favourite childhood book?'

'Let me see, probably The Lion, The Witch, and The Wardrobe.'

'That's a good one,' says Pete, kissing the side of my neck. 'So, this is it. We've graduated. You and me. Rosie and Pete. No longer soppy students, getting pissed every night of the week…'

'Wait a moment. When did you ever get pissed every night of the week?'

'Fine, maybe that was just you, but with jobs and responsibilities, life is going to be different.'

'OK Mr mood dampener, chill out on the responsibilities stuff. I'm still only twenty-one and just because I'm working, it doesn't mean I can't get pissed on a school night. In fact, from what I've heard, in publishing they sort of expect it.'

'We'll see.'

We both take a moment to soak in the views and enjoy the moment. It's a strange time this moment after university and before work. It's like we're sort of trapped in this moment between childhood and adulthood. We're in a place that doesn't really exist and all we can do is relax and enjoy this bubble of time for what it is. It's a break from life. We don't have to worry about exams and learning and we don't have to worry about work. It's a holiday from life and it feels good. This moment, sitting here with Pete, might be the last time I ever feel like this and I'm trying to capture it. I'm trying to remember every tiny detail, every thought, feeling, and everything I can see.

'So, what does the future hold?' I say after we've both eaten some food and had another glass of champagne. I take out a cigarette and light it, blowing the smoke high into the air.

'For me or us?'

'Let's start with you. Where you will be, I don't know, ten years from now?'

Pete takes a moment before he replies. He's sitting up with his legs out straight and I'm lying with my head in his lap looking up at the cloudless cerulean sky.

'Ten years, wow, I'll be thirty. God, can you imagine me that old?'

'Balding with a little pot belly.'

'Oh, that's lovely. I imagine that by thirty I'll be a full-time solicitor and we'll be living in a nice little semi-detached somewhere in south London. A little garden, maybe a dog…'

'Oh, what sort of dog?'

'Something small. Maybe a Jack Russell or a Beagle.'

'Perfect, carry on.'

'We'll go away for weekends together to Paris and Rome.'

'Copenhagen? I've always wanted to go to Copenhagen.'

'Sure, Copenhagen. We'll be thinking about kids, of course…'

'Of course.'

'But maybe we'll wait a few more years until we have more money and can buy a bigger house. Perhaps somewhere in the suburbs. Surrey maybe. We'll be very happy, still having lots of sex.'

'And how will our wedding be?'

'The wedding will be magical. We'll get married in one of those huge mansions in the country and all our friends and family will come and spend the weekend. Then we'll honeymoon somewhere tropical like Bora Bora or the Seychelles.'

'Sounds perfect.'

'So, what about you, Rosie Golding, what will your life look like in ten years?'

'I'll be married to you, like you said, but I'll have a toy boy, obviously.'

'Obviously,' says Pete with a smile.

'I hope we get to go travelling together before we get too settled. I'd like to take a year off in our late twenties and travel for a year. We could rent the house out and really enjoy ourselves. Just like this but all over the world.'

'Sounds good.'

'I'll be successful at work. Maybe I'll be a commissioning editor by then with a string of bestsellers under my belt. I'll be one of those women other women see and think, how does she do it? A successful career, a happy marriage, and I'll be in good shape physically…'

'Unlike me apparently.'

'Unlike you, I'll join a gym and pop there after work for Pilates or something. We'll live in a perfect little cottage in Putney, by the river. Maybe I'll take up rowing and Sundays we'll spend in the pub with our good-looking friends, talking, laughing, eating amazing food, and reflecting on how lucky we are.'

'Do you know who these good-looking friends are

because I'm thinking about our current crop and none are that attractive if I'm honest.'

'We'll have to get new friends. I'll probably meet a whole host of beautiful girls in publishing and you'll meet loads of well-heeled public school boys at the law firm. Maybe we'll matchmake a few of them and they'll become our circle of friends. I'll get a Mini Cooper with a Union Jack on the roof and drive it around town.'

'And I'll get one of those little Italian mopeds.'

'Ah the life we will have,' I say, looking up at Pete.

Pete leans down and gives me a kiss on the lips. We sit here like this for a while, just enjoying the view and the feeling of freedom that having nothing to do gives you. I know how lucky I am. How lucky we are. Lauren's still interviewing for jobs and she just moved into a house share with a bunch of strangers. She has no idea what her future holds and if she doesn't get a job soon, she'll be forced to move back home and I know that's the last thing she wants to do. I know our life isn't settled and talking about the future is just fun and games because who knows what the future really holds? I hope Pete and I make our dreams comes true. I hope we make it, get married, go travelling, have successful careers then eventually a family. I'd like two children, one girl and one boy. All of this is just talk because right now I'm happy lying here with Pete, looking out across London with nothing to do but dream, drink, and revel in the fact we're young and the world is ours for the taking.

The End

Acknowledgments

This is my sixth novel and I want to thank a few people for helping me get this far because despite being a wonderful job, it's also extremely hard and you can't do it alone. So, from the beginning thank you so much to Harriet Bourton for believing in me, for Hodder and Stoughton for publishing me, for fellow male authors Mike Gayle, Matt Dunn, Nick Spalding and Andy Jones for helping me, laughing with me, and sticking together because what we do isn't easy. Thank you to my editor Aimee Swann, who is doing a great job and makes every one of my books better. Thank you to all my friends on Facebook and Twitter, some of you I know in person and others I don't, but your continued support and encouragement means the world to me. Thanks to my family and friends, who have not only helped and supported me, but continue to make me realise that none of what we do achieve means anything without love. Thanks to all the readers who keep buying my books and writing such lovely things about them. I don't know if readers appreciate how much authors love getting good reviews. We write books alone and yours is the feedback that makes it all worth it. Lastly, a huge thank you to the love of my life, Kristin. She is my everything and honestly without her I couldn't do this. She makes my life infinitely better. Thanks baby, I love you.

This is my sixth novel and I hoped you loved it. This was a different novel for me and I took a bit of a gamble that my male fans would still want to read it and my female fans wouldn't say in disgust, "why is a man trying to write a book from a female perspective?" I hope it worked and touched you in some way. Because no matter what sort of book I'm writing, my goal is always the same. I'm trying to connect with people, make you think, make you laugh, entertain you, and make you live another life for however long it takes you to read the book. Life is about living and reading gives us the chance to live more than one life, so keep reading, keep searching, exploring, dreaming, and thank you for giving my little book a chance.

30155807R00188

Printed in Great Britain
by Amazon